Bérénice 1934–44

PETER LANG
New York • Bern • Berlin
Brussels • Vienna • Oxford • Warsaw

Isabelle Stibbe

Bérénice 1934–44

An Actress in Occupied Paris

Translated from French by
Zack Rogow and Renée Morel

PETER LANG
New York • Bern • Berlin
Brussels • Vienna • Oxford • Warsaw

Library of Congress Cataloging-in-Publication Data

Names: Stibbe, Isabelle, author.
Rogow, Zack, translator. | Morel, Renée, translator.
Title: Bérénice 1934–44: an actress in occupied Paris / by Isabelle Stibbe;
translated by Zack Rogow and Renée Morel.
Other titles: Bérénice 34–44
Description: New York: Peter Lang, 2019.
Identifiers: LCCN 2019002664 | ISBN 978-1-4331-6705-8 (paperback: alk. paper)
ISBN 978-1-4331-6707-2 (ebook pdf)
ISBN 978-1-4331-6708-9 (epub) | ISBN 978-1-4331-6709-6 (mobi)
Subjects: LCSH: Comédie-Française—Fiction.
France—History—German occupation, 1940–1945—Fiction.
Classification: LCC PQ2719.T53 B4713 2019 | DDC 843/.92—dc23
LC record available at https://lccn.loc.gov/2019002664
DOI 10.3726/b15850

Bibliographic information published by **Die Deutsche Nationalbibliothek**.
Die Deutsche Nationalbibliothek lists this publication in the "Deutsche
Nationalbibliografie"; detailed bibliographic data are available
on the Internet at http://dnb.d-nb.de/.

Original title: *Bérénice 34–44*
© Serge Safran Editeur, 2012
Published by arrangement with Agence littéraire Astier-Pécher
ALL RIGHTS RESERVED

© 2019 Zack Rogow and Renée Morel

Peter Lang Publishing, Inc., New York
29 Broadway, 18th floor, New York, NY 10006
www.peterlang.com

for my father

PART ONE

· 1 ·

She won't tell about the knowing glances, the conspiratorial smiles. "Oh, there's no such thing as chance," "It was inevitable"—she overheard those trite phrases hundreds of times. They were the origin of the family legend that her calling for the theater, which caught hold of her at the age of six and never let go, was because of her first name: Bérénice—like the play by Racine. Only one person had a point of view that differed from this belief, through conviction, derision, or more likely because she just had a mind of her own. "It's a good thing you didn't name her Sappho, or she would've become a lesbian," joked her Grandmother Mathilde, who was educated and had a sharp tongue, occasionally adding this variation: "You think if you'd named her Isabelle she would've become a Catholic?" This allusion to Isabelle the Catholic, that cursèd queen who expelled the Jews from Spain, was guaranteed to toss lightning bolts into this group—Catholic being, in the hierarchy of the Capel family's values, almost more reprehensible than lesbian. But it was neither Sappho nor Isabelle, it was Bérénice, *Gott zei dank*—thank God—well, almost.

She won't tell her grandchildren or even her children that she entered the world on the 28th of June in the year of grace 1919, even more grace given that it was the year, not to mention the actual day, of the Treaty of Versailles. During the early twentieth century, France was trying to convince itself that the League of Nations, just created, would bring peace to the world. "It was rough, but this was the war to end all wars, we've suffered enough, it's over, Europe will be at peace," or so said her father, and how many thousands like him, all in unison.

On that Saturday, June 28, 1919, five years to the day after the assassination of Franz Ferdinand in Sarajevo, France was hanging on every bit of news, experiencing through the newspapers or radio waves the arrival of the plenipotentiaries in the Hall of Mirrors, the whole country pregnant with expectation to hear about the historic ceremony at Versailles, solemnly awaiting the signing of the treaty that would wash away the humiliation of France's defeat in 1871. It wouldn't bring back the dead, it wouldn't erase the cold, the worms, the suffering, the hell, but still, "they" would pay dearly for it.

Although he had fought right from the beginning in 1914—and proudly served France, mind you, since what could be more honorable for a Jewish immigrant—and though he came back with two wounds, military honors, and the Croix de Guerre, Monsieur Capel had other things on his mind that day than the fate of the Boches: would his wife give birth to a boy or a girl? If it was a boy, they would name him Philippe, of course, like Marshal Pétain, the savior of Verdun. If it was a girl, they had also made up their minds— she would be named Bérénice. Certainly, like the heroine of the Racine play, yes, ladies and gentlemen! He hadn't read an awful lot, Monsieur Capel, but during the war, he became buddies with an elementary school teacher. A great guy, a young man who had read mountains of books and knew entire poems by heart. Hugo, Baudelaire, Verlaine—especially Verlaine. A long time ago, in the *cheder* in Russia, Monsieur Capel had a *chaver* like that who could recite the Torah by heart. You would give him the number of a chapter or a verse, and *voilà*! he would rattle off the passage without ever making a mistake. Even the rabbi, he was impressed. The "teach," he was a goy and an atheist (maybe even a freemason—which goes to show, that can happen even in the best families), so he exercised his talents on French literature—which, come to think of it, is an even more remarkable feat than the Bible. Not only that, he was easygoing, not in the least pretentious, didn't object to mess duty, a real pal, know what I mean? Louis was his name, a good French name, a king's name.

In the stultifying trenches, to pass the time, to escape the fatigue, the heebie-jeebies, the hunger, they would tell each other their life stories. Those two got along well, even if, on the surface, it looked like they didn't have much in common, one from a French family that could trace its roots way back, the other Jewish, exiled from his native Russia for not serving the czar whose army was notorious for its virulent anti-Semitism. That didn't prevent Monsieur

Capel from enlisting in the French army on the day war was declared: "Here, they let me be Jewish, they let me work to feed my wife, it's my turn to make my contribution to France."

As a rule, Louis was someone who liked to have fun, always ready to make a joke, to kid around or tell funny stories, but sometimes, when it was freezing or there was nothing to do, when the routines of military life dragged them down, when the confinement of the tunnels, the piles of sandbags became too oppressive, then he let slip in the presence of Monsieur Capel this phrase, so enigmatic: "The day will begin and the day will cease …" just those words, avoiding the ending, always with just a hint of a sad smile, tinged with irony, as if he himself was surprised by this jest from his own unconscious. Realizing that Monsieur Capel didn't understand the allusion to Racine's verse, Louis told him the story of the tragedy of *Bérénice*, of Titus's passion for Bérénice, the promise of marriage that the emperor of Rome made to the queen of Palestine, and his renouncing it so as not to disobey the laws of Rome, and the sighs of Titus and the lamentation of Bérénice, and everything that makes Racine, Racine.

He also told him about the context of the play, how the former student of Port-Royal was actually talking about the love of Louis XIV for Marie Mancini, the niece of Mazarin, and the king's giving her up for the good of the state, a renunciation that Alexandre Dumas echoed in *The Vicomte de Bragelonne*, romanticized of course, when he added to the lovers' actual meeting, the figure of d'Artagnan and the musketeer's contempt for the prince's cowardice. French literature, thought Monsieur Capel, was definitely fascinating … Cross his heart and hope to die (as his friends would say), if he ever got out of this war alive, he would read all the books he would never have known about if not for that teacher. "The day will begin and the day will cease …" it really was hot stuff, it sounded so French … "And Titus will not see his Bérénice." That concision of the French language: just one sentence could say everything. A shame that there weren't more books in the barracks library. There were no plays there, so Monsieur Capel had to ask Louis to tell him the plot of *Bérénice* again and again, like children who beg for a bedtime story, always the same one, and the adults aren't allowed to change even a comma.

In the end, without realizing it, "Bérénice" became their code word for peace, the dream of a return home, a return to a normal life, the caress of the quotidian, when they could once more fold their wives in their arms, practice their professions again, one would find his students again, those raggedy little rascals, with their gray smocks, their pranks and their ink stains, the other his furs and his customers, those bourgeois women bedecked with their pearl necklaces, their haughty air, their minks, their demands.

And then ... Monsieur Capel congratulated himself silently, Bérénice, hahaha, she was the queen of Palestine. Not that Monsieur Capel had ever thought of living there like those meshuganahs who wanted to rebuild a homeland there and bring back to life a dead language, *oy a broch!* He wasn't crazy, oh no, but still, the land of milk and honey, "next year in Jerusalem," repeated each year at the end of the Passover seder, that meant something, so he loved that Racine for making a Jew the heroine of his play. But he couldn't say that to his pal Louis, he wanted to show him that he was assimilated, that he was French before he was Jewish. But it was his little secret, and it made him happy.

Yes, no doubt about it, Bérénice was the most beautiful name in the world for his little daughter. It would have made his teacher friend happy, his friend who died in the trenches in 1918, just a few days before the war ended. Poor guy! He was only twenty-five and left a widow, a sweet girl whose photo he had showed him. Twenty-five, what a shame. The best always go first. Louis won't ever see again the kids in his school, the little brats—so endearing, Monsieur Capel felt as if he already knew them, the teacher had told him so much about them. Camille, the little carrot-top whose papers were flooded with spelling mistakes but was so clever and good as gold; Charles, that big oaf who had grown too quickly and whose pants, never long enough, ended up looking like shorts; Léon, who showed off because his father had lots of dough and owned a convertible; cross-eyed Victor ... Louis would never know what would become of those little guys once they grew up. Fucking war!

It was the day of the Treaty of Versailles and it turned out to be a girl. The young mademoiselle was delivered in good health, a pudgy, seven-pound baby with immense eyes that took up her whole face, hair as thick as a week-old baby, and the cutest fingernails, so long and smooth that it looked as if she'd just had a manicure. And that scream, that scream ... No question, she would be a real Capel, a girl with her own opinions who wouldn't let anybody boss her around. Nah, she won't take any crap from the boys, thought her father delightedly.

When she discovered the sex of the infant, her mother feared for an instant how her husband might react. In Jewish law, doesn't the morning prayer say, "Thank God, I wasn't born a woman"? Monsieur Capel knew it well, he had often heard that prayer in synagogue when he was young, but even if he hadn't studied for long, he wasn't backward enough to believe in such foolishness. Girl or boy, what did it matter, he would love his child the same. After the pogroms, the death of his first wife in Russia, his difficulty finding work in France, everything seemed good, finally. His second wife was hardworking and attentive, and now he had a little girl who would grow up in the country known for the rights of man and Zola, this country where they wrote revolutionary ideas and melodious poems, where a Racine could write about a Jewish woman and his play could become a masterpiece, where a terrific guy like Louis the teacher could exist, where you could go where you liked, laugh, and sing without Cossacks or the czar's police on your back. Hallelujah, the time of the pogroms was over and done with, soon the Workers' International would definitely win the general elections. What more could you want? He was, as the saying goes, "happy as a Jew in France."

On his visit to the neighborhood civil registry office to declare and recognize the birth of little Bérénice, something strange happened. When he became a naturalized citizen, in 1892, Maurice was granted permission to make his name more French. Instead of being named Moishe Kapeluchnik, difficult to pronounce for those who were not Russian and too redolent of his immigrant past in the shtetl, he became Maurice Capel. But on that June 28, 1919, either because of haste, negligence, or bad eyesight, the civil registry officer made a mistake in recording the baby's family name and the "l" was suddenly transformed into a "t." The new father realized it right away and was about to point out the error to the clerk, but after thinking it over, he kept silent. Or rather, he talked about everything and nothing, the weather, the clerk's military decorations—What battalion were you in oh same here I was also in the infantry, Monsieur—about the Treaty of Versailles—the Boches asked for it—anything to distract the registry office clerk and prevent him from realizing his mistake, too thrilled by the prospect of bequeathing to his daughter, on top of her Racinian first name, the family name of kings of France. Ah yes, even for a die-hard republican like him, that name had a prestigious aura, bringing visions of the exploits of the valiant knights of the Middle Ages, the justice that Saint Louis distributed under the oak tree, and the majesty of the Sun King. No less than that, yes sirree!

Bérénice Capet. There it was, written in black and white, signed, sealed, stamped, validated, registered. That day, leaving the registry office, Moishe Kapeluchnik, son of Abraham Kapeluchnik, Russian tailor, and Myriam Rabinovitch, housewife, felt he had the soul of a Gaul.

He returned home triumphant, brandishing his family registry booklet. Even more moved than at the baby's birth a few hours before, he kissed his daughter, using the fact of his head being buried in the cradle to hide the tears that were welling up in his eyes. Bérénice Capet. The first of the Kapeluchnik family to be born on French soil. The first Kapeluchnik to bear a typically French name. Always the troublemaker, his mother-in-law mocked, "Your parents would be spinning in their graves to see their name massacred like that. *Your* daughter, a *true Frenchwoman*? My friend, you forget that for your belovèd Frenchmen, we will always be Jews. Look at poor Dreyfus!"

Oy, gevalt, what didn't she say? It was the beginning of a bitter argument that lasted hours and from which no one emerged the winner. Although he never admitted it, the Dreyfus affair had always perturbed Maurice Capel. Despite all his faculty for self-deception, extraordinarily well developed, he had difficulty explaining away the anti-Semitism of some French people. But this glorious day wasn't for arguments. To hell with his mother-in-law's quarrelsome disposition, to hell with the anti-Semites of every country, French, Russian, or Chinese; a little girl had been born, the first in the long line of Kapeluchniks who had become a Capet, thanks to a badly calligraphied "l." *Mazel tov!*

· 2 ·

Chez Capel was not the Rothschilds', that's for sure. Moishe Kapeluchnik was born around 1870 in a little Russian shtetl. His father, Abraham, had tried his hand at a little of every profession, depending on what heaven decided to send his way. That's how, in less than thirty years, he worked in turn as a delivery boy, peddler, herring salesman, tailor, shoemaker, grinding machine operator in an umbrella factory, and even a beadle, but by the time Moishe entered the world, he had become a furrier and most likely remained so to the end of his days. His mother, Myriam, had already given birth to eight children when little Moishele made his appearance. From his birth, he was a tough and scrappy baby who had made up his mind to carve a niche for himself in that large family. At the Kapeluchniks' there wasn't enough money for the children to be educated so Moishe just learned to read and write with the rabbi, at the *cheder*.

It all seemed natural to him at the time, because he had no other reference point. It was only later that he realized that his parents' marriage must not have been happy. His mother, aged prematurely by varicose veins and miscarriages, turned more and more to religion as she grew older. Fast of Yom Kippur, fast of Esther, fast of Tisha B'av, fast of the first-born, she never missed a single one and strictly followed the rules of *kashrut*: one set of dishes for meat, one for dairy, abstinence during her monthlies and the day before and the day after, the ritual bath, the prohibition against wearing leather shoes on Yom Kippur, and then the rule against using the lights on Shabbat … What a headache for her husband! He was reasonably pious. "God will forgive me," he said, making excuses when he was caught eating a piece of cheese after a meat dish. "With all the evil people running around in the street, doesn't God have better things to do than to worry about what I put on my plate?" His arrangements about religion were not to the taste of his wife, too superstitious to laugh about such things. "The way you act like some unbeliever, you'll bring the evil eye down on us," and the argument was off and running. At the drop of a hat, his parents would make a scene, hurl insults, slam doors in each other's faces. The only respite began on Friday evening because you weren't allowed to argue during Shabbat. Undoubtedly for that reason, Moishe's favorite time was this magical day that silenced his parents.

The last-born early on revealed himself to be a mischievous and clever boy. His friendly face and his gift of gab soon convinced his father to bring him along when he met with clients. The kid made them laugh with his chatter, and how proud he was that his father brought him along. His brothers and sisters were not entitled to that privilege. What's more, meeting people at the shop was a lot more fun than learning Hebrew in school under the stern gaze of the rabbi who watched every move they made. That's how, little by little, he learned the trade, by imitating, by intuition, on the job. In a few years he became the best furrier in the shtetl.

Life was going well for him, but there, too, it was only later on, when misfortune struck, that he realized it. As they said in his village, "It's only when you lose one arm that you realize how lucky you are to have two." At the beginning, everything went well. At seventeen, he married the rabbi's daughter, a pious young woman, pretty as a peach, *and* he was in love with her. He promised himself not to recreate his family's arguments and turned himself inside out to make her happy. A little compliment here and there, a bouquet of flowers on Shabbat, a new dress when he earned a bit more than usual. Their marriage ceremony was simple but filled with joy. A few months later, his wife became pregnant. Moishe could not have been happier. He almost forgot that one day he would have to do his military service. It was around this time that the village started to hear rumblings about pogroms. At first it was just a rumor, but it was still very worrisome, all those horrible stories about what they did to the Jews. And then one day, when Moishe was coming back from the market … Well, that's all we know. Moishe never wanted to talk about what he found that day when he came home, or the terror he felt when he saw his house devastated, or what happened to his beautiful wife, the pearl of his life. We only know she was wearing that day her new navy blue dress that he had bought her for her birthday. We also know that from then on he was a widower and that no one knew whether he would have been the father of a boy or a girl.

After that, maybe one or two months later, he decided to leave Russia. It was out of the question that he should serve the czar, out of the question that he should join the army with all those drunken and anti-Semitic Cossacks. He wanted to get to France, there at least, you were treated well. Without any means of transportation, without a visa, he trusted his only allies: his feet and his iron will to reach the homeland of the rights of man, that land that a gentleman who came by from time to time to order furs for his wife had described to him as paradise on earth. He had even showed him a postcard of Paris—now, *that* had made an impression on him, Moishe Kapeluchnik. When he arrived in France, the two most beautiful days of his life were when he saw Notre-Dame in person, exactly as it had looked in the postcard, and the day when he was finally naturalized. The two most beautiful days of his life. His life after. In Paris.

"It's not a good thing, a man by himself," he often heard at the *Pletzl*, the Marais district where he loved to reconnect with the surroundings of his childhood. "You have to take a wife, you're not old, it's a sin not to remarry, it's contrary to the Torah." For a long time, he covered his ears. Marry a woman other than the pearl of his life? Start another family after what had happened? *Genug*, stop talking about it! His life was fine the way it was, his shop was doing well, he succeeded in selling a fur coat a day thanks to clients from the court of Queen Amélie of Portugal, money was coming in … What did he need with a wife?

It's not clear what finally won him over. It might be that the desire to have children was the strongest factor, at least to perpetuate the Kapeluchnik name, even in its French form—Capel. Maybe he thought it would piss off the bastard anti-Semites to put one or two more Jews on the planet. Whatever it was, one evening during the high holy days he agreed to meet the Valabrègue family. They were an old Jewish family that dated back to the Comtat-Venaissin, a haven for their people in the area of Avignon during the Middle Ages. The Valabrègues had lived in Paris for five or six years. The parents were shopkeepers and they had a daughter to marry off. Of course she was much younger than Maurice and much less pretty than … well, you know, the pearl of his life, may her soul rest in the hands of God.

Esther, when you looked carefully at her, you realized that she had a high forehead, so high that it made you think of a skating rink. Well, a high forehead is not so bad, it can even be charming with bangs. And that's how he ended up getting married again. The ceremony took place at the civil registry office of the 10th Arrondissement, and then at the synagogue on the Rue des Tournelles, near the place of business of his new in-laws. As for the synagogue, he didn't give a damn, after what had happened in Russia he didn't believe in God anymore, but his new in-laws insisted. So he was fine with the synagogue. And the hundred thousand gold francs in her dowry.

Every day Maurice thanked heaven for letting him live in France. He became passionate about the language of Molière and made it a point of honor that no one should find out that he was a foreigner. In fact, he had succeeded in learning to speak French like a true Parisian. There remained only a few spots here and there where his accent could be detected, but really nothing to speak of, truly nothing. O.K., now and then, maybe, a slight Yiddish accent surfaced. But it was when he was angry, or on purpose, to make Bérénice laugh—she loved to hear him say, "So, vid me you come to the roo des Rosiers? Vee gon' sell some furs dere, huh?"

He certainly did know how to make her laugh, his Bérénice. That story about the train, just for instance. You know it? So, one day two men are sitting opposite each other on a train. The first one, just to make conversation, he says, "Bonjour, monsieur!" He says it real polite, see, but the other, pfft! He doesn't answer even a word. So the first guy persists, "Excuse me, monsieur, but could you tell me the time, please?" Still no answer. Annoyed, the first guy ends up losing his temper: "Listen, monsieur, you could at least be polite. I say *bonjour* to you, you don't even answer. I ask you what time it is, you still don't answer. Is that any way for a Jew to treat another Jew?" So, the other guy looks him right in the eye and says, "No, I don't feel like answering you. You know why? Because if I answer, then we're going to start talking. I'm going to tell you I've got a daughter. You're going to tell me you've got a son. I'm going to tell you that my daughter is of a marriageable age. You're going to tell me that your son is, too, that he's a good student, that he's a fine boy … But why would I want a son-in-law whose father can't even afford a measly watch?"

"Another story, papa, another!"

And Maurice Capel tells his little Bérénice, sitting on his knee, stories about the shtetl, the village idiot, who slept during the day and woke up at night, keeping the villagers awake with his endless chatter, and the lamplighter who would never part with his hat, even when he washed or slept, so they said, and then there was the butcher, who, because his daughter married a goy, tore his jacket ...

"Why did he tear his jacket, Papa?"

"Because that's what you do when you're in mourning."

"But his daughter wasn't dead."

"But it's as if she was, it broke the butcher's heart that his daughter didn't marry a Jew, and he acted as if she was dead."

And so Maurice recounted how the poor father tore his jacket, cursing the flesh of his flesh, refusing to hear anyone speak of her, renouncing her in a great malediction that made his daughter cry liters of tears until the river overflowed.

"Papa, was there a theater in your shtetl?"

"It wasn't a real theater, there were traveling actors who came through from time to time to put on plays in Yiddish, or to improvise in the village square, for weddings or holidays, acrobats who also were partly dancers and musicians."

Sometimes, all of a sudden, Maurice Capel would stop, not out of nostalgia for that period, but because it was too painful to revive those memories of his father, his mother, his brothers and sisters, whom he had no news from, perhaps dead now, or they might just have remained there, too far away in any case for him to have any hope of ever seeing them again. Then Bérénice, perched on her father's knees, asked him more questions, the ones she knew—the little girl was already aware—would make her father happy to answer. "Tell me, Papa," she asked, placing one finger on his left shoulder, "tell me again how you got that," and Maurice Capel, explained proudly how he went to war for France, how proud he was to set out, a flower in his rifle, to defend the homeland of the rights of man, so that other generations could also tread the soil that gave birth to liberty. "Right there is where the bullet hit me at the start of the war, and there—look—that's the second one, not too far from the heart, huh? any closer and there would have been no more Maurice Capel, and no Bérénice."

That idea weighed on her heart, especially at night, when she couldn't find her way to sleep, when her imagination engendered fears and monstrous guilt, she saw her father being hit with a bullet, he dropped dead on the spot, in one motion, like a board that's been dropped, and she started to cry in her little bed, silent and powerless tears that she didn't dare tell anyone about.

Other than that, life was simple in the Capels' home, at least at the beginning. They woke up early in the morning, they ate breakfast as a family, they sent Bérénice to a school next to their home, she walked there with her best friend and neighbor Colette. Friday night the sweet smell of challah filled the house. More often than not Grandma Mathilde joined them—she lived alone in the Marais ever since she had been widowed. Bérénice was very fond of her, except when she bickered with her father. Sometimes she told herself she would have liked to have had a little brother or sister, but her parents never succeeded in having another child.

The Capels often welcomed guests. There were always people in the shop or their home. Friends, neighbors, family enjoyed dropping in without notice, always sure to find a warm cup of tea, sweets, and a good story. In short, they were so used to their lifestyle that they didn't even realize they had recreated a little shtetl in the middle of Paris. The only difference was, French was spoken, on the strict orders of Monsieur Capel, even if a word of Yiddish escaped his lips from time to time, and his wife borrowed a few Yiddish phrases, but in time, he spoke it less and less and forgot—or wanted to forget—that it was his mother tongue.

· 3 ·

"What do you want to be when you grow up, Bérénice?"

"An actress."

"An actress?"

"Oy, *gevalt*," Monsieur Capel objected, "an actress! That's no profession for a Jew. Have you ever seen a Jewish actress? Greta Garbo—does she look Jewish to you? Elvire Popesco, is she Jewish? Gaby Morlay, is she a Jew? That's not a job for us!"

"What about Rachel, wasn't she Jewish?" Grandma Mathilde set the bait.

"Rachel, Rachel … that's ancient history."

"But Papa, why isn't it a profession for us?"

"Tss. Those actresses are all shiksas. How do they say it? Every one of them is a cooker."

"I think you mean 'hooker,' Maurice," observed Grandma Mathilde with her deadpan humor, removing a cake crumb from the corner of her mouth.

"That's what I meant, hooker! My daughter is not a hooker. Theater is all well and good, very high-tone, Racine is a great man, but it's not for my daughter. My daughter is going to be like nice French girls from good families: she's going to study at a *lycée*. Not the local elementary school, mind you, a *lycée*, and then she'll become a teacher or lawyer. A teacher is better, it's more decent for a girl than spending time around thieves and murderers. Then she'll marry a good Jew and they'll give me lots of beautiful grandchildren. You think you're going to have children if you're an actress? What kind of normal husband would marry a woman who kisses other men on stage? What Jew would want a wife who sleeps with directors to get parts—a *schande*, a shameful girl?"

Everyone agreed—case closed. Sometimes a person who was not a family member, a neighbor, most often, or even Grandma Mathilde in her better days, persisted in asking, "Why do you want to be an actress?" "I want to act, I want to be famous," Bérénice answered spontaneously. Now, that was Grandma Mathilde's favorite moment. "Famous? Tss. Landru is also famous." The girl looked daggers at her, wounded by that sacrilegious comparison. Landru! A serial killer! She talked art, and her grandmother answered with crime. Adults were always asking the stupidest questions. Did she know why she wanted to be an actress? Why worry about that? Do they ask water why it's wet? The real question, the one that actually mattered, was why everyone else did *not* want to be an actor. Or maybe grownups were just lying. Frankly, who didn't want to appear on a movie screen with a beautiful face in black and white? Showing up in newsreels swathed in a thick fur coat under which you can just glimpse a gorgeous dress, definitely waking up late and drinking champagne, having at your disposal an automobile with a chauffeur, a country home and servants, being adored by all, getting recognized in the street, receiving hundreds of letters and signing autographs ... Could a school teacher aspire to that? Better to die than work in a humdrum job, Bérénice promised herself. She, she would be a star: the great Bérénice Capet, more sassy than Louise Brooks, more divine than Greta Garbo, more of a femme fatale than Marlene Dietrich.

While waiting for glory, like all children, she mugged in front of the mirror, draping herself in a bath towel to pretend she was wearing a Roman toga, posing for imaginary photos. I think this is my best profile. Would you light a cigarette for me? In the recess yard, she always kept the best role for herself and directed her friends; while in class, she was the first to volunteer to recite lessons at the blackboard. Unlike her friends, who were eager to rush through any required recitations, and regularly butchered La Fontaine or Ronsard with their choppy diction, she took her time from the day when she heard it said that the mistake of the inexperienced was not to respect silences; she projected her voice so that she could be heard at the back of the classroom, speaking with the proper "intonation," and sometimes even "making gestures." Her teachers were thrilled: "20 out of 20, thank you, Mademoiselle, you may take your seat again." She was so happy to make use of her talents in front of a live audience that she ended up overdoing it, gladly hamming it up, as in that memorable version of "The Cicada and the Ant" that became in her rendition a humorous ditty more epic than the death of Roland at Roncevaux, till the news of her performance made the rounds of the school and she had to do a private encore for the headmistress. That year they even asked her to recite poems for the graduation ceremony. Her father beamed with pride, seeing her in a little white dress reciting "How Good Are the Poor" by Victor Hugo without making a single mistake, in front of all the notables of the neighborhood and even the local deputy mayor, who had donned his tricolor sash.

Yes, at school she had a much better audience than at home. At home, the spectators consisted of furs that she pinched from the shop, all lined up on her bed, in her room. "Come here, Colette, I want to introduce you to my admirers. There, in the first row, is Monsieur Fox Stoll. You see those puppy dog eyes? That's because he's so in love with me, he comes to clap for me every evening and brings hundreds of white lilies when he visits my dressing room. I don't dare tell him that their aroma makes me sneeze, I don't want to hurt his feelings. To his right is Madame Astrakhan Pillbox, you know, the drama critic. So harsh ... She always finds something to comment on—when it's not the lights, it's my way of walking or the script that she finds wanting ... You know she just uses her pen to get revenge because she doesn't have any talent of her own, but she's so influential one can't ban her from the theater. There, in the box, right in front, Monsieur and Madame Beaver Coat, an elderly bourgeois couple, always dressed to the nines. One suspects that they only attend plays to be seen; to tell the truth, the theater puts them to sleep, the husband is always stifling a yawn, the woman is thinking of her next meal, and they never have anything to say after a performance that seems original or even intelligent. Oh, I almost forgot, in the presidential box, Princess Ermine Cape. Yes, of course, the Italian princess, the divorcée. Despite her scandalous life, she has a true passion for the theater. They say she has hundreds of photographs signed by Jacques Copeau, Louis Jouvet, Charles Dullin, Henry Bernstein ... all the theater greats."

Yes, you laugh, you think this calling is trivial, the game of a child with a vivid imagination. Maybe. Maybe, in fact, this calling would only have been a flash in the pan if it hadn't been fed by a combustible material more powerful than these dreams of glory tinted by narcissism. Her true calling materialized differently, and somewhat later, at age eight.

An elderly client of her parents, the elegant Madame de Lignières, a resident of the very chic 7th Arrondissement when she wasn't staying at her chateau in the Loire Valley, knowing Bérénice's dream of becoming an actress and wanting to thank her for a small service she had done, invited her to the Comédie-Française for her eighth birthday. For days before, they had lectured to the child about how to behave at the theater and not embarrass her family. No Kapeluchnik, not even a Valabrègue (her mother's family), had ever set foot in the House of Molière. She had to promise to tell them every detail: what dresses the women were wearing, and their hats, and the chandeliers, and the gold leaf on the walls, I've heard they even have a peanut gallery up at the top, is that true? The warnings that Bérénice had to act like a lady were multiplied many times over since they had no idea what the proper etiquette was in a theater. For the occasion, they bought Bérénice a fashionable dress, in navy blue satin taffeta cut in the flapper mode. "It cost an arm and a leg, but she can always use it on holidays," her father insisted, to excuse this folly. It took many hours to straighten her long mane of brown hair and discipline it into two braids rolled up and solidly pinned to each side of her head. "A real princess!" commented Grandma Mathilde.

June 4, 1927, the Théâtre-Français was performing Alfred de Musset's *Lorenzaccio*. When she saw that the role of Lorenzo was to be played by a certain Marie-Thérèse Piérat, Bérénice burst out, "A man's part played by a woman! That's just stupid!" But she didn't maintain that know-it-all attitude for long. Was it the architecture of the hall designed by Victor Louis, the red curtain with its noble folds, the cupola painted by Albert Besnard? What she experienced at the Comédie-Française was akin to the writer Paul Claudel's fabled conversion at Notre-Dame Cathedral. The only thing that mattered was that sensation, terribly strong and simple at the same time—the fact that she was in her element and it felt good.

She no longer wanted to speak. Her hands became damp, thinking of the actors who were about to enter the stage, who were just a couple of steps away, in the wings, preparing, maybe even peeking out through a hole in the curtain at the hall filling up little by little. She was with them, by their side, their stage fright was hers, too. Without even realizing it, she had imbued these red and gold surroundings with the aura of the sacred. From then on, the world was divided in two: on one side, the priests of the theater—the righteous assembly of ministers, composed of the performers—on the other side, the infidels: those people around her fanning themselves with their programs, chatting about hats and hairdressers, dinners around town, the auto show at the Grand Palais …

Madame de Lignières was surprised when she looked at her, hardly recognizing the voluble little girl that she was used to seeing at the shop. A sort of religious awe had settled over Bérénice. If she had been asked at that moment to leave her seat, she would simply not have been capable of it: it's as if a force held her there, firmly attached.

When the lights dimmed and the first lines sprang forth, it was just the opposite. She had to violently restrain herself from jumping onto the stage and speaking instead of the actors. Her desire to set foot on the stage was so intense that several times she was afraid she couldn't control it: what would happen if, in spite of herself, she started to speak out loud? What a scandal! And yet, it would be so easy, it would just take one word, one gesture … and bam!—there she would be on stage.

She was so absorbed that she paid very little attention to the décor and the costumes. Yet they were splendid, remarked Madame de Lignières to her during the intermission—she seemed to like the direction of Émile Fabre, the executive director of the Comédie-Française. While the elegant, elderly woman greeted her acquaintances in the lobby, Bérénice preferred to stay in the theater, walking up toward the stage, observing the musicians tuning their instruments. It was with a sort of superstitious fear that she dared to run her hand over the crushed velvet framing the pit. Tears rose to her eyes. It seemed to her that the velvet was transmitting to her a magical fluid, that it was going to speak to her to explain the mysteries she was discovering. But the audience returned, she had to go back to her seat. The last act went by in a cottony haze. When her parents pressed her with questions on her return home, she responded mechanically, feeding them only the scraps of information she had gathered from the program or remarks made by Madame de Lignières that she had memorized without realizing it. They say that Marie Bell covers herself in jewels in real life. They claim she said, "I can't be a bourgeoise with only one pearl necklace—I need twenty." The family had a good laugh at that. Twenty necklaces! Tss, how extravagant! Bérénice hoped the interrogation would end there.

She almost succeeded, in a little while they would let her go to sleep, since, after all, it was quite late, she could be alone in her room, bring some order to her thoughts, to review the evening and envision her future seriously, tomorrow she'd talk to Colette about it, together they would cook up a plan, everything would be easier from then on, when suddenly, someone—she couldn't remember who—maybe her grandmother, always hitting the nail on the head, unless it was someone else who just innocently wanted information and didn't intend any harm, someone asked the question she was dreading: "Do you want to go back?" *No*, she heard herself say forcefully, afraid of the volume of her own voice. *No!*

That's it, it's over, *mazel tov*! she's not interested anymore, her parents congratulated each other, it wasn't a mistake to let her go. Fight fire with fire, as they say. Bérénice was dumbfounded by the force with which she said no, by the intensity of her refusal when all she hoped for was to go back. Something vaguely told her that she couldn't repeat that pain of sitting in the theater without the possibility of going on stage. She didn't know yet how or when, even less what roles and what path to take, but she knew her place was there.

· 4 ·

Knowing where you want to end up doesn't necessarily mean you have any idea how to get there. Of course she'd heard of that institution called the Conservatory, but at age eight, she didn't have any clue how you got in. Her confidant, Colette, though she was clever, even brazen, didn't know any more than she did. While waiting, the certainty that a day would come when something, someone would change her life, allowed her to remain true to her hopes. With that determination of ambitious children who never doubt for a second that the world will be favorable and shining for them, Bérénice got it into her head to read every single play she could lay her hands on. She regularly bought plays with her modest savings, she borrowed them from the library of Colette's parents or took them out from the school's collection. Always with a play in hand, learning the texts by heart, training her memory, only breathing through the theater: that was Bérénice's childhood. Her parents knit their brows again, finding this passion much longer lasting than the usual infatuations of children, but they saw one advantage in it: it was a tranquil passion.

Bérénice began methodically, which is to say in chronological order. First the classics, Molière, Racine, Corneille, and even those forgotten ones like poor Rotrou, whose complete works she found at school. After that, Voltaire and the romantics, Hugo, Musset, Dumas, and finally, more contemporary playwrights: François Coppée, Porto-Riche, Henry Bernstein, and Jean

Giraudoux. She won't tell her grandchildren or even her children, "Oh, you're still too young, my little ones, my munchkins, to know all these names, but those writers were very important back then, and their works were performed all the time." She won't explain to them that sometimes she had to deviate from the strict rules she'd imposed on herself, that she depended on a variety of sources, and her method escaped them, but she still couldn't afford to turn up her nose at them.

Instead of the usual hobbies collecting stamps or butterflies, Bérénice began to assemble all the press clippings that should could glean about the Comédie-Française. Each article, each photo was meticulously cut out and pasted in a large scrapbook where she had traced on the label on the cover, in beautiful, round letters: Comédie-Française. The names of the performers soon held no secrets for her. She kept up to date on the company's personnel: the newcomers who had just signed their first contract, the principal actors who were retiring, the ones promoted to principal actor. Some day, it would be her, perhaps … She memorized the terms used at the theater and Colette tested her on her newfound knowledge. The head was called the executive director. The dean was the longest-standing principal actor of the company. The board of directors was composed of tenured members, including the dean. They were called into session by the general administrator and they were consulted on all questions that the latter judged important for them to consider. That committee decided on the nomination of new members, the distribution of the company's shares, examined the budget and the accounts, made decisions on the termination of contracts.

Bérénice's greatest pleasure, when she visited the home of Colette's parents, was to immerse herself in Le Figaro, whose pages on the theater she considered to be much more informative than those of Le Populaire, the paper her father bought. If Maurice Capel had known that his daughter devoured that "right-wing rag," that "fascist mouthpiece," he would really have scolded her! But what a treat to discover the judgments of the drama critics on their evenings at the Comédie-Française, the quotes from the starlets, the chronicle of Paris's theatrical life. And those were also new treasures to paste into her scrapbook.

During those years, she gave herself a solid foundation in drama, entirely confined to books, since she never attended the theater. Her parents never went and she rejected all the invitations of Madame de Lignières, who finally gave up asking her. Though she could recite the entire biography of the actress Marie Ventura by heart and knew everything about her Romanian origins, the names of her professors at the Conservatory, the roles she first appeared in, if she assiduously followed the career of René Alexandre or the latest about the dean, Dessonnes, she only knew of them what the critics said or what photos could convey. Their voices, their tone, their diction, their gestures? She relied on her imagination to create them. Cécile Sorel, Berthe Bovy, Colonna Romano, Béatrice Bretty, Georges Leroy, Jean Yonnel, André Brunot—these names, in her highly flammable imagination, acceded to the level of demigods, mythological figures braving the limelight just as Ulysses or Hector slew the cyclops or enemy armies, acclaimed and crowned with laurels at the end of performances like triumphant heroes returning from an epic battle.

Unconscious onomastics made her imagine the denizens of the House of Molière in a highly personal way. The honorary principal actor, Raphaël Duflos, surrounded by the angelic aura of his given name and with his family name redolent of flowing liquid, seemed to her one of the seraphim with blond curls as luminous as those of Venus rising from her scallop. Madame Segond-Webern sounded so Second Empire. She seemed like an old lady, a bit rigid and severe, her clothing retrieved from an out-of-fashion armoire—maybe she still wore crinoline. Charles Le Bargy? No doubt an old gent behaving bizarrely but always with class, owing to his "y"! If Bérénice had met these characters in the flesh, she would have been as astonished as when one discovers how an announcer on the radio actually looks.

One day she finally resolved to do something, so she got up the nerve to phone the Conservatory. This was no mean feat, since it had to be planned far in advance, down to the smallest detail. First she had to go to the home of Colette, whose parents had a telephone, then she had to find the exchange of the Conservatory in the phone book ("Yes, of course, my sweet peas, you don't even know what a telephone exchange is, back then, telephones were very different …"—But of course, Bérénice never said that to her grandchildren, or even her children, she couldn't), then wait till the adults left them alone in proximity of the phone, post Colette on guard duty, and finally not stammer while reading the script that she had prepared, since she was so terribly afraid: "Hello, Madame, am I speaking with the Conservatory of Music and Dramatic Arts, please?" By chance, on the other end of the line was a secretary who was well acquainted with the history of that institution and with the rules, an elderly woman, to judge from her voice, who no doubt, in order to answer with such authority had worked in those noble halls since the dawn of time, and dredged out of her impeccable memory the case of Béatrix Dussane, an actress who was admitted through the entrance examination at the age of fourteen in 1902 and left with a first prize only one year later. "My hopes are possible, then," said Bérénice, delighted. "There's not much longer to wait, fourteen years old, that's a lot closer than twenty-one, when you're legally an adult." Meanwhile, other information gleaned during the course of this phone conversation and gathered from the same erudite lips plunged Bérénice into despair: to take the examination, a minor had to have parental permission. What dunces, what idiots, how naïve they had been! To think that she and Colette had imagined, that they had foolishly thought they could show up at the Conservatory and enroll Bérénice just like that, by themselves, without her parents! It was no good. Useless for her to put on makeup, wear high heels—she could never pass for an adult.

Wait, and then wait some more. At fourteen, she decided to reveal her plan to her father. Fourteen years old, that was serious, and then there was a prec-edent, there was Béatrix Dussane. The entire week before she intended to ask him, she was absolutely charming, ate everything on her plate, even the beets she detested, she pretended to be interested when her father placed his orders, she helped her mother with the cooking, she came home punctually right after school. "Papa, I have a little question I'd like to ask you," she ventured slyly.

"Oy, *a broch*! She's at it again! Life is difficult enough if you've got a reli-able profession, have you even noticed that we don't have as many clients since the Depression started? Rising unemployment—does that ring a bell? Who is this Béatrix Dussane? Who the heck is she? What the hell does that goy have to do with me? If she wants to act like a shiksa, that's her problem." Bérénice didn't listen to the rest, his usual refrain about Maurice Capel the martyr, how expensive life was, children's ingratitude, the professions for Jews and the professions for the goyim, decency and shame—she knew every argu-ment by heart. Farewell to her dreams of the Conservatory, the glories of the theater. So, she would have to wait till she reached the venerable age of her majority.

Dismal years flowed by where nothing happened, a degree obtained fairly brilliantly, but which, far from giving her pleasure, worried her because it forced her to decide. Her father insisted that she begin serious studies, he spoke to her more and more often about a teaching credential, extolling the advantages of the profession. "A civil servant—now that's a serious profes-sion." Then what? Scrape by till she turned twenty-one? And in the mean-time? She could no longer do what she did at age eight, arranging the fox stoles and mink pillbox hats on her bed to make them her spectators. She needed a real audience, she needed professors to instruct her, she needed friends to stimulate her. Many times she thought about running away, but it wouldn't solve her problem of having a legal guardian to enroll her in the Conservatory. Maybe there was a solution, but she couldn't see one, and no one could help her. Even for Grandma Mathilde, who was quick to stir up trouble and thumb her nose at her son-in-law, the idea of her granddaughter having a career as an actress might have been even more shocking to her than to him. She came from a different century, after all, where women stayed at home and kept silent. Bérénice ended up convincing her grandmother to act as her ambassador, which resulted in an epic battle, but the only result was that her father dug his heels in a little deeper. True to form, Maurice Kapeluchnik was even more stubborn than his daughter.

The worst was the summer of 1934. The Capels didn't have enough money to go on vacation at a resort on the Riviera like Colette's parents, Bérénice had to stay in Paris where idleness, exacerbated by the heat, provoked thoughts of suicide or murder. Then one morning, when she was leaving the bakery, she ran into Madame de Lignières. In a confidential moment, she unburdened herself of all her sorrows, speaking too quickly, wanting to pour everything out at once, stammering with emotion—without realizing that her whole wheat bread was dusting her dress with flour. The elegant aristocrat was surprised to hear all this. When Madame de Lignières realized the violence of that passion she thought had spent itself, Bérénice's intensity moved her: "The first thing we have to do is to find a theater professional to listen to you. Give me a few days, let me think about it."

Less than a week later, this unexpected ally found a pretext to come by the shop and take Bérénice aside. "Why didn't I think of this before? You know I live on the Rue Barbet-de-Jouy. Would you believe that, not long ago, a member of the Comédie-Française moved right nearby? She's agreed to see you. I made an appointment for you for a week from Wednesday."

Véra Korène. The gorgeous Véra Korène, a member of the Comédie-Française since 1931, after she was hired at the Odéon Theater by no less than Firmin Gémier himself. The leading role in Louis Valray's film *La Belle de nuit*, playing opposite the famous Aimé Clariond. Véra Korène … An enigmatic and fascinating beauty who seemed the very incarnation of "The Passerby" in Baudelaire's poem. A long and supple body, with an aloofness in her expression, dominated by those enormous and mysterious eyes—in short, a vamp. Would she be as stunning as the photos in Bérénice's scrapbook?

In the wrap-around apartment on the fashionable Rue Barbet-de-Jouy, Véra Korène was not merely an icon who appeared in fan magazines, or a flat face on a movie poster, even less a mere name which, in any case, was only borrowed, her real name being Wiera Koretzsky. A butler had ushered them into this opulent living room scented with lilies, roses, and jasmine, revealing Véra Korène lounging on a blue velvet hassock. Her pose was so elegant! Her gestures were so graceful! While Bérénice looked on in admiration, the statue came to life, the woman breathed, giving off a fragrance with a subtle, peppery aroma, she spoke: "Do you know what my little niece just said to me? 'Aunt Véra thinks she's always right because she talks louder than anyone else!' Now there's a lesson in humility for an actress!"

Bérénice didn't know how to respond. For the first time, she was going to recite a text in front of a professional. What terror when she realized that her right leg was trembling and she couldn't stop it. She discovered stage fright, the panic of forgetting one's lines, the savage desire for a fire to break out to prevent the show from going on.

It passed. She acted her scene and the emotions surged back to her, her face was on fire. Bérénice was so agitated she could barely concentrate on the conversation between Madame de Lignières and Véra Korène, had no idea how she'd done, hardly heard the words, "a natural," and "original," and also something about her voice, "astonishingly serious." With a huge effort, she managed to overhear, "I'm joking, but I understand you much better than you think. Imagine! My parents wanted me to go into medicine. My brother was taking advanced classes in physics and chemistry, my sister was at the conservatory studying classical piano, and I was supposed to become a famous doctor! Can you believe it! I often go to the doctor now, but a doctor of the seventeenth century, on stage, in plays by Molière! You can't imagine what obstacles my parents put in my way to keep me from going on the stage. If they were finally persuaded to let me take my chances at the entrance exam for the Conservatory, it's because they were sure I was going to fail!" Bérénice's eyes were shining. Now she had an idea.

· 5 ·

The Capel family lived in a working-class neighborhood in the 10th Arrondissement, near the Faubourg Poissonnière, the nerve center of the fur industry. A small, dark courtyard of the apartment building on the Rue d'Hauteville: upper-class women whose purposeful look indicates they didn't just wander in. They knew that on the fourth floor of this building, a lowly tenement made grimy by time, was the shop of Monsieur Capel, a furrier who worked out of his home—alterations, repairs, dyeing. His ability to find the most beautiful pieces, his skill at trimming the pelts into long strips, the quality of his finishes, and his punctuality with deliveries had all made his reputation. He also knew all of his clients' habits, and how they could become outright liars when it came to walking away without paying for their orders. To protect himself, he made them sign the pelts they had selected. If there was ever a dispute, he merely unstitched the linings—their initials betrayed them.

Monsieur Capel loved to tell Bérénice about his work, how he chose the pelts, matched the colors, taking the time to assemble the pieces, savoring this task that he compared to a puzzle: "Look, you think this jacket is made all from one hide, when actually it's made up of lots of different ones. See this—I'm picking out sections with hairs that are the same thickness, ones that have the same shade. The most difficult part is the flanks, the edges of the pelt, because the skin is thinner over here and lighter over there."

He was less fond of making the cloth pattern used to shape a particular style. More often it was Esther who took charge of that. Then he gave the skins to a master craftsman who styled the furs to the clients' specifications. When there was a great deal of demand, a flood of orders, Monsieur Capel added two or three workers he paid by the piece. At those times you could hear the noise of nails they hammered to shape the hides. That day, no extra workers were needed: in summer, work stopped altogether: the studio serving only as a storage place for coats. Unaccustomed to idleness, Madame Capel kept busy sewing scraps of mink that she used to trim winter coats. Seated at the serger machine, she focused on the tweezers that she used to push back the hairs of the fur between two pieces she was sewing together, while Monsieur Capel, at his desk, was grimacing at his oversized accounts book. He hated bookkeeping.

When that brilliant member of the Comédie-Française, the beautiful Véra Korène, appeared in the studio of Maurice Capel, he understood right away what was going on. Her name was already familiar to him: Bérénice had often spoken to him about her to prove that actresses who were Jewish could become respectable members of the Comédie-Française. Despite the honor of receiving this beautiful woman in his shop—he could already hear his neighbors saying how impressed they were—he barely gave her time to greet him. And to top it off, he put on his outraged patriarch act, the Maurice Kapeluchnik routine, somehow rediscovering his Yiddish accent that he accentuated to the max:

"You think I don't know why you're here, Madame Korène? My harebrained daughter has probably made you take pity on her. I bet she played on your sympathies, I bet she told you I was born in Russia, just like you. I know my daughter, all right, she probably pestered you like crazy, reciting poems for you. With the chutzpah she's got, she probably roped you into pleading her case: 'Please, please, Madame Korène, help me convince my father to let me try out for the Conservatory.' And I'm sure you're going to tell me she's very talented. You're going to tell me it would be a pity for the theater to lose such a promising talent. You're going ..."

"Tsk, tsk, tsk, how you go on, Monsieur Capel," the beautiful Véra Korène shot back. "But you're so far off the mark."

Despite all his arrogance and his self-possession, Maurice Capel lost his composure. He tried to catch his wife's attention, hoping to understand where his analysis had gone wrong:

"No? You didn't come here to ..."

"I admit, your daughter did let me know about her artistic ambitions. I listened to her attentively … and I agree she has some good qualities."

"Ah hah! I told you."

"Child, would you run out and buy me a pack of cigarettes at the corner store? That would be sweet of you. I forgot mine at home. Here's some money. Listen, Monsieur Capel, I like you, and now that we're alone, I'm going to be completely honest with you. Your daughter has a certain kind of self-confidence that can give the illusion of authority. She has an interesting physique, a fine temperament, an indisputable sincerity, but I'll put it to you bluntly: it takes more than that to succeed in the theater."

"You think she doesn't have the talent?"

"No."

"Even though she got twenty out of twenty on her recitations?" Monsieur Capel ventured, now a bit wounded, the proud father. "She was chosen to speak at graduation before some very *highly* respected officials."

"Of course, a school assembly, that's all well and good, but the theater demands loftier qualities. These young people think that their passion for the theater is enough to enthrall an audience, but with bland articulation, tense hands, stiff posture—try acting for two-and-a-half hours like that."

"She could learn!"

"That would not suffice. Her voice is too weak. Technique isn't everything, you know, the overall appearance one is born with counts for a lot in this profession, and the competition is so stiff … To make such an effort and obtain only a mediocre result—is it really worth the trouble?"

"*Nu, nu,* I trust you, after all, you're a professional, but … I hope you handled all this delicately? She's only fifteen, you know."

"Oh, I know that, dear Monsieur Capel. As a woman, one senses these things."

"I'm embarrassed. She must have made an awful nuisance of herself. Really, you didn't have to go to all the trouble of coming here."

"Let's just say that … Look, she believes I came here to speak to you, the way you described at the beginning of our conversation in order to … well, you know—the Conservatory. She's got it into her head that she just has to go there and I'm afraid that she might break with you irreconcilably if you prevent her from even trying out."

"That's actually what I had in mind—now even more so. I don't want her to be ridiculed."

"Certainly not. But think about it …" Pause, readjusts her veil, glances at him out of the corner of her eye: "… ridicule never killed anyone."

"Ri-ri-ridi …" stuttered Monsieur Capel, who was starting to catch her drift.

"So, my dear Monsieur Capel, let her take her exam! She'll fail the first time, but at least you won't be responsible for having clipped her wings. She'll understand she's not cut out for the profession, and in time, she'll forget all about it."

"Oh, I see you come from the same place we do! A *yiddische kopf*! Isn't she, Esther? Ah, here are your cigarettes. Can we get you anything else? Some tea, coffee, or maybe a shot of something hard?"

"No, thank you, I'm in a bit of a hurry."

"Of course, of course. Thank you so much, Madame Korène, if you need anything at all for the winter: a stole, a pillbox hat, a muff … I have a magnificent fox that just came in …"

A few days later, Monsieur Capel himself accompanied his daughter to 14, Rue de Madrid to enroll her for the admission exam to the National Conservatory of Music and Dramatic Arts.

· 6 ·

One classic scene, and one modern scene. That's what Bérénice had to perform at the November entrance competition. She didn't have a partner, but
she was assured she could find one that day—a second- or third-year student
who would give Bérénice her cues. What text to choose? Véra Korène had
suggested scenes from *Don't Fool with Love* and *Iphigenia* that leant themselves
to virtuoso performances. "Great classics, with material that can shine, even
without experience, but be careful, it's all or nothing: a good reading can win
the day. On the other hand, the jury can be more severe with these show-stopper
bits that they've heard a thousand times. Watch out for the bell ringing!" The
bell ringing? Bérénice learned that the jury could use that to stop a candidate's
performance, sometimes after only one verse. The bell meant they showed you
the door.

July, August, September, October. Four months to prepare, without ever
taking a course or attending a class at the Conservatory or following the custom of the aspiring actor presenting a scene in front of each of the professors
to get their suggestions before the competition for admission. Bérénice only
had Véra Korène's few directions, her own will to succeed, and her faith in her
lucky star. "After all, to get here Papa somehow crossed Russia almost entirely
on foot," she sometimes told herself for encouragement. End of August, the
faithful Colette, back from vacation, helped her rehearse her lines: "When

you say, 'Is your love like money, that it can pass from hand to hand until it dies?' it seems to me that ... that ... you can't say it any more truthfully than that, you know? Camille—it's simple—you *are* her. You own the part!"

Finally that Monday in November 1934 arrived, the day of the competition for admission to the Conservatory. Approximately two hundred candidates were there to try their luck, just as she was. The number actually reassured her—so she wasn't alone in being drawn to this profession. Mothers accompanied their children, smothering them with suggestions, straightening their limp collars, taming their rebellious hair. Neither her mother nor her father had made the trip, only the indispensable Colette was there to support her friend. She was the one who had counseled her on what she should eat in the morning to avoid sudden fatigue, she was the one who loaned her the outfit that she declared appropriate for an audition: a black skirt topped by a pale blue blouse that brought out her large, light eyes. She was also the one who did her hair, and Bérénice didn't realize how much her black hair with a virginal part in the middle made her look like a Madonna. Yes, a painting by Leonardo, except for her nerves, far from the serenity of young Italian virgins.

In the general commotion, it was Colette again who succeeded in finding a student to give Bérénice her cues. A second-year pupil of André Brunot, he introduced himself, proclaiming with a military air: "Name: Robert Manuel. Age: nineteen. Profession: second-year student, first honorable mention in July for Uladislas in Musset's *Barberine* and Lauriane in Courteline's *The Idiot*. Pleased to meet you, Mademoiselle!" His beaming face and his social skills spurred Colette to ask him to help Bérénice. He accepted without hesitation, hoping after the audition to share—at least!—a coffee with the two young ladies. "Honey, let me fill you in!" he began, but Bérénice ran to the women's room for the third time that morning and threw up what remained of the café au lait and croissants in her stomach.

When she reappeared in the entrance hall, saturated with sweat and nerves, Colette looked for her, concerned. "One more ahead of you and then it's your turn!" Panicked, Bérénice hurried into the small space that served as a waiting room. Her hands were cold and clammy, her fingernails had turned purple. Through the half-open door she caught a glimpse of the room where the competition was taking place, a promised land she was so happy to gain entry to, despite her stage fright, that she idealized the décor, finding stylish the antiquated pomp of *The Oath of the Horatii* hanging on the wall, and the grandeur of the lugubrious, garnet velvet that framed the windows.

Her turn. Catastrophe! Just before her entrance on stage, the announcer mixes up the names and the title of the play in a hot mess: "*Don't Fool with the Stove*, by Alfred Manuel, with Bérénice Musset and Robert Capet." She is appalled by the announcer's frivolous tone, which to her is a high crime and misdemeanor of the theater. With a squeeze of the hand, her comrade tries to make her understand that she shouldn't worry, chiding himself for not having warned her that the announcer often made that sort of blunder. As if the immense horseshoe-shaped table where the renowned actor/director Louis Jouvet was seated was not imposing enough! Who had the right to be so sloppy when she was staking her whole life on this role? What a nightmare: the muddle caused by the announcer makes the jury smile, she hears their stifled laughter, she spots their mocking glances. The outsized mouths of the members of the jury are drawing nearer to her in a frightening way, they spit in her face their bursts of sardonic laughter, making fun of her right before her eyes. All is lost. They aren't taking her seriously, they're going to send her packing, tell her that her place is not here but in the fur shop, with her father Maurice Capel, she can already hear the bell, ding ding ding ding ding ding. That can't be, she hasn't done all this for nothing. The Comédie-Française sticker on her binder whirls before her eyes and then she stands up straight, disdaining their laughter, so out of place within these sacred walls. With authority, she lets fly the first words: "Lift your head, Perdican! Who is the man who believes in nothing?" Not one of them thought again of laughing.

At the end of these two scenes, as in Véra Korène's living room, the emotion that seizes her is so violent that she can no longer see anything, hear anything. She isn't aware of the surprised expression of her partner, she can't plumb the depth of the jury's silence. She can think of only one thing: "They didn't ring the bell."

As it was every evening, the Rue d'Hauteville was full of the clatter of dish-washing and the odors of cooking, and as it did every evening, it exhaled a sweetish aroma, a mixture of onions and vegetable soup. The office clerk who lived on the second floor had just turned his key in the lock, the space-heater salesman on the fifth floor had parked his bicycle in the courtyard, the common folk of Paris had put on their slippers and were anticipating that night's dinner.

On the third floor, in the Capels' apartment, Maurice was ensconced in his favorite armchair, reading the newspaper brought by his errand boy who went downstairs every day to buy two irreconcilable publications: the left-wing *Le Populaire* for his boss, and the ultra-right *Action française* for himself. As was his custom, Maurice took a devilish pleasure in saying that his assistant handed him the socialist newspaper as if it was poison. He nudged his wife with his elbow and then plunged into reading the speech that Blum, the leader of the Socialists, had given in Narbonne. A shame that Bérénice missed that, he would tell her all about it when she got home, that would give her a good little laugh. Not Blum's speech—he knew she didn't give a damn, but the errand boy's irritated expression—now that was funny!

Maurice Capel was looking through the classifieds: he read them conscientiously, line by line, in order to prolong reading the newspaper. Esther had finished preparing dinner just a moment ago, the table was set, they were only waiting for Bérénice. In order to get a head start on the next day, Madame Capel took her sewing box and set herself the task of darning her husband's socks, but her thoughts were elsewhere, she had definitely noticed that Maurice was stealing glances at the clock more and more frequently. Finally he couldn't stand it anymore:

"She doesn't have the courage to come home. She must be so ashamed that she doesn't have the courage to come home."

"Maybe you should just have forbidden her to enter that competition. What if she did something foolish?" asked Esther, soothed at finally being able to pour out her heart.

"She had to find out for herself. That's how you learn, by making mistakes. Look, when I was a kid, my father knew I was going to fall out of the tall cherry tree in front of our house, but he let me do what I had to. I climbed, I climbed, I was so proud of myself, I thought I was a *mensch*, and then I fell and I understood."

"I know, I know, you've told me that story a hundred times. But with girls it's different, especially Bérénice."

"Tss, what can we do now? The damage is done."

They fall silent again. He resumes reading the classifieds, but honestly, does he really need a 40 RENAULT 1,200 to 2,500 kilograms, vans and chassis you can haul away low price, or a moving sale Gaveau grand PIANO moderately priced?

"How about baking her favorite cake tonight?"

She sighed: a cake, that's more work, it's really too late to start baking, to light the stove … Fine, a cake, why not?

She went into the kitchen, dragging her feet. What a worry children are! Oy yoy yoy, why does Bérénice have such strange ideas? None of the other children I know wants to go on the stage, why did this have to befall our daughter? What did we do to our God to deserve this? It's not in this cabinet, it must be in the other. Oy! Where did I put that cake pan? This one's too big, it's for brioches, I need the other one. The Feuerstein girl, she's not as pretty as Bérénice, she doesn't act out any dramas, she's happy she'll take over her parents' grocery store when she grows up, here it is I found it how did I manage to put it there I must be losing my mind, and the Zussman girl who wears those funny round glasses she's a good student, with a little luck, she could become a secretary, even Colette who's a real Frenchwoman, she doesn't want to go on stage she wants to be a hat maker, hats are refined, they're fun, they're useful, but the theater, that's not a job. What a crazy idea that was to call our daughter

Bérénice, that stuffed her head full of strange ideas, I never liked that name, no one in my family ever had a name like that, you never saw a Bérénice Valabrègue, that Racine, with his *goyishe* name, he could choose whatever name he liked for his books but us, why would we need to call our daughter a name like that? When she was born, I said yes to please Maurice, he should be more careful, he's getting too big for his britches, something could happen to him, *vey ist mir*, that's all we need, what would happen to us without him? it put crazy ideas into her head to be named Bérénice, how many eggs do you need again, I always forget, I get it confused with challah, what could she possibly like in those cock-and-bull stories? The other day when I secretly tried to read *Iphigenia*, it had fallen under her bed, all those books she reads, I realized that's what's riling up her brain, who can believe in those stories of gods and tempests, and all those characters with difficult names you can't remember, 150 grams of flour, 300 grams of sugar, how do you even pronounce it, Chalcas or Calcas, how would I know, I was ashamed to ask Bérénice, she would have made fun of me, kids today, they don't respect their parents the way we did, I have to remember to clean the windows tomorrow, my grandmother could make a cake without even glancing at a recipe, she didn't have to measure anything, she knew exactly how much to put in without even looking, she hasn't come home yet, oy! I hope nothing has happened to her, there, not a single lump, it's because I sifted the flour, I can put it in the oven now, ow! that burns, I have to watch Maurice and make sure he doesn't eat too much, he can barely fit into his pants anymore, I don't know how I'm going to keep him in clothes this winter, and his socks too, I've got to buy him some, Madame Zussman told me the Magasins Réunis are having a sale, we should invite my mother for dinner but that's going to create a scene with Maurice, why are things always so complicated here? In other families it's easier the children are nice to their parents, respectful, Bérénice never listens, she only does what she gets it in her head to do, I didn't answer my parents like that, when my mother talked to me I peed my underpants I was so scared, Bérénice laughs when I tell her that, what a shame that I couldn't have more children, I wanted so much to have a son, boys are sweeter to their mothers, just look at that son of Madame Glazer, he always has a kind word for her, he tells her endlessly that she's the most beautiful mother in the world while everyone can see she has a nose as big as a potato and gunky eyes, you can bet she's going to cry tonight, like when she peels onions, I should have told her what Madame Korène said, Maurice didn't want to but it would have prepared her, little by little, we would have told her so nicely and now she left thinking … That Madame

Korène was a real beauty, there it's all ready now, and to think that she came from Russia, Koretzky is her real name but her parents are rich, she's not from some shtetl like Maurice, where is she from again? Baku? No that's not it, I'm getting old, I'm forgetting names, I have to ask Maurice, forty minutes for the cake, I think there was a *k*, and Bérénice not even home yet, she's going to be the death of me, I just hope she didn't do something stupid with those crazy ideas of hers, you never know, Bakhmut, it came back to me, she was born in Bakhmut, I knew there was a *k*. Oy! why is that man coughing? It's those damn cigarettes, I told him a hundred times to stop, it's true she's really beautiful but she's a shiksa who smooches everybody in the movies, her dress must be from Patou but what a strange job, we don't have the means to spend money on clothes like that. Bérénice is also a beauty, it's going to bring the evil eye on us, earlier when she left you would have said a fashion plate with those clothes of Colette, nice girl even if she is a goy, are those flies going to go away, they are keeping nice and warm in the kitchen, and the concierge's dog that never stops barking, don't they ever give it anything to eat Oy, he's coughing again, I'm going to have to tell him to quit smoking, ah, finally, *Gott zei dank*, she's here.

· 8 ·

Bérénice returned to Colette downhearted. Complete disaster: first the mess with the announcer and then, at the emotional climax, she was out of breath, and besides, she had noticed a member of the jury, who before that had remained unmoved, jotting down a few lines in a notepad. "They've killed me, it's all over." Robert Manuel tried to reassure her: "Dear girl, number one, this isn't the first time the announcer has made a mistake like that: for instance, if you had played Mary Tudor, he would have said, 'Mary the Door,' or 'Marry Tutor.' My word of honor, he's done it before! We're so used to it that I didn't even think to warn you. Number two, I assure you that you were superb, a true tragedian. You see, I wanted to be a tragedian, but look at me: I have the soul of Hamlet but the mouth of Scapin. I just have to accept it, I was born to make people laugh, and in the end, it's even harder to make them laugh than to make them cry. In any case, you, you have both the temperament and the looks. I'm not even talking about your voice, which is made for tragedy. You give the verse its fullness—it flows, like honey …"

Poor Robert, who was trying so hard to convince her. She only remembered the flaws in her performance, she went too fast over, "What is the world?" She suddenly recalled having said, "My whole entire life is on my lips," instead of, "My whole life is on my lips." But her new friend wasn't lying to her, he wasn't trying to flatter her, to console her. He knew. Even with only a year's experience, he knew that she had them eating out of her hand, as they say in the business. He knew that her pale beauty, her noble pride, her poetic presence, her musical voice, her inventive acting had pulsed blood into the proud Camille. Of course he also knew how arbitrary a competition could be, even unjust, there were so many other candidates, and the girl, with her ingenuity and wild streak, was disconcerting enough in the way she stood out—enchanting as it was—to displease the more conservative judges.

"It's criminal to make us wait this long, do they want us to have a stroke?" you started to hear from the mouths of the impatient candidates. The minutes ticked away, the wait became more and more nerve-wracking. Bitten nails, lined faces, hysterical laughter, feverishness, and finally, the moment of the results, the doorkeeper posting the lists, the rush to the bulletin board, the name someone thought she saw but didn't actually find, some in tears, distraught faces, others screaming with joy, the happy few selected, looked on with admiration, envy, or hatred. Bérénice was admitted, her name at the top of the list. "I told you, you were a hit," Robert Manuel trumpeted.

They clapped for her, gave her an ovation. Colette cried with joy. They hugged her hard enough to break every bone, they practically carried her in triumph on a chair, like a Jewish wedding. The young fiancée with the sapphire eyes and the face of a Madonna had just married the theater, with all her fervent youth she swore faithfulness and fidelity to her lord and master the theater, today, this red-letter day, her true birthday, this virginal day, inauguration day, she sealed her union with the stage, for better or for worse, but there couldn't be a worse in the theater, she thought, muse of the theater, I pledge myself to you until death do us part, I'm taking the oath, I'm all yours, and if I forget thee may my right hand forget her cunning let my tongue cleave to the roof of my mouth, if I no longer think of you, if I don't put the theater above all other joys. "You're one of the gang now," Robert Manuel declared more prosaically. She was admitted at the top of the list. All hopes are permitted. Top of the list. Her life begins.

She just had to go to a café to celebrate her victory with Robert Manuel, Colette, a few of the other admitted students, her new friends who had also been admitted—she had bonded with them in the blink of an eye, also some older students, ready to chaperone her, to nurture her. Her heart was brimming with joy. Even in her wildest dreams she hadn't imagined that the universe of the theater was so full of joy, the thespians' tables so full of bluster, the anecdotes so juicy, the one about Julie, the daughter of a famous actor, born at ten minutes to eight, just before the curtain went up, so that she could be passed to her father to hold right before his entrance. Or Martin's fatal memory lapse before his first walk-on role on the stage of the Salle Richelieu, his shame when an honorable member of the company indicated with a decided thumbs down that Martin had flopped.

How incredibly different from the conversation with her family or her parents' friends, what a new world, Rue de Madrid. Here camaraderie was king and foretold horizons filled with promise, where you were no longer ashamed to give your life over, to lay bare your doubts, qualities, or faults and then make fun of them, to speak loudly, to say you loved each other and you loved your happiness. Night began to fall, she had to leave this new paradise that welcomed her as the first among its own, she had to go back home, and all the way home, zigzagging, bumping against passersby several times, holding back from screaming with joy, she was tortured by thoughts of whether to reveal her joy to her parents or to fool them into thinking she had failed.

Damn it all! Her intoxicating happiness made her abandon all prudence. Maybe she also wanted to prove to her parents that she had been right to insist. She didn't suspect that the words she was about to speak would weigh heavily in her life, that years later she would ask herself what would have happened if she had minimized her triumph. "I was admitted at the top of the list," she announced to them, radiant. No need to proclaim her success: it was written on her face, a glorious face, luminous with joie de vivre and faith in the future, the glorious face of the chosen.

In the ranks of historic wrath, the wrath of Maurice Kapeluchnik, son of Abraham Kapeluchnik, furrier by profession, and of Myriam Rabinovitch, housewife, must have more or less equaled the wrath that came over Moses when he discovered his people worshiping the golden calf.

"You're not going to the Conservatory—it's out of the question. A schande, a schande. Your mother and I sacrificed so you could go to a lycée, we bought you all the books you asked for, you didn't want for anything. That wasn't so that you could throw it all away lightly on a childish whim."

"Papa, this isn't a childish whim; theater is my life."

"Your life? What do you know about life, at fifteen, you little shit!"

"Fifteen is plenty old enough. Grandma Mathilde was already married at my age."

"Don't talk back to your father! Married? Look at her—you squeeze her nose and milk comes out."

"Your grandparents must be spinning in their graves, Those books of yours must've stuffed your head with weird ideas, You're a slut, Cursèd be the day we named you Bérénice, When we're dead and buried, you'll regret this ..." It was even worse when Maurice Capel understood the trick that Véra Korène had played on them. It was too much for him, this was truly the proof that actresses are worthless, respect nothing, not even the honor due to parents. "On stage, they revel in honor and lofty sentiments, but in real life, actors are worthless—absolutely worthless."

"This is what we raised you for? You're not going to the Conservatory, it's not a profession for a Jew, I've told you that a hundred times."

"Then I'd prefer not to be Jewish."

A slap. A resounding slap with so much force it made her stagger.

"I never would have believed I'd hear that from the mouth of my own daughter. That's how we raised you? I barely escaped getting killed by the Cossacks, I lost my whole family before I came here, the world is full of anti-Semites who only want to get rid of us, and Mademoiselle prefers not to be Jewish? Are you forgetting who you are? My little one, remember well what I'm about to say to you: you don't choose to be Jewish—it's something you carry *in* you."

It was the first time that Monsieur Capel had ever slapped his daughter. Bérénice intuitively understood that the force he put into that slap was not just the physical violence of a man pushed to his limits, it was the entire weight of the lack of understanding between father and daughter, formerly so closely allied, the disappointment of a father who had imagined a different life for his only daughter, a more banal life, assuredly, but decent and without risk, something completely different from this profession of an acrobat, this schnorrer's profession that was not even a profession.

Deeply wounded, she showed herself to be even prouder—unless it was her survival instinct that took over, that made her act, stand up straight and look her father right in the eyes, without a tear, even if that cost her, resolved to stand up to him, sensing that she had to, that it was now or never, that if she didn't have the courage now, she would be defeated, so much so that from now on she had to rebel and take the consequences, whatever they might be, because no punishment would be as bad as not being able to act. Her mother, beside herself, tried clumsily to separate them, putting between them her weak body and the arguments of another era:

"My God, stop it, what will the neighbors think?"

"This discussion is over. Go to bed."

Of course, the cheesecake went untouched.

Of course, Bérénice didn't sleep that night. Of course, the next morning, at breakfast, her first words were about the Conservatory.

"If you go to the Conservatory, you are not my daughter!"

"I'm going."

She was surprised that her father didn't scream at her. He said nothing, which was much more worrisome than anger. Her mother didn't say anything either, but a fleeting glance from her made her daughter realize she was embarrassed. Something was brewing, but what? Not receiving a response, Bérénice decided to move on. She left the room to get ready. When she came back, dressed and with her hair combed, it was when she took her purse off its peg that she started to understand. She was almost certain that she hadn't left her purse like that when she had come home the previous night. She wasn't completely sure because she had been in such an emotional state for the last twenty-four hours, but even so, she wasn't in the habit of leaving the flap of her purse half open. She glanced inside. Obviously …

She walked back to her father: "Did you take my wallet?"

"Absolutely. Just try to leave without any money and without your I.D. Are you forgetting that you're a minor?"

She opened the door.

"I don't give a damn. I'm going."

"You're staying here!" he screamed, positioning himself between her and the door.

"Stop!" cried her mother, trying to separate them.

It's like a scene out of Feydeau, thought Bérénice, who took advantage of the confusion to leave. Outside, the winds of freedom were blowing, outside, the world was red and gold.

"You cursèd child, I disown you! Don't you ever set foot in here again, a shame to our family, shame on you …"

Rrrrrip. The sound of torn fabric. She left, slamming the door behind her. She left in order not have to see anymore the torn jacket, she left in order not to hear the sound of that fabric, to obliterate it with the racket of the door slamming, she had never thought that an article of clothing could make so much noise, she left in order not to hear any more of the terrible insults that her father unleashed on her and that dishonored them, she for receiving them, he for uttering them, she left to stem the torrent of insults and not to think any more of those curses like those of the shtetl butcher against his whore of a daughter who had married a goy, she left in order not to retain that vision of her father in his rage, she left in order not to tarnish the image of her father that she wanted to keep intact despite the misunderstanding that separated them, she ran till her heart felt it would split apart, she took the stairs four at a time, not fast enough not to notice the curious stares of the neighbors watching her leave, not fast enough to not feel the eyes of the whole building spying on her, not fast enough to not hear the whispers commenting on their argument. She guessed her mother would be in a panic about the scandal. For the neighbors who didn't miss one word of the argument with those walls as thin as cigarette paper, her mother would end up making excuses to put a good face on it. *She's the one who's going to act a part*, Bérénice thought, furious, *she'll act the part of a martyr to show how unhappy she is, she'll say everything is fine and no one will believe a word, and at heart, she won't even want them to believe her, she'll want them to pity her.* The girl ran without stopping to the rhythm of the high-speed thoughts hurtling through her head. What to do without money, she didn't even have enough for a metro ticket. She ran to the home of Colette, who would surely lend her a bicycle and a ten-franc bill. There would be time later on to think about how to survive. She ran faster and faster as if her life depended on it. She couldn't be late for the Conservatory.

· 9 ·

The paving stones of this street seem to be magnetized, thought Bérénice. She was back on the Rue de Madrid. It was no longer a dream, from now on the street belonged to her, at least number 14, her student identification card proved it. She was already in love with the half-open casement windows revealing a view of the garden full of blue paulownia trees, the hum of instruments wafting from the music classes enchanted her, from the time she entered her literature class, she felt reborn, forgetting the painful morning, the ripped cloth. Immediately she adored her first day at the Conservatory, even the required class that most of her friends did not have to take. Even that course was more worthwhile than the antiquated curriculum she had endured in high school. Everything about Georges-Gustave Toudouze, her literature professor, was theatrical, from his goatee out of a different era, to his impeccable ascot. If that kind sexagenarian tried to impress his pupils with his academic exploits—judge for yourself: former resident of the Villa Medici and author of highly respected works!—his strange claims were actually quite amusing. Whether because of his heredity (a novelist father), or his passion for the sea (childhood in Brittany), during his first class he launched into a diatribe that the standard comic character of Scapin was from Malta. Why? On what insignificant stage direction was he basing his claim? Mysterious! But he wouldn't let go of it: Scapin was from Malta and he should wear the appropriate costume!

The only cloud on Bérénice's horizon was how she would support herself. Colette's family sheltered her during this crisis. Since childhood she had loved her friend's cozy apartment, where the atmosphere was so much more liberal and whimsical than her own. But her friend's parents let her know that this refuge was temporary. They reminded her that she was a minor and that she had to return to her parents' home sooner rather than later. Bérénice was too shy to tell them about the incident of the torn jacket. She knew that her father's curse was definitive, and that going back would be the equivalent of bending to her parents' will, to renounce forever her reason for living—it was out of the question. Paraphrasing Musset, she repeated to herself, "I have suffered often, I have sometimes made mistakes, but I have lived." That's what she explained to Colette, who admired her friend's tenacity, and that's what she was thinking when she was leaving her literature class and by chance ran into Robert Manuel.

"So, how was your first class?"

She was just about to answer him, to tell him what a joy it was to speak only about theater and how she finally felt that she'd found her place, how she couldn't even imagine a life more idyllic than the Conservatory, and how quickly these three years of school would pass, but she didn't have a chance. She had just spotted a familiar face.

"I'll be back in a second, Robert. Madame de Lignières? What brings you here?"

"I'm looking for you, my child. I went by the shop today to get news of you, and your parents pretended that everything was fine. Just between us, your neighbors are much less discreet, one of those good souls couldn't wait to tell me that your father had booted you out of the house. So, here I am!"

"Did they tell you to bring me back?" asked Bérénice defensively.

"Do I look like a gendarme? "I'll pretend I didn't hear that outburst, just come with me. I have to talk to you."

Madame de Lignières spoke and acted quickly. In a few seconds, Bérénice found herself in the car of her parents' rich client. The chauffeur drove them to the Rue Barbet-de-Jouy. This time, Madame de Lignières did not have her climb the stairs to Véra Korène's, but took her to her own apartment. Even though Bérénice had heard about this elderly aristocrat's fortune, she would still never have dreamed that one could have such a beautiful residence. Everything spoke of luxury and taste. On each wall was a painting by a master— at least that's how it seemed to her—heavy drapes on the windows, rugs as thick as three minks, crystals, chandeliers, gilded woodwork …

"Don't just stand there like a statue, take off your hat and sit down."

Bérénice did as she was told. Since the audition, her life had taken an incredible turn. Now a butler in livery was bringing her a little tray with cups of hot chocolate. Silver, porcelain, *Talk about sophistication!* thought Bérénice, who would not confide to her grandchildren the absurd idea that came to her mind while listening to Madame de Lignières. Her host was speaking all by herself, it seemed like a scene right out of a play. Yes, that was exactly what it was like. If it was a play, it would have been written like this:

MONOLOGUE: MADAME DE LIGNIÈRES:
Delivered swiftly and with authority.

My child, I know how unsettled your situation is. You're only fifteen, your father has shut the door in your face. That sort of behavior might merit legal action, but thank God we're not savages. A lawsuit between father and daughter would be very bad form. I was somewhat aware of your passion for the theater, but I didn't quite comprehend the scope of it. To begin with, you finished first in the exam. By itself, that does not necessarily mean that much, a jury can make mistakes, especially those dinosaurs at the Conservatory, but Daunat saw you and saw talent in you. You've heard of Daunat, of course, the drama critic at *Ars Nova*? A remarkable periodical, by the way. He's an old friend, I am personally acquainted with him and I have confidence in his intuition: he has a bite that stings, but good taste in all things. Listen to me, spinning out rhymes! *Anyway*, to speak like the English, Daunat told me that he's just written a short article about you. It will appear tomorrow. So, here's what I suggest. I like helping talented young people. Don't interrupt, just drink your hot chocolate, you haven't touched it. There's another reason. When I was young—I know, you can't even imagine I was ever young—I wanted to be an actress, just like you. Fancy that! Naturally, my parents were not in favor: imagine, in our family, an actress, that would have been a stain on our name! Instead, they married me off to a man who was excessively rich but something of a dimwit, the poor fellow. Not only that, I never loved him. Well, he died young, thank God. Since I've been free, I swore to myself I would only do what pleased me. My children don't understand me at all, they think I'm a crazy old bat, but I can assure you I have all my wits about me. Quite simply, I no longer bother with formalities, I do as I please. My children are a matter of indifference to me, my grandchildren are a disappointment, their parents have turned them into dolts. Now you, you're different. You have personality, talent, passion; that's sufficiently rare for me to help you. I'm rich, you're not, I have a little room on the Rue de Tournon, a sort of bachelor flat, you have no place to live, the apartment is yours. Give me a week to arrange for some renovations and you can move in. In the meantime, you may sleep here, if you choose. I'll give you money every month while you're looking for work. For all this, I have only one condition: that you graduate from the Conservatory with the first prize. That's it. Haven't I sorted this out well? Oh, I forgot, we will not tell your parents that I'm helping you, of course. As for your papers, I know enough people to get you false ones. We can give you a pseudonym, that's quite acceptable in the theater, or look, I could even give you my own name, that will piss off my children—lovely! "Bérénice de Lignières," it has a ring to it, don't you think? Fine with you? Perfect, I'm calling Daunat to get him to change your name in his magazine: this will be your first mention in the press with your stage name! At the Conservatory, you merely have to explain that you are using as a pseudonym your mother's maiden name. I'll pass for your mother, I'll sign your papers, all your worries—out the window!"

In a theater, the audience would have applauded such a forceful speech. Instead, in that vast living room, over cups of hot chocolate, their eyes sizzled. Irrepressible giggles followed this conspiratorial glance. Bound by this scheme, the two women both felt fifteen years old.

· 1 0 ·

Her life was transformed overnight, she was surrounded by fifty new friends, fellow students in the first through third years, bound by a brand new camaraderie. Her triumph made her popular, and to that was added the next day, as Madame Lignières had announced, the news item in *Ars Nova* magazine. Just a brief item—after all, it wasn't about the exit exam, far more celebrated—but it was from the influential pen of the fearsome Jean-René Daunat:

"The entrance exam! Just imagine what anxiety it provokes, what hopes it elicits, what memories it creates! Why? It is of decisive importance: admission is the first step to success, the 'open sesame' to a first prize and then being signed by the Comédie-Française or the Odéon. With failure comes discouragement you never recover from.

"That is certainly not what awaits the beautiful and luminous young lady who appeared for the first time before the Conservatory's jury. Bérénice de Lignières—remember that name.

"Her judiciously chosen excerpts allowed her to dominate the competition. I detected her strong temperament in the role of Camille, combined with born instinct as Iphigenia. I was amazed by the authority she showed in this role, arduous even for more experienced actresses.

"Mademoiselle de Lignières was ranked first among all admitted students. Her beginner's attempt was a masterful attempt. If this young woman with her predestined given name profits from the instruction of her professors, she appears destined to assume an important place among the tragedians of our time."

Huzzah, the trumpets of fame sounded! Colette spent all her allowance to buy copies of *Ars Nova*. Bérénice read these lines over and over—they heartened her enormously. Robert Manuel boasted of "his" discovery.

But this triumph was short lived. A few days later, just before ten in the morning, when she arrived at the Conservatory for her first drama class, Bérénice saw at the foot of the staircase ... Louis Jouvet in person. The master! The one she hoped so much would choose her for his class. Dressed in a tweed suit with a black felt Anthony Eden-style hat, he looked exactly the way he did in the movies, although no film could recreate the scent he wore or the aroma of his English cigarettes. His steely eyes focused on her attentively, seeming to rummage through her heart to gauge the depth of her love of the theater.

"So, you're the girl who finished first?"

"Yes, Master Jouvet."

"No, no, call me monsieur, Louis, or boss, but not Master, I'm not some old prick, you know."

"Yes, monsieur."

"I hear you've never taken a single acting class."

"No, monsieur."

"It shows."

Wounded, a lump in her throat, she tried to extract herself from this confrontation. Jouvet held her:

"Come, now, don't give me that look. Listen carefully: you don't know how to move, you make too many gestures, you don't breathe properly, but there's no question you have something. I'm not speaking of your physique, you're beautiful, that helps, but when it comes to your temperament, you have a sort of inner quivering, a fiery presence. That's quite unusual for a person as young as you. How old are you? Seventeen? Eighteen?"

"Fifteen, monsieur."

"Even more unusual. Maybe it's because you've never taken a class or tried to imitate anyone. With you, it comes from the guts, you have no feminine restraint, one senses an inner necessity to be heard. I don't know what that will amount to, but it's worth a try. Do you get what I'm saying? Do you get it, little mama? Hurry along now or you'll make us late for class."

She was so shaken that she didn't even realize they'd entered his classroom. Welcome to the class of Louis Jouvet.

· 1 1 ·

She won't be able to tell her children or her grandchildren: "Oh, we should watch *Stage Entrance* together," Marc Allégret's 1938 film that she discovered when it was first released in theaters, a film that recalled to her so vividly her three years at the Rue de Madrid, that's exactly the way it was in Louis Jouvet's class, just like in the movie, and of course that scene in the laundry where the boss avenges all the actors whose parents thwarted their passion for the stage. She won't be able to watch and watch again that movie with them, she won't be able to tell them about her first day at the Conservatory, her eyes drawn to the raised platform when she entered the classroom. So this was that wooden platform they would step up to each week for three years to perform for the master. It would be with the help of that backdrop and those wings that they would create the illusion of the stage. And that piano, there, in the corner, she would soon discover that it was for the music students. At the back of the room, far from the platform, a long wooden plank riveted to the wall was set up for the auditors. If Bérénice had not done so well on the entrance exam, she would have sat there, with them, on the wrong side, on the side of those who had not been judged worthy of full admission to the Conservatory. A few days before this, the prospect of even being an auditor would have delighted her. Now she looked on those unfortunate ones with pity.

On this first day of class, a man with a beard and white hair appeared in the classroom. It was Henri Rabaud, recipient of the Rome Prize, composer of the popular operetta *Mârouf, The Cobbler of Cairo*, but most notably, the director of the Conservatory. He cleared his throat before speaking: "Tradition dictates that I should introduce a new professor to his students, and not, as one might suppose, introduce the students to the professor. May I present Monsieur Louis Jouvet."

Why was he doing this? Every single person in that room was there for Louis Jouvet. Everyone knew him from his films. Especially *Topaze* and *Knock*: "Does it tickle, or does it prickle?" All France knew the answer and enjoyed that staccato delivery, this actor's trademark. People in the theater world knew a great deal more. They knew that Jouvet was part of the adventurous Vieux-Colombier Theater with its impresario Jacques Copeau, that Jouvet had been a manager, set designer, assistant, and then actor and director.

Jouvet's arrival as a professor at the Conservatory this year had caused quite a stir. The venerable institution was allowing someone to teach there who had failed the entrance exam three times—because of his stammer, some claimed. "Because of my ugly mug," he remarked ironically. They say that when he was officially named to the faculty, he yelled, "I got those old fuckers this time!" Unlike most of his colleagues, Jouvet was not a principal actor of the Comédie-Française, he maintained an ambivalent relationship with that theater, attraction mixed with contempt. It's true that in 1934, that ancient institution did not have a good reputation: the executive director, Émile Fabre, was blamed for a lack of boldness, the sloppiness of the troupe, dusty productions, insufficient funding, the decline in revenue ... Not only that, the moderns were turning away from that institution, which seemed to live only on its past glories. For a long time, true theater had not been practiced at the venerable House of Molière: the avant-garde came from the Comédie des Champs-Élysées, run by none other than Louis Jouvet; Charles Dullin's Atelier; the Théâtre des Mathurins headed by Georges Pitoëff; or the Théâtre Montparnasse of Gaston Baty— in short, what was called The Cartel. To add to his scandalous reputation— at least at the Conservatory—Jouvet programmed not only classic plays with productions that were more modern than at the Comédie-Française, but he also had the nerve to be interested in contemporary authors. Most notable was his admiration of Jean Giraudoux, whose work was soon to be staged at the Athénée, where Jouvet had just become the artistic director.

If the students were already very aware of the facts of his biography, they had not yet discovered their professor's little quirks. Astonishingly, given that Jouvet was considered "modern" in the theater world, he reinstated in his classroom customs that dated to the period before World War I. On the moleskin benches framing his little table, the girls were seated on the right, by the window, while the boys were on the left by the pegs where the students hung their coats. That, along with the silence that followed the artistic director's little lecture and along with Jouvet's visible emotion, gave to this first class the air of a religious ceremony. The impressionable Bérénice was even more struck because the separation of the students reminded her of the configuration of a synagogue: men on one side, women on the other.

The profane nevertheless burst through. A little dry click, a faint sizzling. The "boss" opened the drawer of his little table to snuff out his cigarette butts. During the entire class he never stopped opening and closing it.

"Come here, we're not in the Sorbonne! You, what've you got for me?"

"Vasili, Master Jouvet, from *The Swan Song*."

"That Chekhov! He never earned a single franc … What's your name?"

"Jean Meyer," stammered the student, a bit disconcerted by the master's attack.

"Begin."

"'Here's an adventure for you! Here's a story! I fell asleep in my dressing room at the theater. The play had ended a long time ago; the entire audience had left the theater, and there I was snoring away so peacefully! Ah, old fart! Old sheep dog! …'"

"Is this some kind of fish story? Are you pulling my leg? If this is what the Conservatory is like, I'm going to grab my hat and clear out of here."

"But, master …"

"Why are you constantly jerking at your scarf? Start from the top!"

"'Here's a story for you! Here's an adventure!'"

"Look, you're getting yourself all tied up in knots with your lines. Do this again for me when you actually know it by heart."

"I knew it just a little while ago."

"But you don't know it now. You haven't worked on this scene. You think I wake up in the morning to hear this? Sit down. The little one, over there, the one who placed first in the exam, where is she?"

"Me?"

"Who else? So, what are you doing for me?"

"The Infanta's monologue."

"Let's see it!"

"Shall I hear you again, high blood of ours,
That makes a crime of my love?
Shall I hear you, love, whose tender powers
Make my generous heart against it move?
Poor Princess, to which of the two
Must you devote these hours?
Rodrigue your valor proves worthy of me;
But you're no king's son, despite victory."

"You, over there, what do you think? Nothing? Nobody here thinks? No, you wouldn't dare rat on a friend, so I'll tell you myself what's not working here, little mama. You cry easily but no one gives a damn about your real tears. Save them for the movies. In the theater, tears distract the audience. First learn to breathe or your talent will be stuck in your boots! What's magnificent in this passage is that if you breathe the way you should, if you have enough breath to make it all the way to the end, if you don't pant, you will succeed in achieving, little by little, a rhythm, a ..."

Her apprenticeship at this profession, her gorging on work for a period of three years, and how early she arrived for her classes, especially when the instructor was Louis Jouvet, who ruthlessly locked the doors of his classroom the moment the bell rang. The sermons of Bossuet projected at the top of her lungs to develop her breathing, her jawbone hurting from the pencil chomped during the articulation exercises, those Betty Botter bought a bit of butters that unbettybottered themselves to the point of nausea ... Voice gymnastics she practiced day after day, at home or at the Conservatory, making use of even a minute waiting on line to train, much to the amusement of the passersby who heard her stringing together these absurd phrases as quickly as possible: "A big black bug bit a big black bear and the big black bear bled blood," "Which wristwatches are Swiss wrist watches." It was only much later that she understood how important technique was, especially for a tragedian playing roles that can wear you down because of the density of the text, with their mournful moods, and also because of the length of the verses, where you have to get all the way to the end without choking, needing to know how to breathe from head to toe right to the tip of your skull despite stage fright which can consume at least twenty percent of your energy and the costumes from the seventeenth century that corset your lungs even more.

Her bedrock in these moments of doubt was the joy of acting. It never left her, and this joy actually increased with every challenge she withstood.

Despite her having been admitted as an "advanced female lead," she wanted to try every part: flirtatious ladies, soubrettes, lovers, ingénues, duennas, comics, women, even men, old men, cross-dressers … This born tragedian had a thirst for comedy as well as serious drama, classics as well as moderns. She strove always to follow to the letter Jouvet's recommendation to work on every scene as if it were her audition piece. Despite her gifts, she worked like a coal miner. When not at the Conservatory, you would be sure to find her at the Athénée Theatre where the students of the boss were lucky enough to rehearse in the afternoons with his collaborator, Pierre Renoir.

Her nerves were so rattled she often speeded up her delivery and then raced. "You're going like a bat out of hell," yelled Jouvet, mercilessly. She had to steel herself, calm her jittering limbs and tongue. She also had to limit the gestures that in her excessive enthusiasm she tended to use immoderately. She was learning her trade.

At the tables for six in the dining hall she picked the brains of the trumpet players to find out what methods they used to develop their breathing, discovering in the rigor of musicians an inspiration for her own studies. Solitude became her friend, her identity asserted itself, little by little she became aware of her feminine powers of seduction, her volcanic temperament emerged. Now that she knew where she belonged, she blossomed.

And then there was the Comédie-Française, which her status as a student at the Conservatory gave her access to as often as she wanted. Here in the flesh were the names she had learned by heart. There was Madeleine Renaud and Marie Bell and even André Brunot, the assistant head, who, as her professor, called her "tootsie." Here was the actual House of Molière that she always spoke of with veneration, to the great displeasure of Jouvet: "What? You love that dusty old museum full of bureaucrats who couldn't even pass the exam for the postal service?"

Jouvet and his idiosyncracies, his cigarettes during class, his disturbing attacks on modern theater, the authors he detested, and also his training as an apothecary that would suddenly emerge, even more so because he had narrowly escaped that profession. He prescribed medicine for his students when they caught colds or "some other crap." Here's what he'd say:

"What's the matter with you? You sick or something?"

"Yes, sir, I've got a sore throat and a cold."

"Any fever?"

"Yeah, it kept me up all night. I didn't close my eyes once."

"O.K., come with me, we'll get you something."

They didn't know if they were in Jouvet's film *Knock* or Molière's *The Imaginary Invalid*. Having Jouvet as your professor put you in a special league at the Conservatory, he was so famous and talked about. But even if his students felt they were the aristocracy of the Conservatory, their greatest fear was to hear him yell, "Now, that would totally flop on stage!"

· 1 2 ·

He ran a finger over her naked skin, never tiring of following the curve of those inviting hips he knew by heart, breathing in the scent of that finely textured skin, digging his hand into her red mane of hair. "Your body is like a Berlioz symphony: stormy, provocative, hyperbolic." She laughed with that big, throaty laugh of hers. Even in an intimate setting, her voice projected, with a well-rounded timbre. A soprano voice, dazzling and sonorous, that filled the cozy room.

She stretched out on the linen sheets. "Mmm. I slept marvelously last night."

"My red tiger," he whispered, nibbling her ear, "my beautiful Agnès."

Like a conqueror she looked him over, her talented musician she had lived with for three years and who had finally composed an opera for her. The premiere had taken place the night before, an admirable success for a new score. They had come back late, drunk on champagne and fatigue—the garments scattered on the thick Persian carpet testified to their haste.

"I wonder what Daunat will write," said Agnès. "Would you pass me my dressing gown?"

"He snuck out like a thief, didn't say a word. He must have detested it, as usual. You know the critics, you can never please them, though they couldn't write a fucking measure themselves," grumbled Nathan, lighting a cigarette.

"It seemed the audience liked it, no? Give me a drag. They made me sing an encore of my second aria."

"Oh, the French! What do they know about music? Mozart was right: 'The French are jackasses, they're not capable, and they always need to rely on foreigners.' Isn't that also why I'm in your bed?"

"How gallant of you, bravo, Herr Adelman! And your Ravel—is he also a jackass?"

"No, luckily, there's Ravel. At least he knows how to write a score for orchestra."

"Where the hell did I leave that slipper? Oh, here." She recovered it from under the bed. "Your music might be too modern for them but they can't say anything about my voice. I was perfect yesterday."

"You were divine," Nathan agreed.

He repressed a smile. Nathan knew she was going to bring the subject back around to herself. Even off stage, she always had to be the focus of attention, talk about herself, of her voice that she was used to hearing praised since she was very young, proud of her successes, of her sizzling reputation, of her male conquests. Sometimes Nathan was a bit weary of this permanent performance, he would have preferred a bit less egotism, especially at a time when his own work was being tested by public opinion.

"I'm so hungry," he declared, throwing back the covers, "I could eat a cow."

"You'll have to make do with croissants." Agnès rang for the chambermaid.

The soprano got out of bed, wrapped herself in the dressing gown her lover handed to her, and threw him a bathrobe. She quickly yanked a brush through her long red hair, which fell almost to her waist. A few minutes later the maid came in, carrying a platter with breakfast and the morning mail.

"Thank you, Rose, you may leave now."

Nathan noted that Agnès looked at her lady in waiting with irony: he was sure that she suspected him of having an affair with her. Yes, he had hit the nail on the head.

"Did you see how she was smiling in your direction? If she makes one step out of line, I'm firing her, she can return to her hometown in Berry, that little slut. Ah, *Ars Nova* is here, let's see the review." She snatched the newspaper. "Here it is: '*Scheherazade*, Opera in Five Acts, after the *Thousand and One Nights*, libretto by Alain Béron, music composed by Nathan Adelman.' ... Oh, not bad, get a load of this, honey pie: 'The character of Scheherazade provides Mademoiselle Agnès Grangé with yet another lovely part. What nuances this light soprano voice has treated us to with her trills and cascades! What a science of color in the midst of highly challenging, vertiginous vocalizing!'"

"Magnificent, my beauty," said Nathan, coming near to her. "So, nothing else?" he asked sardonically.

"Yes, of course. I'll read the whole article from the beginning: 'Do you know what strikes me with regard to Monsieur Nathan Adelman, since his scandalous *Theseus* at the Berlin Opera five years ago?"

"Great, what's he going to talk about?"

"Be patient! 'It's that, far from imitating Wagner's leitmotivs, as so many other composers of his generation, far from eagerly copying the impressionism of Debussy or being led astray by Schoenberg's atonality, Monsieur Nathan Adelman has found a language that is his alone. Let us remind our readers who are as yet hardly familiar with his *oeuvre* that Monsieur Adelman comes to us from Berlin, where he studied at the Hochschule with the likes of Franz Schreker and Paul Hindemith. He was quickly noticed by the conductor of the orchestra, Wilhelm Furtwängler, whose assistant he became, but he is currently almost exclusively devoting his attention to composition. Numerous orchestral musical scores preceded his arrival in France, among them the remarkable *Concerto for Piano in D Minor*.

"'Like many of his Israelite compatriots whose music was banned there, Monsieur Adelman left Germany in 1933 to seek refuge in France. Barely thirty years old, he seems to be at the height of his powers. His teaming up with the poet Alain Béron, who was his collaborator for *Aeneas*, his previous opus, has definitely put him on the road to maturity.

"'These coauthors have drawn their inspiration from oriental magic: Scheherazade is the princess in *A Thousand and One Nights*, known to, and appreciated by, the French public since Antoine Galland's translation.

"'The librettist has pared down all that is not workable on stage and has added fanciful elements of his own invention, and despite the liberties taken with the text, they do not at all betray it. As usual, Alain Béron has chiseled the characters and shaped them with the poetic flair that is his alone.

"'Now we come to the music, and let us acknowledge that Monsieur Adelman has succeeded in recreating an ideal Orient, at the same time that he has made the characters of these ancient tales completely modern. We appreciate the clarity and irony in his score—which does not in the least exclude, on certain pages, a nostalgic *je ne sais quoi* that touches the soul. Although it boasts many instruments, his orchestra never overpowers the voices, a treat that is now rare at the Opera, while those audacious rhythms have now become the signature of his work.

"'I don't pretend, however, to defend this work in its entirety. To deny its weaknesses, here and there, would be as false as it would be ridiculous. The audience, I might note, noisily displayed its boredom at the end of Act I, closer to a symphonic poem than to an opera. Certain audience members reacted with alarm to the tritonal development of the prelude to Act II. A subscriber in the parterre exclaimed, not without reason, 'The man is stark raving mad!'

"I would've put money on their not being able to make sense of that passage."

"Don't interrupt, this is where he talks about me: 'the French nightingale,' etc. Oh, no, wait till you hear this: 'We will not omit congratulations to the delicious Madame Henriette Duval. Her incisive and expressive voice is moving in the extreme.' How could he see any talent in that Henriette? Daunat is losing it!"

The telephone rang in the next room.

"He praises Rouché's direction, etc. I'll just read you the last part: "Let us wish *Scheherazade* a long run at the Opera. That would be a just fate.'"

"Get the phone, I'm sure it's Alain, he probably read the review."

Agnès went to pick up the phone. She spoke for a moment with the librettist before passing Nathan to him.

"Yes, I saw. Daunat is in a great mood these days, he must be in love! ... Yeah, yeah. I agree, he's behind the times when it comes to music. We were just talking about it during rehearsal. Here's what I suggest, old man: are you coming with us tomorrow to The Masked Owl? It's Agnès's night off and a former student invited us. He wants us to hear a friend of his, they say she's fantastic. ... What are they performing? You know, the kind of music they do these days, realiiiiistic, traaaaagic, as if Monsieur Hitler weren't poisoning the world enough. ... I know, I know. ... She also sings some Kurt Weill, I hear she's terrific. I'm curious, just want to hear some of it. ... So, join us, afterwards, we'll dance the fox trot, it's always fun at The Masked Owl. ... You're in? Great, see you tomorrow, we'll come get you around ten."

The composer hung up and rejoined Agnès, who was seated at her dressing table.

"I'm still hungry," he said, leaning toward her. "Very, very hungry," he added, eating her up with kisses.

She laughed again and they ended up in bed to continue the pleasures of the night. It was already eleven, but who cared? They still had time before that evening's rehearsal at the Opera.

· 1 3 ·

The Masked Owl was the newest trendy cabaret. Opened in 1930, its proximity to The Bluebird, long established, created problems when it opened. The competition was fierce. The Masked Owl had trouble finding clientele, it wasn't unusual to see just two or three spectators taking in the floor show. It was only since the recent change in ownership that it had acquired a certain notoriety. The owner knew that the young and well-off would flock without hesitation to whatever was new. He understood that you had to flatter the taste of this fickle audience. First he brought in young, unknown singers that he gambled on, often successfully. Then he skimmed all the working class neighborhoods to recruit exotic dancers with black or mulatto complexions. His boa-wielding strippers had finer and more supple bodies than the other nightclubs, their faces had more character. This did the trick. In 1934, The Bluebird faded while The Masked Owl was in full swing.

When Nathan Adelman, Agnès Grangé, and Alain Béron entered this hotspot, it was already late in the evening. Waiting for them at a table was Jules Puech, a student of the horn at the Conservatory, who had taken private composition classes with Nathan. The two men had become fairly good friends, and Jules often called the older one to let him in on his Paris nightlife discoveries. This evening, he was accompanied by a woman friend slightly older than he was.

"This is Fanny, my fiancée. She's a flautist, we met at the Conservatory. Quick, sit down, sit down, the show is about to start. Wait till you see the chanteuse—she's sensational."

"Champagne all around?" asked Nathan. "What's the singer's name?"

"Lou."

"*I'm writing to you, oh my Lou* ..." joked Alain Béron.

"Aha, the poet is already cobbling together an elegy," said Agnès, who didn't get the allusion.

"That's not mine, my dear, it's Apollinaire."

The lights dimmed, a voice with a microphone introduced the chanteuse. Silence fell over the room, a silence broken by the conversations that continued at some of the tables. Nathan always found that intensely annoying. *Stille!* he wanted to yell at those fools. And then, from the break in a black curtain appeared the hand of a woman followed by a face in profile adorned with a blue wig. Total silence. Then, slowly, mysteriously, the silhouette of the chanteuse emerged from behind the curtain. She was tall and dressed in a black tuxedo, wearing four-inch heels. She turned ever so slowly toward the audience and when she was facing them, all of a sudden she popped open her huge eyes. The whole room held its breath staring at those cat eyes with lush lashes, so pale that they seemed dead, everything about this woman was enigmatic, with her sumptuous mouth lacquered red. The piano began to play—*heavy left hand, too much pedal,* Nathan noted *in petto,* despite himself.

Then the voice of the chanteuse welled up, softly at first, in a whisper, tender, almost flirtatious. She murmured, "Take back your hand, I don't love you," and suddenly her voice swelled and became savage and husky, it turned wild, biting, as if it was surging from the depths of the earth, catching you unaware, reaching your fault lines and fissures, and there she was giving you everything and you realized you were walking by her side, that you were breathing in unison with her, that you were panting in rhythm with her, that you were no longer breathing because she had carried you away to her world where when you say "I don't love you" you love her to death and when you say "I'm on my knees" you have only one desire, to kiss her feet and become her slave. And then she sang another song, this one in German, and even if you didn't speak German you still understood, you knew she was speaking of shared love and unrequited love, you knew she was speaking about your life, your hopes and your regrets, of your smashed dreams and your wildest desires, you knew she was speaking about your laughter and your sorrows, your youth and your seventeen-year-old self that will never return, and you knew that this woman could do good and evil, be embracing and maternal and hostile and a succubus at the same time, that she was all of those things at once, and how delicious and dangerous at the same time, that desire to go there and the fear of going there, like that fear you have as a child discovering what's hidden in Bluebeard's chamber, the fear of being face to face with a tiger and the fascination of wild animals. And for Nathan it was even worse, because he was German and knew perfectly well what she was saying, every single word, and the one thing he couldn't understand was how a Frenchwoman could sing German so well, it wasn't just the accent, it was her intimate comprehension of the language, it was how she had just the right inflection on the appropriate words, it was the atmosphere of the cabarets when he was twenty years old, it was the city where he was born, his lost Berlin, the one before 1933, it was his Conservatory and his teachers, it was his childhood friends and his first loves, his father and mother, it was the Germany he had to flee, it was his nostalgia for his native land and sometimes when Lou's eyes rested on him he felt so sick he could die, as if a knot had formed in his stomach and he had to restrain himself in order not to be consumed by the emotion.

"So, what did I tell you, she's incredible, right? She's like Damia and Lotte Lenya rolled into one," Jules Puech exclaimed.

"She's better than that," Alain Béron muttered. He looked at Nathan and the two friends knew that they had seen the same thing in this woman with the blue wig and the black tuxedo.

"I'll never be able to hear 'I Don't Love You,' sung by anyone else," Nathan declared, pouring himself another glass. "Kurt just absolutely has to hear her."

Jules Puech had the glow of an impresario, he was so pleased with "his" success, he kneaded his fiancée's hand, filled everyone's glass, became very excited, gesticulated, no one had yet noticed Agnès's silence, so unlike her. The soprano hated the way the men had looked at that girl. She suffered to see Nathan devour her with his eyes, she'd been jealous at seeing how excited even that overly serious Alain Béron had become while he hadn't said a single friendly word to her the night before about how she had created the role of Scheherazade. She found that woman's voice indecent, her training in the canons of opera made Agnès find nothing but fault with that voice, that tessitura, an ample range but lacking consistency between the high-pitched register and the low, and she didn't like those notes that sometimes broke and that fuzziness in the higher register, with no understanding that what was unacceptable in opera was exactly what made the timbre and emotion so unique. How could she appreciate this voice so different from her own, Agnès's voice, so round from one end to the other of its range? In any case, she couldn't understand what people saw in Kurt Weill: it was too German, this music: vulgar, that was the word for it.

Caught up in his enthusiasm, Jules insisted on bringing his friend from the Conservatory over to their table. She did come over to join them, looking even more beautiful than before, when she was singing from afar surrounded by a halo, as if the heavens, charmed, pointed her out to the audience, saying: she is favored by the gods. Heaping superlatives on her, Jules introduced her to his friends.

"Congratulations, Mademoiselle," Alain Béron said to her. "Now we have some idea of what Ulysses heard from the mouths of the sirens."

"Champagne?" Nathan quickly offered, serving the young woman. "That was magnificent. How long have you been singing?"

She didn't have time to answer, to find out more precisely whether he meant how long she'd been singing at The Masked Owl or how long in general. She didn't have time to answer because Alain Béron's compliment and Nathan's attention to her had just added the final straw. Agnès, jealous, had slid into her serpent's skin, her voice turned into a hiss, she had to inject her venom now. She did it insidiously, speaking first of the decadence of the century, characterized by a slackening of technique: "Take ballet, for instance: ever since Isadora Duncan, pseudo-dancers have invaded our theaters. It's not even dance anymore, it's not pantomime, it's a sort of sub-art." And then she really got down to it: "And with singing, exactly the same thing has happened." With a disingenuous smile, Agnès began deriding Lou and her pretensions of being a singer, accusing her of copying Fréhel in her repertoire, criticizing her for wavering between two arts, singing and tragedy, flawed in both because of her failure to choose between them. Agnès wasn't satisfied until she thought she had scored a knock out of her victim.

Lou was wounded, but, faced with this danger, she mustered her courage, she answered with pride, invoking Greek theater which mixed the two arts, mocking the soprano for her narrow-mindedness that left no room for innovation and experimentation, accusing her of hiding in tradition and producing only a sclerotic art, throwing in her face the lack of natural expression in classical singers, their inability to act their roles except by planting both feet on the ground and placing a hand over the heart. Then it was the other woman who staggered under the weight of this rebuke, the soprano idolized by all of Paris had lost her ability to parry. She started to answer but Lou stood up and left the table, meaning that the joust had ended, and that she would take this pointless contest no further. She cast a defiant glance at her rival and her entourage, lumping them all together, those who would associate with such a friend and say not a single word to silence her.

With Lou gone, Nathan turned to his companion: "What got into you just now? That was rude and it was wrong. You're not jealous, by any chance?"

"Me, jealous! As if a diamond could envy zircon! If you're taking that attitude, you two can stay here and be the ladies' men, I'm going, I'll leave you to swoon at that steamboat whistle voice."

She got up and headed toward the cloakroom to get her coat. Nathan made a what-can-I-do gesture to his friends. Grudgingly, he followed her.

The mood was ruined. Alone with Jules and his fiancée, Alain Béron sipped his drink. He excused himself a few minutes later.

"He must be thinking of a new poem," Jules's fiancée ventured, not at all displeased to find herself alone with her lover.

· 1 4 ·

"Your honor, yes, it's true that Paul Bloch committed a crime. Paul Bloch violated his deportation order. But who is being accused today? A man who traffics in flesh? A lewd man? A drunk? A murderer who deserves to have the hand of justice smite him with all its force? No! Just look at the defendant and you will understand a great many things that the law fails to take into account.

"Justice is blind, the prosecutor tells us, it must be applied to everyone in the same manner. The truth is, it would be all too convenient to use this neat phrase to sidestep problematic cases. When I think of Paul Bloch, I know personally that this man didn't have a choice. I know that he couldn't leave France as his deportation order demanded because Paul Bloch is, in point of fact, a stateless person.

"Let me remind you who the defendant is: this forty-year-old man has lived a life without a blemish on his record. Son of a wealthy German industrialist, he has a solid academic background in philosophy and literature from the University of Berlin. In his homeland, which he loved, he became a journalist for the social democratic newspaper, the *Vorwärts*. Nothing suggested that this honest journalist would one day find himself before a French court. No doubt he would have lived ignored by history if Hitler hadn't come to power.

"The new regime does not appreciate his pen: that newspaper is banned. Paul Bloch is sent to a concentration camp where he suffers brutal treatment, abuse, and humiliations. By a miracle, he succeeds in escaping, with only one thought in mind: make it to France. Within a few weeks, he succeeds in getting here. There he is, in our country, where he obtains a passport, and where he succeeds, thanks to his enthusiasm and his perseverance, in finding a job at a printing company. He has no difficulty getting along with his co-workers, he gets engaged to a young Frenchwoman, he is waiting to improve his circumstances before his wedding. That is the life of Paul Bloch, a life of exemplary work, I think you will agree.

"But then, because of an ordinary parking ticket, the authorities serve him with a deportation order. He receives an order to leave French territory, his passport is taken. What does Paul Bloch do then? Respecting the law, he makes the rounds of the foreign consulates to obtain a visa that would allow him to leave France. Each time he is told that this visa has to be affixed to his passport, the very document that was confiscated from him. Precisely that!

"How was he to react then, knowing that any step he could take would be in vain? What would you have done in his place? Would you have illegally crossed the border, at the risk of being thrown in prison in another country? No, of course not: *impossibilium nulla obligatio est*—no one is obliged to do the impossible. You would have stayed in France by your fiancée's side. Exactly what Paul Bloch did.

"So, I ask you, could he have done anything differently? If he had traveled to a neighboring country, he would have risked being arrested for entering illegally. If he had returned to the country of his birth, his life would have been in danger. This is why I tell you that the defendant is in fact a stateless person: he is at home nowhere; everywhere he goes, he is a stranger.

"The situation of stateless persons is truly tragic. To expel them from France goes against both common sense and the most basic principles of justice and humanity. How long will we allow this scandal to continue?

"My distinguished colleague the prosecutor just reaffirmed it: violating a deportation order carries a sentence of one to six months in prison. We all know, your honor, that's it's not within your power to change that law. It's true, you could lawfully sentence Paul Bloch to prison. He knows that, this banished man, and he accepts the risk. And yet, I beseech you, your honor, do not add internment to the nightmare of deportation. Rather show your humanity, and acquit the defendant. May I remind you why Paul Bloch came to France? Because he believed he would find in our country a land of refuge and liberty. This idea of France, which we won at such a terrible cost during the Revolution, which we proclaimed before all nations, which has inspired so many other peoples, this idea is our pride, this idea is our honor. But this idea will remain an abstraction if it is not embodied in individuals, and that individual is named Paul Bloch, who prefers French handcuffs to German barbed wire."

"Bravo!" yelled someone in the audience.

Alain Béron had just rested his case. *If this man in the first row who keeps fiddling with his gloves now transfers them to his right hand, then Paul Bloch will be acquitted,* he told himself. Despite his Cartesian outlook, the defense attorney couldn't help having this sort of thought—absurd, you might call it—magical, in any case, precisely in moments of extreme self-control, as if superstition took pleasure in taunting him, the better to demonstrate the fragility of reason. He knew then that it was impossible to escape it, that all logical arguments amounted to nothing. Those peccary gloves of that man in the first row functioned as a barometer for Alain Béron throughout his speech. Perhaps because his clothing revealed his membership in the middle class, it seemed to him that this man he did not know represented the average Frenchman. When the lawyer got carried away and observed that the man squeezed his glove more tightly, he knew he couldn't go any farther, that the antidemocratic and xenophobic propaganda cranked out by publications such as *Candide* or *Gringoire* had already gained too much ground in their country. If he didn't moderate his statements, he risked shocking the court and having the opposite effect from the understanding he was counting on. So he softened his remarks, found nuances, beating a retreat where necessary.

He went outside to smoke a cigarette. The fresh air invigorated him. A half hour later, the judge announced his verdict: "Given that the presence of Paul Bloch in French territory on the date of his arrest stemmed from his inability to leave it because of a series of circumstances out of his control ...

"It is therefore resolved that, in ruling for the defendant, we acquit the aforementioned Paul Bloch of all charges and dismiss his case without prejudice or costs."

The pair of gloves hadn't lied. Acquittal it was. The tribunal followed the attorney's argument point for point. A total success. Alain Béron's face relaxed, his eyes lost their feverish look. He warmly shook his client's hand and slid over to him a piece of paper on which he had just scribbled a few lines. He nodded in the direction of the judge and the prosecutor, and then rapidly left the courtroom.

Outside, having shed his attorney's robe, which he left in the cloakroom with his cylindrical black cap, he felt suddenly bereft. Despite his success, a huge sadness descended on him, as it often did when his level of adrenaline fell. He lit a Gitanes and sped up his pace. The image of the gloves of this unknown man in the first row would not leave him. To be completely precise, he would describe their hue as chestnut verging on an orangey beige. As always, colors struck his consciousness with impressionistic touches that he no longer tried to control. The brown of the peccary gloves, the off-white, Roman-style cloak of a colleague where they paced up and down in anticipation in the vast hall of the Palace of Justice, the gold of trees in fall that he associated with the aromatic crust of a baba au rhum. It was that association of colors and sensations that then gave birth, through a mysterious process, to the words eventually transmuted into poems.

The streets passed by, right foot, left foot, turn left, turn right, pedestrian passageway, change sidewalks. In leaving the Palace of Justice, the attorney had veered to the left, in the direction of the Gare de Lyon. A few minutes later, he was seated in a train en route to Aix-en-Provence. The carriage was practically empty, the landscape so monotonous that it seemed to be in hiding. Alain Béron went back over his closing statement. The court had accepted his argument, including the basic premise—fairly bold—that this was a case of force majeure, but he knew his victory was fragile. He had been fortunate to have a sympathetic judge, a man of the left known for taking courageous positions on behalf of foreigners. If the case was taken to the next level, there was a risk that the judges of the appellate court would be less lenient. For several years now he had defended stateless persons (the heimatlos, as they were called in judicial jargon). At first, he had just taken the case of a friend of a friend. When they heard about his first success, Russians, Armenians, Germans came to him, full of hope. Even if legal doctrine was largely favorable to his ideas, the judges most often objected to resolving a dramatic situation that should rightly have been remedied by legislation.

His daydreaming was interrupted by a person sitting near him, intrigued by the copy of the legal journal Dalloz sitting on the seat, and said:

"Are you a magistrate, Monsieur?"

"No, Monsieur, I'm a lawyer."

"Ah, an excellent profession, excellent!"

"And you, Monsieur?" he asked, purely out of politeness.

"Me? I'm s stockbroker."

"Very nice. Would you excuse me? I have an article to write."

To avoid any further disturbance, he pretended to be immersed in reading his magazine: "Accident—Responsibility for an accident occurring on the stairway of a movie theater. While walking downstairs in a movie theater, C., a young woman, took an unfortunate fall and broke her right ankle. The Court of Paris (7th Chamber), in an order dated 17 November 1933, denied the application of Article 1384 of the Civil Code, considering that, 'When the role played by the object in question is entirely passive, it cannot incur a legal responsibility on the part of its owner, and it is obviously necessary ...'"

He stopped reading, his thoughts wandered. He thought about his mother, whom he was about to see in the home where he had grown up in Aix-en-Provence—she would be waiting there for him. A hundred times he had insisted that she not wait for him to eat, she never listened, too impatient to see him. He was eager to speak with her and to return the very next morning to that table where he would work in monastic seclusion, the beloved wooden table of his youth, which his adult body had outgrown, but which he still loved to write on, as if these roughly hewn pieces of wood assembled by his grandfather murmured exactly le mot juste that had brought him the best results, from his first compositions in French class to the prizes he had won for Latin and Greek in the nationwide student competition. It was at this modest table that he had composed his adolescent poems, it was always there that he wrote his poems and opera libretti. Not a single opening or closing statement, however—he preferred to write those outside the house, in cafés, for example, maintaining that he needed to fill himself with other people, with all that made up their humanity, noise, habits, foibles, conversations, as if better to absorb their motives.

He tried to focus again on the magazine: "... and it is obviously necessary that the detrimental contact of the victim with the object that caused the damage should be the result of a destructive or harmful movement or action on the part of the object ..." His fellow passenger had left, no doubt he had found his way to the dining car. He looked at his watch. Nine o'clock. At the Opera, they would soon be starting the performance of Scheherazade, he himself would certainly have been there if he hadn't had to return to Aix, the overture was one of his favorite passages. "... of a destructive or harmful movement or action on the part of the object ..." He glanced again at his watch. Five minutes past nine. It was still too early for The Masked Owl. "... and not a voluntary or unconscious act on the part of the victim ..."

I definitely am not concentrating, he thought impatiently, crumpling his empty cigarette package. But responsibility with regard to material objects was a subject he was passionate about and one where he had followed the progress of legal precedent with interest since his university days, even if he only argued criminal cases now. The court's solution is absurd, he analyzed. Let's recap: the judges assigned the responsibility on the part of the theater based on Article 1382 of the Civil Code. In estimating that the theater is only half responsible for causing the accident, they ruled only to award the victim half the amount of the damages. That poor Mademoiselle C.! Not only did she have to prove that the owners were at fault, but she had to be content with 32,500 francs when she should have been awarded twice that sum if the judges had applied the presumption of responsibility in Article 1384. And what is the meaning of that "destructive or harmful action on the part of the object"? It seemed as if the court wanted to resuscitate the concept of danger-ous and not dangerous objects, even though it was categorically rejected in the Jand'heur ruling. ... Absurd! I would almost like to write an article on this subject —but that's completely out of the question: my publisher is waiting for me to submit my next poetry collection, don't get distracted by legal matters ... He glanced at his watch again. Nine-thirty. "Lou," he muttered, "Lou. By now she must have received it."

· 1 5 ·

"It's me, Monsieur Francis! Good evening."

"Good evening, Mademoiselle Lou," greeted the concierge, opening the door of The Masked Owl for the young woman, as he did every night when there was a stage show.

Lou liked to arrive early, around eight o'clock, in order to have time to get ready, put on her makeup, exchange a few words with the other performers, feeling the mood build little by little in the club, so different each night, obeying the mysterious laws of the theater, which were even more noticeable in a cabaret where the audience can get distracted so easily. As he did every night, the elderly concierge brought her the fan mail and the gifts from her admirers. "The flowers are in your dressing room," he added. The old Parisian would have gladly gossiped longer with the beautiful Lou, but his wife reminded him as sharply and as she always did, to feed the cats. If he could have talked to Lou longer, no doubt he would have told her, as proud as Punch, that he had been very tight-lipped, very discreet, and to all the gentlemen who had asked him if she had a lover or if she was as beautiful without her makeup and elegant outfits, he had said nothing: "They slid me their ten franc bills for nothin', they could even have given me a thousand, it would still be: mum's the word! You know me, when I want to be mute, there ain't nobody muter than yours truly!"

Quickly she ran up the stairs, greeted the dancers who were pulling on their stockings amidst a rustle of feathers, tulle, and sequins, closed the door of her dressing room, ran her hand over her black tuxedo hanging on a coat rack, and finally thought about looking through her fan letters and the gifts, but she was in no hurry. Ever since she had created this character of the vamp at The Masked Owl, requests rained in from everywhere, each night she received praise from men, invitations to go out, a whole armful of flowers, one night it was Jean Gabin in person making a pass at her and he was even more seductive in real life than on the big screen. But she wasn't there to flirt with the boys, to listen to their declarations of love, receive their presents and finally to wake up in their beds, she was not a tease, and in any case, she had to get up early the next morning for her class at the Conservatory. She told her friend Jules not to introduce her anymore to people as unpleasant as that Agnès Grangé. She would urge him one more time to keep her secret, her true identity—he was the only one who knew it. She was not at all sure that the Conservatory would have looked favorably on her evening occupation, even if it didn't make her late for class. She needed to earn a living in order not to rely exclusively on Madame de Lignières. It wasn't just about the money, she had gotten caught up in her own game, which was not without its benefits: tame her stage fright, each evening face an audience demanding that she capture their interest the second she stepped onto the stage for fear of being mercilessly catcalled. And then it was such fun to embody in the flesh the character of Lou.

The last package in the pile was wrapped in plain brown paper. She crumpled it into a large ball on the table where she took off her makeup, loaded with eye shadow and blush, and discovered a printed folio of textured paper. It was a collection of poems by Alain Béron with the enigmatic title: *The Bending Crown*. The title page bore a dedication, traced with a firm hand in blue ink: "To the siren with the sapphire eyes." Under the signature, the poet had drawn an eye rimmed by long lashes. She remembered the man from the night before who had looked deeply at her, his upright bearing in his impeccably tailored three-piece suit, his sadness, which seemed to come from somewhere far away; she remembered more clearly, contrasting with the disagreeable impression of last night's quarrel, the gesture he had made with his hand to hold her back when she wanted to leave the table after having made her final verbal stab at Agnès, the calming effect that the warmth of that large, protective palm had on her. For the first time, she wondered if she should write a note of thanks.

· 1 6 ·

Bérénice had just left her theater class. The boss had not been nice to one of her friends who had acted the role of Sylvette in Edmond Rostand's *Romanesques*. He had criticized her because she hadn't worked hard enough on her scene. As he often did, he made misogynistic comments and then threatened to quit the Conservatory. He had changed his mind and upset his class by suddenly claiming that direction did not exist, that scenery was useless. What a paradox, what an act of provocation on the part of someone who was about to be praised for his production of Molière's *The School for Wives* at the Athénée with the marvelous sets of Christian Bérard.

When she entered the dining hall, Bérénice was swept up in a group of students who were leaving André Brunot's class—he was the main topic of conversation. Robert Manuel, an excellent raconteur, had an affection for his professor that bordered on veneration, reinforced by a mutual predilection for andouille sausage, beef boiled in coarse salt, and Beaujolais.

"The other night, we were invited to the home of an Italian princess. Despite her aristocratic origins, the lady was—how should I put it?—'as stingy as somebody from Auvergne.' ... The 'feast' we were offered consisted only of tiny sandwiches and instead of the wines we had anticipated: fruit juice! General despair! Melancholy glances from Brunot! 'Don't worry, kids, I'll lift the siege.' he whispered to us. We were getting ready to clear out when our hostess made the mistake of exclaiming, 'Leaving so soon? At least promise you'll come back and dine with me again. I'm counting on it. When would be good for you? —'Why not right now, Madame?'"

"No!"

"Scout's honor."

"It's all true, I was there," confirmed a student in the company.

Everyone laughed even more. At the next table, the sound attracted the attention of Jules, Bérénice's horn player friend.

"Hey, gorgeous, I've got two tickets for *Rigoletto* on Sunday at the Opera. Will you join me? Fanny isn't free, she's got a rehearsal."

"I'd love to."

"While we're on the subject," Robert Manuel interrupted, "did you know that the Comédie-Française is looking for extras for *Lorenzaccio?*"

That was great news! Bérénice went home very excited: so, only two short months after her admission to the Conservatory, she could hope to act on the stage of the House of Molière? And in *Lorenzaccio*, no less! The same play and the same production that she saw when she was eight years old, a commemorative revival on the occasion of the centenary of the play's publication. "You'll meet Monsieur Jans," said Robert Manuel, always well informed—he had had his first role as an extra several months before in *Coriolanus*. She remembered the stir the play had caused in February 1934. Certain lines, which criticized the decadence of the Roman republic, had been interpreted as subversive on the eve of the violent events of February 6, 1934, at the Place de la Concorde. "They're trying to encourage the fascists, Shakespeare is threatening the regime!" The executive director, Émile Fabre, who had run the Comédie-Française for twenty years, had almost lost his job—to tell the truth, he actually had, but only for twenty-four hours! Bérénice regretted not having been present for that modern version of the battle over Victor Hugo's controversial *Hernani*, which Robert Manuel recounted so well: "Oh la la, in the theater, they were dropping telephone books from the balconies, no one had ever seen such a commotion." But back then, she was still moping around her parents' home, wondering if she could ever take the entrance exam.

A few days later she found herself facing Monsieur Jans. The person in charge of the extras was tall and heavy set, his dentures were loose, but Bérénice took his corpulence for joviality, his homeliness for kindness. If it hadn't been for her theatrical myopia that embellished everything around her, she would have realized that the interview took no more than five minutes.

Who cares! She was hired. Ten francs a performance, what luxury! She would need to inform The Masked Owl the next day that she had to cut back to three or four nights a week. Monsieur Francis was going to be very disappointed not to see her every night walking up the stairs to her dressing room! When she had to go back for rehearsals, she discovered Mounet-Sully Hall, where the other Conservatory students were assembling, also extras. She would meet the well-known actors Jean Yonnel, cast as Thomas Strozzi; Marie Ventura, who was appearing in *Lorenzaccio* for the first time; René Alexandre portraying Alessandro de' Medici, and his wife, Gabrielle Robinne, in the role of the Marquise de Cibo. Some of the principal actors confided in her, delighted to have a new audience for their anecdotes, like those of Jean Yonnel—he immediately seemed likeable to her because his father had cut off his support when he learned that his son was taking acting classes: "My debut was at the Monceau Theater in *The Hunchback of Notre-Dame*. One night I was playing my scene with Esmeralda, who was sitting on my lap, with her back to an open window where Claude Frollo suddenly appeared. From the top balcony, a woman yelled, 'Look out, kiddo, here comes that preacher guy. He's gonna carve you up.' I was stabbed by the knife and fell. The woman was beside herself: 'I told you so, you little dipshit!'"

She encountered the sloppiness of the Comédie-Française that Jouvet had repeatedly warned her about: the absent directors, the principal actors showing up late, their being understudied by prompters and sometimes even the chambermaids, and worse, ladies performing with white cotton gloves so as not to besmirch their hands with the stage props. On the other hand, she was struck by the strict hierarchy: if the principal actors were allowed to get away with anything, the novices from the Conservatory were only allowed in the "puppet theater," the little makeshift dressing room at stage right. Nor were they allowed to take the elevator.

Before that, before she discovered this new world, there was the soirée at the Opera. The only previous time she had set foot in a theater where singing was performed was at the Light Opera, Favart Hall, for *Malvina* by Reynaldo Hahn—the play seemed rather weak to her. As for the opera records that she had heard at Colette's apartment on the family phonograph, they had filled her only with boredom and sarcasm: what a crazy idea to repeat the same phrase ten times! She had actually counted no fewer than twenty-two "Funny sort of people these" at the beginning of *Carmen*. She had nevertheless accepted her friend's invitation—he had succeeded in getting hold of two comps in the dress circle. After all, opera was theater, she could certainly learn something. She arrived at the Opera knowing nothing of the libretto except that it had been inspired by Victor Hugo's *The King Amuses Himself*. She discovered in the program that Agnès Grangé was playing the part of Gilda, the heroine. Bérénice had to admit that she was a bit curious to hear what sort of voice she had.

Since the famous evening at The Masked Owl, she had not had a real conversation with her friend Puech. She didn't blame him for the soprano's outburst, but had remained more than skeptical about Jules's admiration for the composer: "Look, Nathan's there, you see him, in the orchestra stalls, yes, with the white scarf." Bérénice did recognize the composer who, standing, in a suit with tails, was talking with a couple seated in the row in front of his. Perhaps he sensed that he was being observed at that moment, because he turned in their direction, noticed the enthusiastic gestures that Jules was making to him, and recognized his friend. He doffed his hat, nodding to her. Bérénice turned away, testily. "I'm warning you, there's no way I'm going to say hello to him during the intermission. You go by yourself if you're so keen on it."

Despite herself, Bérénice thought of Agnès, who must be busy in the wings. To judge by the program, she wouldn't appear on stage till the second scene. What do opera singers do to get themselves ready, Bérénice thought. Do they have special exercises, like actors who repeat over and over, "Serious decisions several musicians" to warm up their voices? In the hallways of the Conservatory, she often ran into young singers who would vocalize at the drop of a hat, visibly proud of showing off their lovely voices. Displaying their throats for all to view had always seemed to her as vain as it was indecent. Downright pathological, as synonymous with singers as lead colic is to painters.

Though hardly inclined to indulgence, Bérénice had understood since the first notes of the overture why opera fascinated so many people. What a difference from the records! The sheer numbers of the orchestra, the power of the voices, formed a sonorous mass that seemed to penetrate her and whose force felt as invincible and unstoppable as a raging sea. She also understood that the melody could multiply the emotion and compensate for the mediocrity of the text. Above all, there was the voice, pushed almost to the limits of the possible, allowing it to sing the highest pitched notes or to project to the very last rows with a sort of Dionysian fervor. That was what she wanted to work toward as an actress, she wouldn't be satisfied until she succeeded, through the amplitude of her voice, by the variety of its colors, to make the audience feel the difficulty of being, how madness and death lightly brush against each other, that moment of swaying, so subtle, where each person could suddenly pass to the other side of normalcy. Art doesn't have to be realistic, she thought, it has to amplify life.

During the intermission, true to her vow, Bérénice did not walk down to the lobby with Jules. Experiencing an emotion almost as violent as her first play at the Comédie-Française, she remained in the empty theater, nearly prostrate, staring blankly, still under the spell of the terrible curse uttered by the old Count Monterone.

Suddenly she realized that she wasn't alone in the box. A man had entered—it was Alain Béron. "Good evening, Mademoiselle Lou." He extended his hand.

She didn't have time to be upset: she found again in the poet's handshake the inexplicable warmth she had felt at The Masked Owl. The deep and timbered voice of the poet had the same calming effect. He explained that he had recognized her in the theater and wanted to say hello. Bérénice didn't attempt to shy away. At least he knew how to talk about art, as evidenced by his poems—their lyricism and depth had been striking to her, even his most hermetic verses had a poignant beauty. She told him all that, and something knotted between them, born from a mutual recognition, a collusion of their sensibilities.

His presence stirred something very strong in her, a desire to cry and open up, a desire to confide and be reassured because—she suddenly realized—the path she had chosen was long and difficult. It was while talking to him that she could feel the weight she had taken on her shoulders, and all at once she missed her parents terribly, the lost rapport with her father, the conversations with her mother. Why did she have the feeling that he understood all that she kept to herself and that they resembled one another despite their twenty-year age difference? He also couldn't explain that sudden desire to lay down his weapons and his baggage in her presence, to abandon the mask of social interaction and to finally be himself, as he only was when he wrote in silence and contemplation. The audience began to filter back into the theater, the lawyer-poet had to take his leave of her, they promised to see each other again. Before that, he made her cry without meaning to, simply by evoking *Rigoletto*, because the way that he spoke about the musical theme of the curse made her think of the sound of torn clothing. Her father had cursed her, and her shame was so great that she didn't confide her secret to him, but he understood that she carried within her an immense pain and perhaps that was what bound them together.

· 1 7 ·

During the early days of June 1936, the Conservatory was boiling over with turmoil. For once, this bubbling was not about an upcoming entrance or exit exam, or an audition. Nor was it about the sensation that a student or professor had caused, or a bit of gossip. The cause was politics. And yet, the students at the Conservatory were ordinarily not terribly curious about political matters. More preoccupied with themselves than with the workings of the world, the fate of Spain or the colonies held little interest for them, newspapers put them to sleep unless they were talking about the theater. Financial scandals and the replacement of cabinet ministers went right over their heads. In truth, reality did not weigh heavily in their minds. At most, they hoped that the winds of history would blow in a direction that was propitious for them and their intimate desires.

Now, however, something different was happening: the leftwing Popular Front had just won the elections and a wave of enthusiasm, close to euphoria, passed through the Conservatory. Many students cracked open a bottle of champagne on hearing the results: "Did we cream them or what!" they crowed. Only a minority of the students commented bitterly about a Jew, Léon Blum, taking over as president of the Council of Ministers. They all repeated the incident that had taken place in the Chamber of Deputies, the words of a certain Xavier Vallat, a representative from the Ardèche region, a deputy of the extreme right: "Your accession to power, Monsieur le Président, marks a historic date. For the first time, this ancient Gallo-Roman country will be governed by a Jew." Édouard Herriot's response was superb: "I know neither Jew, nor Protestant, nor Catholic. In this Assembly, I know only Frenchmen."

This political transformation could have serious consequences for the theater, delighting these performers in the making. Wasn't Blum a former drama critic, the author of nearly a thousand articles between 1897 and 1914, an admirer of André Antoine and his naturalistic and rebellious Free Theater? Things were going to change, that much was certain. In a few weeks, the students found out more, especially those who, like Bérénice, were students of Louis Jouvet, because the boss was regularly summoned to the Rue de Grenelle, home of the Ministry of Education and Fine Arts, headed by Jean Zay. Rumor had it that the minister had proposed Jouvet for the post of executive director of the Comédie-Française. But Jouvet declined the offer, little disposed to leave the Athénée, where he had become director two years earlier, even less disposed to be recruited for the House of Molière, so difficult to govern, encumbered with tradition and its principal actors. Out of the generosity of his soul, he nevertheless suggested to the minister that he choose Jean Giraudoux, but that playwright also refused. The two friends then proposed the name of Édouard Bourdet, author of such successful plays as *The Captive*, *The Weaker Sex*, and *Hard Times*.

Would Bourdet also bow out? He took time to reflect. Retreating to his house in Tamaris, in the South of France, he weighed the pros and cons. Bourdet ended up accepting but with a triple condition: he would chose the works he staged, he would name four men to the title of Director (Louis Jouvet, Gaston Baty, Charles Dullin, Jacques Copeau), and finally he would obtain from the Board of Governors a pledge of non-interference in the affairs of the theater. And so he was named executive director on August 13, 1936, one hour after the resignation of Émile Fabre. "He's not one of ours," Léon Blum remarked to Jean Zay. What did it matter? Even if he wasn't a leftist, Bourdet had important qualities for the post: he was a man of the theater with proven taste and he knew the profession inside and out, a scrupulous and independent man. Bérénice caught a glimpse of him at the Conservatory where he had a meeting with Henri Rabaud. A severe mien and steely blue eyes that inspired respect, even fear. "Oh, he's a tough one, all right," Jouvet commented, rubbing his hands together. "He'll give the old boys a run for their money."

Summer 1936. With the blossoming of the Popular Front, an elation close to jubilation spread throughout France. People savored their first paid vacations, they applauded the forty-hour work week, they clinked glasses to the revolution, even the actors of the Comédie-Française joined in, at least those whose heart tilted to the left: Marie Bell fraternized in a silk dress and a wide-brimmed, white organdy hat with the strong-armed porters at Les Halles in their bloody aprons, the principal actors greeted factory occupations with enthusiasm, went to read poems to the occupiers, generously contributed the money that they had on them to the strikers' cause.

While the workers of Suresnes or Puteaux were packing their bags to leave for the beach or to go camping, Robert Manuel passed his end-of-the-year exam. He was brilliant in his portrayal of the title role in Molière's *Scapin the Schemer* and Lui in *Fear of a Beating* by Courteline. Journalists and friends alike warmly celebrated his triumph. Jouvet offered him a contract at the Athénée. He refused: like Bérénice, he was dreaming of the Comédie-Française. The deal was concluded on July 10, the day when he signed a one-year contract in the office of the executive director for roles of "young comic lead, butler, comic lover, and various minor parts."

Just two weeks later he made his official debut in *Scapin the Schemer*. Official debuts involved a moving ceremony where the torch was passed to the next generation. The young member of the troupe was surrounded by all the oldest principal actors, arranged according to their roles. One couldn't help but sense in the transmission of this secular art the spirits of the illustrious men and women who had come before them, names such as Rachel, Talma, Mounet-Sully, Sylvain, Lekain, and even—for good measure—the benevolent shadow of the patron of them all: Jean-Baptiste Poquelin, otherwise known as Molière.

Robert was delighted: his professor André Brunot kept his promise and returned specially from Saint-Jacut-de-la-Mer in Brittany where he was spending his vacation to play Sylvester and support his young student. A supreme honor: he loaned him his Scapin costume, the role that he had owned. "He's like that, Brunot, he loves to help young people," Robert Manuel commented, jubilant. The night of his debut, the theater was sold out. Even the minister Jean Zay attended, accompanied by his principal private secretary, Marcel Abraham, sitting next to Henri Rabaud, the director of the Conservatory, as well as all the critics, writers, and artists of Paris.

That evening, like everyone else, Bérénice was completely focused on her friend's success, and like everyone else, she applauded the debut of Robert Manuel, without realizing that in the heat of the action, he lost his pants. She heard about it that evening at the Café de la Régence straight from the horse's mouth, when Robert recounted the story of the accident, and how he had to rush to find Pierre Dux's trousers and slip them on while on stage, behind the scenery. That was theater for you, in the midst of the majesty and ceremony, a trivial little event could intervene that upset the beautiful, sacred mechanics, as if in mockery, as if to say, "Remember, this is all a game!"

How many times had Bérénice heard anecdotes like this about the Comédie-Française and its customs at the Café de la Régence, or sitting at the sidewalk tables of the Café de l'Univers, or Chez Ruc? Between sandwiches, bottles of beer, or Vichy water, she was soon up to date on the "war of succession" for the post of executive director. In the course of the next few weeks, you could feel the two factions taking sides: the "Bourdettists," who applauded the modernization plans of the new executive director, and the "Anti-Bourdettists," who felt their ways were threatened and constantly spoke with nostalgia of the good old days of Émile Fabre.

In October 1936, the controversy came to a head when it was disclosed that Bourdet, nicknamed "The Fabre-Swallower," cancelled all the contracts. The old guard screamed, "Who does this guy think he is—Napoleon? Even in the middle of his Russian campaign, Napoleon thought about our House and instituted a rule that the major roles in the repertoire had to be played by 'tenured' actors, and here comes this little worm, Bourdet, this author of boulevard trash, and he sweeps all that away! This punk thinks he's better than an emperor."

"But look, The Cid played by a principal actor who's sixty years old—it's just not believable! It's ridiculous. The audience today won't put up with the part of a young man being played by some bedridden actor. Everybody howls when Perdican asks, 'How old are you, Camille?' and Marie Ventura answers, 'Eighteen,' when everyone knows she's seen fifty springs."

"My dear fellow, Sarah Bernhardt played the Eaglet, Napoleon's son, when she was seventy. I've never heard that anyone had a problem with that. Because of your damn cinema, you've forgotten that we're in the theater. Would you want sixteen-year-old adolescents playing Romeo and Juliet? Do you think at that age you have the emotional depth? Why don't you push realism to the point of having a negro play Othello, while you're at it? Of course, with all those new professors that they've saddled the Conservatory with, there's no danger that standards are going to be raised. ... Imagine, Jouvet! A stutterer! And they complain that the theater has become decadent! I only hope he doesn't contaminate his students with his awful diction."

Bérénice laughed up her sleeve, she thought about her friend Jean Meyer who did such a good imitation of the boss. Her mind was made up. Without knowing the new executive director, she felt she was a committed "Bourdet-tist," realizing that with a man like that, young people might get their chance before their hair turned white.

A year later, the Popular Front was waning, it had abandoned Spain, prices kept going up, unemployment was continually on the rise. Bérénice hardly took notice: it was now her turn to take the exit exam. The situation was serious: rumor had it that Bourdet was refusing to preside over the jury. They said that he was asking to serve on the jury with three of his directors, Jacques Copeau, Charles Dullin, and Gaston Baty, and that the director of the Conservatory refused. Bérénice and several other students ran to find Jouvet to get clarification:

"That's exactly right, there won't be an executive director of the Comédie-Française on the jury this year," Jouvet told them.

A few days later, Édouard Bourdet himself confirmed this in *Le Temps*: "The director of the Conservatory is in charge in his own house and has the right to constitute the examination jury as he sees fit—that is a fact that I do not contest for a second.

"When I appealed to his good will and asked him to include on this jury the directors, my collaborators at the Comédie-Française, and because he agreed to my request to include Gaston Baty, but not Jacques Copeau and Charles Dullin—Louis Jouvet being a professor and therefore not eligible to serve on the jury—we find ourselves, Baty and myself, if we agree to serve on the jury without them, in an objectionable and awkward situation, and that is another fact that I hope Henri Rabaud will appreciate the importance of, out of common courtesy.

"Although I reiterated my request about the exit examination, he did not grant it. The consequence is this: he is completely within his rights, as we are, Gaston Baty and I, to recuse ourselves. That is the whole story. In itself, it is not that serious. What is serious, though, is that the students, in particular the graduates who are justified in hoping, in certain cases—even though it is not at all a right—for a contract with the Comédie-Française, the students, as I said, are the ones who will suffer as a result of this incident. But they should be completely reassured. Appropriate measures have been taken and will be announced in due course, so that the perfectly legitimate interests of the students can be thoroughly protected."

"Can we hope to get a contract? What measures are they talking about?" Bérénice anxiously asked Jouvet.

"Here's how it stands. Auditions will take place at the Comédie-Française. They are scheduled for July 2, four days after the official competition.

Third-year students and those who participated last year can take part. You'll be among them. But, my little mama, as far as the exit exam for the Conservatory, don't expect to get the first prize. Since Bourdet announced that he would not take into account the decisions of the jury in offering contracts for the Comédie-Française, I would bet that the official jury will refuse to award one."

"No first prize?"

It was a catastrophe. What about her promise to Madame de Lignières? How could she explain that circumstances had prevented her? Even before her first day at the Conservatory, that was the dream she had aspired to. Like the majority of her friends, the *cursus honorum* was clear for Bérénice: the Conservatory, first prize, the Comédie-Française. Second prize—that would be a disgrace!

Bérénice made up her mind: "Would you hold it against me if I didn't enter the official competition?"

"As you wish, my child. But you'll have to go for broke at the audition for the Comédie-Française. And believe me, even with me on the jury, it won't be a piece of cake."

In fact, no first prize was awarded in the exit exam for the Conservatory in June 1937. In the category of tragedy, Jean Chevrier and Mademoiselle Riddez both received honorable mentions, while in comedy, Jean Meyer, Moulinot, and Renée Faure all were awarded a second prize.

"So," exclaimed Jean Meyer as he prepared to audition all over again, this time for the Comédie-Française, "now that we've gone through the impossible ordeal of the first test, let's get ready for an even more excruciating one!"

· 1 8 ·

Simul et singulis
1680–1937
The Executive Director,
The Members of the Board of Directors,
and the Principal Actors of the Comédie-Française
request the presence of Mademoiselle Bérénice de Lignières
for an audition,
Friday, the Second of July, 1937, in the Salle Richelieu,
at 10:15 a.m. sharp

Bérénice held in her hands the card embossed with the famous emblem "1680," the date when the House of Molière was founded. It seemed to her she was gambling with her life for the second time. What would she do if she failed? She wouldn't even have the satisfaction of winning a second prize at the Conservatory, since she hadn't taken the exam. Would she continue in the same profession or return to her parents' home, her dreams of glory shelved like those of so many others before her? The idea crossed her mind, but she knew it would be impossible. If it wasn't the Comédie-Française, she would be terribly upset, but she couldn't give up the theater. She would act elsewhere. At the

Athénée, perhaps, as Louis Jouvet was urging her to do. Or she might even join a traveling company and go on the road. During her studies, she had met passionate and adventurous young people, like that Jean-Louis Barrault, who had staged an amazing production of Cervantes's *Numance* at the Antoine Theater. Tradition or avant-garde—in the end, what did it matter? The main thing was to act. Although, the Comédie-Française. ...

She kept thinking about something she had heard Jouvet say many times when the trembling young actors had summoned all their courage and interrogated their instructor at the risk of annoying him, and received straight from his golden mouth a phrase that they would internalize and cherish: "A calling is only a persistent choice."

She often thought about this. Maybe there is no such thing as a calling, she said to herself at the time, maybe it's just a word to try to grasp the mystery of a life, in the same way that her family often used her given name to explain her love for the theater. At first a calling is only a desire, and then, through work and tenacity, it can take a form that deserves to be given the name of a calling. If we were honest about it, we would admit that we've all had a calling, as a child or an adolescent. One person might have wanted to write, another to sing, one might have dreamed of being a boxer, still another imagined becoming a teacher or a lawyer. But ultimately, how many succeed? The majority don't persevere long enough, they get distracted, and if they don't have a breakthrough, they give up. Instead of becoming an actor, you become a stage manager. Instead of a singer, you become a journalist. Instead of a writer, a professor. Instead of becoming a lawyer, you run a business. And then you find justifications: a family to feed, the training lasts an impossibly long time, bad luck, anything not to lose face, in order not to tell your children later on that you missed out on your dreams. And sometimes, as in the circus, the ultimate pirouette: life has the last laugh on us, and the one who dreamed of being a writer becomes a famous director—a fate that many would dream of, except the one concerned, eternally frustrated at not having the satisfaction of fulfilling that initial calling.

She will be an actress because she wanted to. She will join the Comédie-Française because it was there that her love for the theater was born, it was there she felt she was in her rightful place, more than on any other stage, because it's the House of Molière. And because it would impress her father. *There, I said it, I hadn't thought about it before, but yes, if I have to be a whore, at least let it be in the only theater that has the word* français *in its name. Comédie-*Française, *that has to mean something, even (and above all) for Maurice Capel, born Kapeluchnik. I have to succeed tomorrow,* she told herself again and again.

On July 2, 1937, at ten a.m., about forty young people arrived at the Rue de Richelieu. Bérénice no longer heard anything, not the sound of the vacuum cleaners in the hallways, and not the shouts of her friends who were looking for a dress or a lipstick or a wig. She felt as if she gone back three years, less knowledgeable than when she had entered the Conservatory. In the end, what had she learned in those three years, how to synthesize what she had received? Some of her friends were able to theorize about their education. Not Bérénice. It seemed to her that all of her apprenticeship had seeped into her little by little, almost without her being aware of it, without her even knowing how "it" had happened.

Not the right time for daydreaming. The auditions were starting. The first candidates retreated to the wings after their performances, greeted with an avalanche of questions:

"So, who's on the jury besides Bourdet and his three musketeers?"

"Is the one in the middle actually Dessonnes?"

"Did they say anything to you at the end?"

"What's Marie Ventura like? She looks meaner than her photos."

"They say that Pierre Dux and Fernand Ledoux were the most lenient, is that true?"

"How much time did they give you?"

"Hey, Bérénice, it's almost your turn. What are you performing?"

"… myownlilac," she muttered.

"Huh? What? Lilac?"

"Hermione's soliloquy from *Andromache*," she burst out, infuriated.

For God's sake, make them shut up, let me concentrate, make sure everything's in order. Wig: secured. Makeup: eyes, cheekbones, rouge, nothing overlooked. A fire, let there be a fire, let it devour me the way it killed Jane Henriot in this very place. No, I'm crazy. This is it, it's my turn. They're all there, at the table set up by the sixth, seventh, eighth row of the orchestra. Eight, that's my lucky number. How many are there? Eleven or twelve? My vision is getting blurry, I can't even count. Oh la la, it's just like a jury in a criminal court deciding my fate, the guillotine or life. Help me, dear Comédie-Française, that I've dreamed of for so long, help me, dear red and gold theater, you I love so much, help me dear stage that smells so good from all the velvet, woodwork, and sawdust of the sets, help me my kind, my dear Molière, you who know what this profession is like and what it is to love the stage, help me both of you, my sweet Comédie-Française, my sweet Molière, let me be worthy of you, let me remember my lines, may I not choke, please, please, let my tongue unstick itself from my palate, oh, my God, I'm going to be the only one who is shamed because she can't speak …

"It's your turn, Mademoiselle de Lignières!"

I never loved you? What then was my deed?
I scorned for you the vows of other princes,
I found myself adrift here in these provinces;
Still here, despite your infidelity,
My Greeks are ashamed of my mercy.
I ordered them to hide my injury.

"She's impossible, that girl," murmured a stage manager in the wings. "Usually, they all scream at that point. Not this one—she's smiling …"

Waiting, then more waiting. By the end of the day, they had not yet announced the jury's decision. The candidates all had to go home without knowing anything of their fate. Why did it seem to Bérénice that Louis Jouvet wouldn't make eye contact with her? They told the candidates that Édouard Bourdet had left for his villa in Tamaris to think it over.

"Tamaris, what the heck is that?"

"It's his wife's seaside home, near Toulon."

"When's he coming back?"

"Well … in about ten days."

"Ten days! That long?"

· 1 9 ·

Listen, Comédie-Française, arrange it so I'm invited to join the company, you're the one, the only one that I will sacrifice everything for—youth, family, children—what do those matter if you allow me to become part of you, to be one of yours, House of Molière, my blessed one, my glorious one that I love with all my heart, with all my soul, and with all my ability, I recognize you, living and righteous queen, my beloved, I will listen to your commandments and I will give you all without stinting, my fervor and my love, accept me as your own, adopt me as one of your children, I will toil toward your glory so that you will shine ever more resplendently, I give you my oath, I will not fail, I will not betray you, when I go to sleep, when I awake, I will speak of you, I will honor you always even if my home crumbles, if illness strikes me down, if my children turn their backs on me …

She won't repeat to her grandchildren or even to her children the prayer that at every moment, in the street, at home, at the movies, at her friends' homes, in the metro, at the International Exposition of Art and Technology, in a café, while shopping, in bed, she spoke under her breath for those ten days, the prayer that culminated on July 13, 1937, the day before France's national holiday, when her landlady shouted that she was wanted on the phone. She flew down the stairs four at a time, jostling her elderly neighbor who grumbled, "these young people have no respect," Bérénice's hands became sweaty when she picked up the receiver and she recognized Jouvet's voice. "The director wants to see you. Bring your mother, you're a minor." She understood that she was being asked to join, she didn't dare scream her victory out loud since nothing was in writing yet, you never know, she might be dreaming or get run over by a bus, the jury might change their minds, the executive director might change his decision, they might discover that she was not the daughter of Madame de Lignières, her father might come and testify that she had lied, that she had falsified her age and everything would fall apart, her three years of study and all her efforts. After barely taking the time to phone Madame de Lignières who—luckily—was free and delighted to pass for her mother in France's premier theater, Bérénice flew to the Palais-Royal.

The same prayer recited rapidly in her head while walking up to the second floor of the Comédie-Française, by the bust of Molière that she stroked shyly, because they say it brought good luck. On the second floor, in the antechamber of the executive director's office, assembled before Émile, the doorkeeper, who congratulated her with his sonorous voice and his warm Burgundian accent, four of them gathered: her friends who had also graduated, Renée Faure and Jean Meyer, but also Mony Dalmès and Nadine Marziano, who had won their prizes a couple of years before. They greeted one another there, congratulating each other with hushed voices, not daring to make too much noise right outside the office of the executive director. She was the youngest so she was also the most intimidated of the five on entering for the first time the holy of holies. Édouard Bourdet greeted them, a severe silhouette in his dark, pinstripe suit. It was freedom that he first touched on in his speech to the new members of the company, announcing to them that they were hired and that their service to the House from now on would demand their complete dedication, proclaiming to them in a tone that precluded any reply that they would quickly become principal actors or they would leave: "I want a young troupe and not a bunch of bitter actors we no longer dare to let go after fifteen years here. We don't work here for the vacations." Vacations? What vacations?

Mademoiselle de Lignières commits herself, in agreement with the Executive Director, to play in the Theater of the Comédie-Française, all the roles assigned to her in tragedies, comedies, and dramas, especially in the role of [handwritten text:] Young female lead in tragedies, dramas, and comedies.

Her signature, which she wrote with a trembling hand, with seriousness and gratitude, and below, in contrast, the initials of Madame de Lignières scrawled in a confident and, it seemed, almost mocking manner; quite a trick she had just played on them. With just her initials she avenged herself on her own parents who had squelched the dreams of her youth, Bérénice's parents,

Jouvet's, all the conformist parents, all the bogeymen from the past and the future who only believe in good jobs and try to teach with their trite sayings that a worthwhile life is achieved through money and a suitable profession even though it is only art that holds the world together.

Bérénice had signed. From now on, she would be inscribed in the archives of the Comédie-Française. At the end of the year, a kind man, Édouard Champion, erudite, historian and man of letters, and in addition, president of the Circle of Clericks, a charming name, though obsolete, or perhaps charming because obsolete. Édouard Champion, therefore, telling the story of the daily life of the House of Molière beginning in 1933, will have the time to write this notice, which will be printed in the volume for the year 1937, on page 12, under the rubric "New hires and debuts," just before he passed away, preventing him from further work on his opus:

15 July, Mademoiselle de Lignières (Bérénice).
Conservatory: enters in November 1934; class of Monsieur Louis Jouvet. Contract signed for one year with the Executive Director, 13 July, to begin on the 15th. —Performs for the first time at the Comédie-Française 26 July 1937, in The Crows (as The Servant). Debuts officially on 10 August 1937, Hernani (Doña Sol). Played various minor roles at the Comédie during her studies at the Conservatory.

It was the principal actor Jean Yonnel who spoke the most resonant words when he came to congratulate her: "Now your real work begins." Yes, it's when you have passed the milestones, the Conservatory, the audition, membership in the troupe, that you can finally start acting with more tranquility, without having failure on your mind, and truly make progress. Still ahead was the step of becoming a principal actor, but the most difficult part she had achieved, the House of Molière had accepted her. That, in essence, is what she would say in the newspaper Excelsior, which reported on the impressions of the five new troupe members and printed their photographs, an interview that one can still find by consulting the archives for the date of 29 July 1937, her first interview—there would be many more. In the paragraph, "Comments of Mademoiselle de Lignières," one finds her remarks on how happy she is to be invited to join the Comédie-Française, fairly conventional remarks, but odd in this instance because those words do not give the slightest glimpse of her true personality, and so, incomprehensible until one remembers that she couldn't reveal the path blocked by her parents, under threat of being accused, she and Madame de Lignières, of forgery and use of forged documents.

On August 10, she would make her debut in *Hernani*, directed by Georges Le Roy. She would discover on the columns of the kiosks the yellow posters with her name on them, posters announcing in red letters the debut of Mademoiselle de Lignières above the exceptional and partly new cast. Jean Yonnel (Don Carlos), Robert Vidalin (Hernani), her dear pal Robert Manuel (Don Garci Suarez), her friend Jean Meyer (the Duke of Gotha), Mony Dalmès (the Marquise), and Renée Faure (Iackez) would be at her side, they would support the young actress in her debut, giving her advice on how to walk in a dress with a train, they would help her master all the stage directions. But even more than having her name on the posters, more than the flashbulbs of the photographers, the curtain calls demanded by the audience and the great reviews, there were all the little welcome notes that she found in her mailbox that delighted her just as much as the smiles of the principal actors after her debut, the gracious presence of Véra Korène, the appearance of the assistant head André Brunot who took her hand to lead her onstage to take a solo bow. They were so generous, her new family!

She would see for the first time her little dressing room on the level called the Rachel floor, also the floor where the head hairdresser was located, Monsieur Georges, the linen maids, the seamstresses, and the dressers. The first piece of furniture she moved in Colette gave to her as a present, a little round pedestal table inlaid with marquetry, that they had found together one afternoon while strolling past the shop window of an antique dealer. Bit by bit she filled it with armchairs upholstered in off-white cretonne, small mirrors from Murano, a secretary, blue silk cushions with a cream pattern, a daybed upholstered in beige and blue, vases, paintings. … A cozy little nest so comforting, it helped her exorcise her stage fright before her cue to enter.

From the time she arrived she was taken in hand by Raymonde, her dresser, who told her all the secret gossip about the theater. Bérénice became the protégée of Béatrice Bretty, called "The Brette," twenty-two years older, who took a liking to her at first sight. Bretty excelled at soubrette roles, was marvelous at playing the maid Dorine or Marinette, roles she had made her debut in back in 1915. "You weren't even born then," she observed to Bérénice, enchanting her with that distinctive laugh that you could recognize from across the room, the laugh of a woman who fully enjoyed life, irresistibly communicative. Bérénice learned that she was the sweetheart of Georges Mandel, the minister for the colonies, she would discover what role they played in 1936 in saving the Comédie-Française when there were only ten thousand francs left in the theater's treasury, a sum that couldn't even meet the monthly payroll, so that Mandel, then the postmaster general, and Bretty, already a principal actress, asked that the Comédie-Française be allowed to broadcast radio programs every day. Scientific progress coming to rescue of the House of Molière, what an inspiration they had! "Everything went smoothly. Last year, we broadcast more than three hundred live programs!" boasted The Brette. The coffers were brimming, the proceeds from the radio broadcasts allowed the Comédie-Française to completely recover financially. Building on that momentum, Jean Zay raised the State's subsidy to the theater at the time of Édouard Bourdet's nomination.

It was with that illustrious principal actress that Bérénice ("You, my dear, have a truly predestined name!" she heard for the hundredth time) sought refuge on the night of her official debut. Her own dressing room was overflowing with flowers, so she couldn't even enter it. While the dresser was busy at her work, Bretty, seated on a modest, lacquered chair with its back shaped like a lyre, ran through the list of the actors of the troupe to give her protégée the scoop on them: The Dusanne, the other great actress in the company who played soubrette roles; Gisèle Casadesus, a charming, petite woman, already a mother; that big giraffe Mary Marquet; the adorable and wild Marie Bell; that insolent Florence Hégué, a member of the troupe hired three years before by Émile Fabre. At the time, Bérénice didn't understand what Bretty meant when she declared, laughing, "As soon as you arrived, the ambitions of that poor Florence went down the drain!" That prospect seemed to delight her. An old feud that dated from the day when the young woman, then a student at the Conservatory, had used the elevator forbidden to the students and even to the regular members of the troupe, forcing Bretty to take the stairs. "If she can throw a stick in your spokes, she'll do it, but she's too chicken to seriously hurt you. And in public—you'll see—she'll act like she's your best friend!" Bérénice didn't pay too much attention to this torrent of information, too happy just to be there, in the dressing room of that more senior actress whom she would not dare ask to keep silent, yielding to the expert hands of Raymonde, who was dressing her in the yellow gown of Doña Sol.

· 2 0 ·

For a long time she kept her first work schedule as a member of the troupe with her at all times, meticulously folded in her wallet. What an incredible joy to possess this document that recorded each day, hour by hour, the sequence of tasks for employees of the theater. Their symbol was a hive and there was no better image to describe the work of these industrious bees. On stage in the Salle Richelieu, the committee meeting room, then the Brohan Foyer … From eight in the morning till eleven at night, the activity never stopped. Bérénice had to arrive by one in the afternoon on stage at the Richelieu Theater for her first tech rehearsal in her capacity as a member of the company.

She felt proud as she crossed the threshold of the stage door, left a humble bouquet of violets by the bust of Molière, an offering to the Boss to ward off failure. When she arrived at the theater, the stage was set. She recognized the massive armoire and the door to the hidden stairwell described in the opening stage directions of *Hernani*. Her dress wasn't ready yet, it needed alterations, the previous actress who had played the role was a bit more full figured. So she just wore her street clothes, a little red summer dress, her hair pulled up in a chignon because of the August heat. The other members of the troupe took their time arriving. She was alone on stage, without her script, remembering—when was it, a year ago?—it seemed like a century—how furious Jouvet was, one day when he had just come from the Comédie-Française for the first rehearsal he had directed of Corneille's *The Theatrical Illusion*. When he saw that the actors had brought their scripts, he challenged, "You don't know your parts yet?" "Not yet," they answered. "I'll come back when you know them." Jouvet put his hat back on.

In the pit, the orchestra was rehearsing the incidental music for *Hernani*. Harmonies she'd never heard before reached her ears, nothing like the usual ersatz Spanish music. Intrigued, Bérénice stepped forward. And then, leaning over the footlights to get a better look at the musicians, she suddenly stepped back, recognizing the conductor, none other than Nathan Adelman, who also recognized her and gave her a hint of a smile, immediately stopped the rehearsal, leaped onto the stage to greet her, and the two of them were joined precisely at that moment by Jean Yonnel and Robert Manuel, who made the introduction: "Bérénice de Lignières, a new member of the troupe— Nathan Adelman, the composer." In a few moments she would finally have her revenge, a way to make the musician pay for the humiliation she'd suffered at The Masked Owl, because the composer was German and had not yet fully mastered the vocabulary of the Comédie-Française: "You've enlisted in the troops? Well, should I congratulate you?" to which she replied, cuttingly: "Yes, as you can plainly see, I'm right here on the front lines," without pity for his confusion between "troupe" and "troops." So much the better if she humiliated him, even if he had broken up with Agnès Grangé, as she'd heard a few months before on the grapevine, she had avenged herself for the insult with ridicule, she could count on Manuel, who left right away, stifling a guffaw, to tell everyone about the incident, which quickly made the rounds of all the floors, from Préville to Talma and even to the topmost level, the Rachel floor, just under the attic, where the seamstresses and the linen maids had a great laugh at Nathan's expense. Bérénice remained alone with Adelman, flattening him with a look of triumph, then turned on her heels. He stood there, stunned, while Yonnel, a bit embarrassed, patted him on the shoulder in masculine solidarity. Later he would reveal to Bérénice that it was at this moment that he fell in love with her, so fragile because of the gaffe he had committed, precisely at the instant when her glance pierced him, her eyes so clear that they seemed strange, almost otherworldly, "That's where I fell in love with you," he told her, fooling himself, because it was actually when he'd heard her sing, "I Don't Love You" at The Masked Owl that he first loved her.

Still later he would tell her how emotionally riled he felt during those final rehearsals, discovering the young woman's acting style, the way she immersed herself in the language of Victor Hugo, which suddenly seemed to him the most French and delicious of languages, conquered by this queen who passionately confronted death and love, jealous of that Hernani whom she called, "My lion, superb and generous," when he wanted her to speak to him alone, almost forgetting the music that he'd composed, hearing only that of the poet through the voice of the young woman with her unflinching gaze, transfigured by that strange personage who had bewitched him at The Masked Owl in her black tuxedo and who was casting her spell again in that little red dress. I will have her, he said to himself, not knowing what part of this impulse belonged to desire, or the wish to protect her, the wish to confront her, the wish to love her. I will have her, my Doña sol, *do la sol*, musical woman, muse woman, a romantic *Lied* in *sol* major, major love, the beginning of a *Lied* in *sol* major that he would complete a week later, caught in an obsession with her gaze and light eyes that haunted him, and then he left the handwritten sheet music in the young woman's mailbox and she glared at it with a haughty look that was already forced, because she had sight-read the melody; in the *foyer des artistes*, the lounge reserved for performers, he would play her his *Lied* on the piano, and not to disturb the august personages in the paintings on the wall, he whispered the words to her rather than singing them. She looked at him suddenly stirred, finally abandoning her resentment to take in his declaration, looking into her dilated pupils he held himself back from furiously kissing her, that fragile porcelain that a fleeting moment revealed to him with all the youth of her eighteen years, making him suddenly shy, hesitating to throw himself into the life of that young female lead fourteen years his junior, asking himself if he had the right, concentrating then on his fingers which he noticed were clutching the keyboard tightly, all his usual easy manner gone, certain then that he no longer even had a choice, that leaving the room, leaving her, not taking the risk was no longer imaginable, and that she also knew it, he read it in her face when he turned his toward hers, the two of them bowled over, his heart pounding, and who knows what would have happened if the door hadn't opened at that very moment, revealing the doorkeeper, Émile, wondering who was playing the piano, and realizing too late that he had intruded, quickly retreating, apologizing profusely, the first witness to their nascent love, which the congenial doorkeeper would boast of afterwards when people began to gossip about the couple, I was there, he would say, it happened right before my eyes in the artists' lounge, they were like two turtledoves, and that phrase, they would hear it a thousand times from his mouth, each time he saw them, "You're like two turtledoves," he enjoyed repeating to them in his Burgundian accent, "I could tell right away in the artists' lounge, you were so beautiful that I didn't dare tell you that the lounge was reserved only for principal actors," but that story they will no longer be able to tell.

PART TWO

· 1 ·

That stab to the heart at a sidewalk table of the brasserie Deux Garçons in Aix-en-Provence where Nathan was winding up his vacation in the company of Bérénice and Alain Béron, when he read in a copy of the *Éclaireur du Sud-Est* left by a customer that the Germans and the Soviets had signed a nonaggression pact. They had just sat down to lunch. The radiant weather of August 23, 1939, on the Cours Mirabeau was so out of sync with this unnerving information. Nathan read out loud the story on page three of the newspaper, suddenly dejected, finding no comfort in having been right to leave the Communist Party out of disgust more than a year ago after the Moscow trials, because he no longer believed in the socialist utopia, because he thought, on the contrary, that Stalinism had torpedoed it once and for all. Not being able to rejoice that history had proven him right, seeing around him only a vertiginous void, finding himself orphaned for a second time, first by his native land, Germany, and then by his promised land, the USSR. Nothing was left, all the gods were dead.

Bérénice just shrugged her shoulders, made fun of politics, seeing only art as being able to bring humanity to the world, mocking his gullibility.

"That Stalin of yours, it doesn't surprise me one bit that he would sign a pact with Hitler. Neither of them is worth a damn, you know it yourself—you left the Party after the Moscow purges."

He tried to explain to her, who belonged to that generation without illusions that was born after the Treaty of Versailles, how he wanted to hope that he had been wrong, and how in his heart of hearts it had comforted him that Russia had proved it had been a mistake for him to believe. Now it was over. He was only an orphan of the left, disoriented.

The plane trees of the Cours Mirabeau, so charming just a few moments before, had lost all their luster and now had an arthritic look. Although more measured in his response than Nathan, Alain Béron had become restive, you could see it in the way he stubbed a cigarette butt and then lit another as soon as he had finished the last. Even though communism had never tempted him, he was just as stunned as Nathan by this dumbfounding news. It was in the name of hatred of communism that Hitler had justified the destruction of the Spanish Republic, and here was their public enemy, now turned ally. This dramatic turn of events was unbelievable. The situation was so serious that you could only think it would lead to war.

"War, war, war," Bérénice said impatiently, annoyed by the repeated scares that had been going on for months. They had come here to sit and talk about their new project, the opera that the three of them wanted to create together, and here was war monopolizing the conversation again.

"Maybe now Hitler will stop and we'll have peace."

"That's a fantasy," Nathan replied, losing his temper again. "You'll see how with their pretty little 'revolutionary dialectic' they'll find a way—without even blushing—to make sense of this pact, even though it's against nature, it's just horse trading, that's all it is. They'll tell us it's a purely strategic decision, that Russia wants to protect its borders, and of course, that the ends justify the means. I know it all by heart: to hell with morality, what difference does it make that they've allied themselves with Hitler, who helped Franco conquer Spain, who allowed Kristallnacht to happen ..."

The people sitting near their table began to stare at them, disturbed by their outbursts. As for Bérénice, she suppressed her own annoyance, suddenly aware of her lover's emotion. She remembered his devastated expression, that vein suddenly bulging, throbbing against his temple, when he announced, the morning of November 10, 1938, that his parents and his sister had been murdered by the SS. He had just received a phone call with the news, a neighbor of his parents had called him, in a torrent of muddled words he had told him that his "Jewish church" had burned down. At first Nathan thought there had been an accident. When he finally understood the disjointed narrative that followed, stirring up memories of his father, the cantor of the synagogue, his mother and sister, and above all his guilt for failing to convince them—despite his warnings, his prayers, his begging—to leave Germany. They just couldn't believe that misfortune would ever befall them, they had made Germany their home. She had listened to the words pouring out of him, seeming as if they would never end, thinking about what her own father must have gone through after the pogrom in Russia, trying to calm him down, affected herself by Nathan's emotions that she absorbed like a sponge—and it might have been that emotional state that she drew on in her triumph as Roxane in the production of *Cyrano* a month later, which led to her being named a principal actor at the annual meeting of the board, only a year after she was first hired.

At the Deux Garçons sidewalk café, Nathan's mood was becoming increasingly bitter.

"It's shameful, a betrayal, a disgrace. I bet they're now going to perform that Nazi anthem, the *Horst Wessel*, in Moscow. Isn't it priceless that Wessel, the author of that 'magnificent hymn,' was shot by a communist? *Kam'raden, die Rotfront und Reaktion erschossen, Marshier'n im Geist in unser'n Reihen mit,*" he began singing, beside himself.

"That's enough, Nathan," said Alain Béron, standing up. "Let's get out of here. And calm down, already."

But Nathan was uncontrollable, the poor orphan who no longer had any ideals continued to sing, louder and louder, the irony in his voice building as he chanted each couplet, shouting those ignominious words, scandalizing the nearby tables, who thought he must be drunk as they looked disapprovingly at that German acting like a savage. "Stop, Nathan, think of your parents," whispered Bérénice. That was like a cold shower. Suddenly sober, he fell silent, relighting a cigarette and rubbing his thumb over the scar on his upper lip. "The world's gone mad," he muttered. His head was filled with trumpets, cornets, and tubas, all echoing and disordered, like a symphony gone out of joint.

A few days later, Bérénice and Nathan were back in Paris. Draft classifications 2, 6, and 7 were called up simultaneously. War had never been so close. September 1, a general mobilization and a state of siege were decreed. The same day, the board of directors of the Comédie-Française decided, in accord with the General Administration for Fine Arts, to safeguard its art collection in the Touraine. They shored up the flooring under the statue of Voltaire by Houdon, which was too heavy to be transported—it was buried under a pyramid of sand. September 3, war was declared.

By telephone they heard the news that Alain Béron was assigned to a factory that manufactured gas masks. At the Comédie-Française, many had received their mobilization orders, beginning with Édouard Bourdet. It was strange to see him in his captain's uniform, hurrying back to the theater as soon as he'd completed the tasks for his military service—he was stationed in Paris. The secretary general, Robert Cardinne-Petit, was transferred to the Office of Censorship, vetting newspapers at night, which also allowed him to continue to work at the theater during the day. As for the actors, many were called up. Pierre Dux had to report to Versailles, Yonnel, or rather Sergeant Yonnel, was assigned to the staff of the first battalion in Meaux as secretary to Commandant Berland. Also required to report for duty were many of her old friends from the Conservatory: Jean Weber and Robert Manuel, as well as Martinelli, Échourin, Bonifas, Seigner, Balpêtré, Julien Bertheau, Le Marchand. The executive director reminded the actors who had been mobilized that in these matters, the Comédie-Française had an honorable reputation. All had in mind the war of 1914.

"Thank you, God, for making me a woman," Bérénice couldn't help but thinking each day when she woke up, parodying the Jewish morning prayer. Because of her sex, she could remain in the theater, practicing her profession as if nothing was happening. They were only awaiting the official authorization to reopen, but they were more or less sure it would be granted. Bérénice was able to take part on September 24, 1939, in the poetic matinee entitled, "To the Glory of French Genius." A program of works by French authors from the beginning through the nineteenth century, inclusive, because, chanted Bourdet in a surge of patriotism: "I believe that in times like this, people are hungry for all that is profoundly French, for everything that evokes the most vital strain, the best of our race." Paul Valéry was speaking that morning. That made up for many inconveniences, such as civil defense classes and having to carry a gas mask. And consider this: ever since a famous fashion designer had offered the young principal actress a superb container fashioned of full grain leather instead of its horrible cylindrical metal case, the gas mask had become less repugnant.

Bérénice also found out that she would be cast in the first play to be staged since the theater had reopened, on Tuesday, October 10, 1939, in her first performance as Célimène in The Misanthrope, directed by Jacques Copeau. The rehearsals had begun and were going well despite the negative atmosphere at the Comédie-Française.

Béatrice Bretty was losing her temper more and more often. Most likely because of her liaison with Georges Mandel, the former ally of the late prime minister, Georges Clemenceau, her political awareness was more developed than most actors. She returned one day from the Café de L'Univers choking on the opinions that Madeleine Renaud had expressed: "It's too much, the little horrors she comes out with: 'Who gives a fuck about Alsace Lorraine,' 'If there is a war, it's the fault of the Jews and the English,' 'What difference does it make if we're German or we're French?' 'We just have to give them what they want, that's not such a big deal, anything is better than this,' And that's not the worst of it … You know what she dared to say about Nathan? 'If he's so against Hitler, why doesn't he just enlist?' She waved in our faces a letter from her Jean-Louis: 'Those guys and the Senegalese are the ones who should be fighting, since France let them in and they didn't have the balls to prevent the rise of Hitler.' She may be an excellent actress, you can't say anything against her there, but you should only talk theater with her, nothing but theater, and definitely nothing related to politics. And the same for that little Barrault."

Bérénice would not admit that, at heart, at this moment, the war didn't impinge on her at all: her best co-star, Jean Yonnel, could appear on stage despite his military duties, the Comédie-Française moved his performances to an earlier time slot since it had become too difficult to go out at night, but that didn't prevent the curtain from going up soon with a program of several classics: *The Misanthrope, Never Say Never, The Traveler and Love, The Imaginary Invalid* … Rumors were even circulating about a tour of the Balkans, and meanwhile they announced the reopening of the Odéon, the Opera, and the Light Opera. A normal theatrical season, in short, while the war was happening far away, in the Sarre, for instance, or in Moselle, where the towns at the front only amounted to disembodied cartographic drawings on page one of the newspapers, where those who were killed in action were only an abstract list of names on page three. All you had to do was not listen to the radio, not read the newspapers. And with modern technology, one thing was certain: the war would be short.

· 2 ·

"Yes, you're German and Jewish, but what the devil is the likelihood that they'll come after you, given all our connections?" she kept telling Nathan. But the devil did get into the mix. He appeared right at their door, at their huge apartment near the Luxemburg Garden, Rue Gay-Lussac. At seven thirty in the morning, the bell rang. Nathan wasn't sleeping. Since the war had started, he was afraid he might be arrested. Several of his compatriots had been rousted out of bed by the police since September 2, they had been detained as "enemy aliens." For weeks nothing had been heard of them, it was only recently that anyone had gotten word of them: it was said they were being held in secret and that they were languishing in La Santé Prison. There were terrible stories and they didn't know whether to believe them. Nathan couldn't explain by what miracle he was still free. Worry had tormented him for a month. Usually he trusted his experience: arrests took place at night, and by daybreak he felt more calm and went to sleep. That particular morning, maybe because of a vague premonition, unless it had to do with having drunk too much the previous evening, he absolutely couldn't stay in bed. He moved to the living room, trying to resolve the problems posed by a triple fugue for four voices, drinking cup after cup of coffee, trying to exorcise his anxiety by substituting the difficulties of work, which, after all, was only a question of arranging notes, and he had almost succeeded while Bérénice was still sleeping, when the doorbell made him jump.

It could have been the concierge, it could have been the mailman, it could have been a neighbor, it could have been a friend who was in the neighborhood and had seen a light in their windows. That's what he tried to tell himself as he walked to the hallway to open the door. In the bedroom, Bérénice woke up with a start and understood from the tone of Nathan's voice that something odd was happening. Worried, she quickly threw on a bathrobe and rushed to join him. Two policemen. Her heart began to beat faster, she started to panic and tried to control her emotion with the breathing exercises she used for stage fright. She calmed down enough to ask, "What's going on here?" in the voice of a high-class lady out of a Feydeau farce. Her air of authority impressed the two policemen. The one who seemed in charge, a man of medium height, about fifty years old, his hair carefully oiled, coughed to regain his composure and began to use his Sunday best words to repeat to this beautiful lady what he had just announced to Nathan, to let her know that they had orders to take Monsieur Adelman to the police station. "I'm sorry, Madame, but you are not permitted to accompany the gentleman."

They gave him a quarter of an hour, the time to pack a bag, which she did as quickly as possible, recovering her sangfroid by taking action, folding first his warm clothing—sweaters and flannel shirts—remembering to include a few provisions, such as salami, chocolate, cookies, and also bananas that she ran to the kitchen to find, hoping that would be enough, thinking at the last minute of Rubiazol, in case he caught a cold. She went with them as far as the outside door of the apartment building, Nathan pressed her hand very hard before leaving, flanked by the policemen. She remained on the threshold a long time, until the worried concierge came out to remind her that she was still in her nightgown. She went back upstairs with leaden feet, collapsed onto the unmade bed, and began to cry.

A little bit later, after quickly getting dressed and washing her face, which revived her courage, she phoned Alain Béron, reaching his mother, whom he lived with, apologizing for disturbing her so early in the morning, asking if her son might be there, explaining that it was urgent, finding out that the lawyer had already reported to the gas mask factory, jotting down the number, finally succeeding in getting through to the lawyer, recounting to him the circumstances of Nathan's arrest, asking him what action they should take. He promised to do whatever he could, to keep her posted, he expressed regret that he couldn't be with her at this difficult time, he was thinking of both of them. A bit reassured, she phoned Colette, finally understanding the void that her friend had faced, left alone since her husband's mobilization, but her friend was lucky enough to be surrounded by her family, who had taken refuge since the war at Clermont-Ferrand at the home of her maternal grandparents. Reproaching herself for feeling envious when her real family, the family closest to her heart, waited for her at the Comédie-Française, diving into a taxi without paying attention that in her precipitous rush she had put on mismatched gloves, it was Florence Hégué who slyly noticed Bérénice when she arrived, pleading with Émile to arrange a meeting for her with the executive director, who made time for her, surprised that she had come to see him on her own initiative, and she, knowing that he could do nothing, but having the need to confide in him, feeling a ridiculous sort of calm in standing in front of the Louis XV desk and the Gobelins tapestries, reassured by the familiar gestures of Édouard Bourdet: the way he chose a cigarette from his box of Laurens, the care he took in rubbing Rosat ointment on his lips while avoiding his mustache.

As for Nathan, he was wondering where the devil they were taking him. Bérénice's last glance—oh, such a look of devastation—reminded him of a passage of the *largo* of Bach's *Concerto for Four Harpsichords in A Minor*. He reproached himself for not having spared her that experience. Why hadn't he followed his instincts, why hadn't he left France for America like several of his friends who had been urging him for a long time? It was weak of him to listen to her when she had persuaded him that his celebrity would keep him safe. He had always known that wasn't true: since the day when war was declared, since September 3, many important people had been sent to La Santé Prison. Their notoriety as a writer, sociologist, or filmmaker had weighed precious little compared to their German nationality. Why had he blindly persisted, like his parents, like his sister, when he had begged them to leave Germany? What guilt did he want to expiate by doing this?

During the trip in the black Mariah, he thought about how he might escape, but the handcuffs were too tight, the policemen were too vigilant. Maybe when they arrived … or so he hoped, all his senses on alert, knowing that he would have to seize whatever chance presented itself. But no chance deigned to appear. He was taken to the police station where he had to wait on a hard bench in the waiting room, next to a drunk, a pickpocket, and another foreigner arrested as he had been that morning. In the afternoon, they transferred him to police headquarters, where he was thrown into a sort of auditorium equipped with a movie screen, no doubt intended for highly instructive lectures for policemen.

He thought intently about Bérénice, wondering what she was doing, having an interior dialogue with her, mocking to himself the national guardsmen, sweeping his eyes over the group of foreigners who had been arrested along with him, looking to see if he knew anyone, champing at the bit, passing the time by tinkering with the fugue that had preoccupied him since that morning, annoyed not to be able to find the right structure, realizing that he'd forgotten his pack of Lucky Strikes on the piano in the living room. About two hours later, another black Mariah arrived, delivering about twenty new arrivals. He had the pleasure of discovering in that group the Hungarian journalist Arthur Koestler whose accounts of the Spanish Civil War in *Le Populaire* had made a strong impression on him. He moved to sit near him and they struck up a conversation, recalling a gala dinner at the Opera when they had been introduced, after which they discussed Mussolini's foreign minister Ciano's visit to Berlin, what France's odds were, the banning of the Communist Party, so that, absorbed by politics, they could forget for the moment the uncertainly of their own fates. At the end of the day, all of them, the men and the women, were assembled in the courtyard and taken to a coal cellar where they spent the night, trying as best they could to get a little sleep, despite the lack of privacy, the coal dust, and their worries about what would happen the next day.

When Bérénice arrived in her dressing room, the first thing she did was take off her shoes. She needed to feel the red carpet under her feet, to draw strength from the bowels of the Comédie-Française, feel the might of the building rise up in her, fill her veins, her fibers, her pores, giving her back energy and courage, calming and vitalizing her. She could go on stage the master of her own will, play the part of Célimène and find new colors in her character. She might be playing the role a bit too darkly, she heard Florence Hégué who was sitting in the theater, although Florence had no business being there, exclaiming in a hypocritical voice, "Interesting, but it's not at all the character." Jacques Copeau let her do as she pleased, even though her interpretation of Célimène wasn't at all what he had in mind. Édouard Bourdet was kind enough to stop by and encourage her, standing by her with his beneficent presence in this difficult moment, astonished, as he confided to her later, by the power of her performance, which, far from being hampered by adversity, seemed instead to be enhanced by it. She, for the first time, found herself in one of those fragile moments that all actors experience at one time or another, where destiny gets into the mix and ruthlessly, cruelly lashes you—but you still have to go on stage, put a good face on it—the show must go on.

After the rehearsal, she went back to her dressing room, where the door was always open to admit one friend or another. The entire company, now aware of the Nathan's arrest, came by to say a warm word, and to ask how they might help. A few of them, without even realizing it, assumed the look of a martyr, like Lavinia in *Titus Andronicus*, whose hands and tongue were cut off, so used to playing tragedy or seeing it on stage that it had become their natural means of expression and it had twisted them, at heart they liked it that the real world now had a tragic note, allowing them to feel they were living more intensely. Béatrice Bretty, more practical and steady, and maybe because she had internalized the soubrette parts, promised to speak to Mandel. He would certainly have some information.

The most difficult part was the thought of spending the night alone. Bérénice foresaw that if she left the Comédie-Française, she would fall apart. She wouldn't be able to stand that apartment, much too big for her alone, the mute piano—especially that. She decided to break the strict rule against actors sleeping in their dressing rooms. She acted as if she was leaving by the door that opened onto the Rue Saint-Honoré and snuck back in through the entry by the Galerie de Chartres, taking advantage of the concierge's inattentiveness. Silently she snuck back upstairs to her dressing room, took care to pull the curtains completely closed, as much to keep from being seen as not to violate the civil defense regulations that compelled Paris to live in darkness. She stayed there the whole night, and for the first time she lived hour by hour the life of the House of Molière, sensing all its nuances, all its sounds. She had taken with her the pack of cigarettes that Nathan had forgotten and smoked them all except the very last one, out of superstition, as if it could guarantee his return.

· 3 ·

The next day, still no news. And yet she had to rehearse for *The Misanthrope*, attend the matinee poetry reading, learn her role as Junie in Racine's *Britannicus*, sit for her portrait by Lipnitzki in his studio on the Rue du Colisée, and at the same time step up her efforts to find out where they had sent Nathan.

It wasn't until the third or fourth day that she finally had some word. Right in the middle of a rehearsal, the main stage manager, Bourny, came to find her to tell her that she was wanted on the phone. Oh, how her legs trembled as she went down the stairs leading to the office of the executive director, and oh! her anxious glance at the bust of Molière. The unfailing Alain Béron was on the line. They had located Nathan at the Roland-Garros Stadium. "Roland-Garros, the tennis stadium?" asked Bérénice, surprised. It was inside an enclosure adjoining the Auteuil Gate, and it was where the French national championships had taken place that June that they had interned five to six hundred "undesirable aliens," as Béatrice Bretty confirmed for her a few minutes later, based on information from her lover.

Under the grandstand of the main tennis court, Nathan felt as if he was at the bottom of an orchestra pit, with that huge ceiling overhead that doesn't really allow you to participate in the opera being performed above, feeling anonymous, understanding the frustration of the musicians relegated to the most distant stands, experiencing a terrible uneasiness spilling over into anguish, and accustomed to his prestigious place as the conductor of the orchestra with the appreciation of the audience and the musicians, he felt dispossessed by this change of perspective.

It was the first time he had endured incarceration, unlike many of his unfortunate companions, who had already experienced Spanish, German, or Italian prisons. For an artist used to living by his own rhythms, isolation was itself an ordeal. For Nathan, this was intensified by a bitter sense of the injustice of being cooped up liked a murderer, yanked out of the social fabric like an undesirable element even though his music was a hymn to liberty and civilization. Koestler showed him a communiqué that had appeared in that morning's paper: they explained that arresting such a large group of foreigners had cleansed Paris of its mud. "Paris, which, under ordinary circumstances, gives refuge to cutthroats from all four corners of the world, has now experienced one month of complete tranquility. Have the cutthroats suddenly calmed down? The answer is simpler than that. They've been arrested."

"We've become the dregs of the Earth," Koestler astutely observed.

"But you're Hungarian and Hungary is a neutral country. What are you doing here?"

Neither of them had any idea.

From that day on, Nathan abhorred tennis. The sight of a white ball inexorably recalled the smell of the damp straw that he was forced to sleep on, as well as the stadium scoreboard that announced the results of the match of McNeill/Harris against Borotra/Brugnon: 4–6, 6–4, 6–0, 6–2, 10–8. These numbers started to haunt his dreams. And the red clay … Two hours a day, they exercised there. The clay began to stick to your clothes, it even got into your nostrils. Luckily, there was not too much to complain about as far as the food. There were even some pleasant moments, like the time they heard floating on the air *Du bist glücklich* from his opera *Theseus*. It was being sung by a bass-baritone whom he had once worked with in Berlin, it was so surprising, so completely unexpected to hear that joyous piece in this place. They recalled their mutual acquaintances, notably "Papa Rouché," the director of the Opera, they went over all the works they had performed before their arrest, they discussed his plans for a new opera, which began to progress, to his great astonishment.

After a few days, Bérénice was able to send him a package—cigarettes, jams, clothing. Visitors were not allowed, but she worked unceasingly for his freedom. "I know him, without his piano he'll die," she kept telling Béatrice Bretty and Alain Béron, who urged her to have patience. Now that all

Germans and Austrians were interned, the government had promised to name a panel that would examine every case and separate the Nazi refugees from the anti-Nazis. Under those circumstances, Nathan would certainly be released, but the panel was slow to be formed. In the meantime, the Nazi prisoners were treated better than the opponents of Hitler, since they benefited from the fear of reprisals against French prisoners of war in Germany.

"We've got to get him out of there," Bérénice kept insisting. "Pull strings," she heard several times. "Money," she also heard, "that's all it takes." Although disinclined at first, she followed Bretty's advice and obtained a meeting with Albert Sarraut, the minister of the interior, trembling that, in exchange for her appeal, he would ask her what her father thought they asked actresses for, not wanting to imagine what she would do if she were faced with such a choice. At the ministry, she received a warm reception from the radical: "Your Roxane last year was enchanting, Mademoiselle. So, how can I help you?" She swore on everything sacred that Nathan was no longer a communist, telling him the whole story. As she left the appointment, she laughed at herself for having believed that such a courteous public servant would ask for her favors.

When she returned to the Place du Théâtre-Français, she was swarmed by friends curious about the results of her meeting. They took her to the Café de L'Univers where they made her eat at least a sandwich, "Look, you're so skinny, eat!" Several friends of Nathan paced up and down outside the Palais-Royal hoping to talk to her, musicians snuck out of the Opera to get the latest information and rushed back up the avenue as soon as they had given her their words of support. She even received a visit from Agnès Grangé, who had remained on good terms with Nathan. She offered to help if it was in her power to do so. "Really nice of her," she admitted to Bretty.

Sometimes when an actor said something witty, she laughed along with the others and felt guilty since she didn't even know what conditions Nathan was living under, if he was being well treated, what his spirits were like. Above all, she began to realize that at the Comédie-Française they had been terribly self-absorbed. But except for the Brette, aware even well before the war of how grave the situation was, who there was seriously interested in politics? She was angry with herself for having made fun of Nathan and his obsession with reading all the newspapers. If by magic he would suddenly appear in front of her, she herself would read all of them to him, his newspapers, she would even take on her "Comédie-Française voice," as he sometimes called it to tease her. She wouldn't get angry, she wouldn't protest that the House of Molière had become more modern since Bourdet, that today the actors were nothing like the pompous Montfleury in *Cyrano*. She would smile at him with love.

· 4 ·

"Look at me. Relax your jaw. That's good. *Click.* Turn your face, no, the other way. *Click.* Good, just like that. *Click.* Try it with your hand over your arm, there, right, like that. No, go back to how you were before, yes, better. *Click, click, click.* Less sad, what's with that sad face? A beautiful girl like you? That's better, I prefer that little smile. Again, no, just smile with the cheekbones. Perfect. Beautiful, beautiful. *Merci,* Mademoiselle, we're done."

That's one thing she could cross off her list, she could return to the Comédie-Française.

"Goodbye, Monsieur Lipnitzki."

"Goodbye, Mademoiselle, I'll have prints sent around to you tomorrow, late afternoon. What are you acting in Tuesday? Ah, *The Misanthrope.* 'That is how a lover with extreme ardor Loves even the faults of the person he loves,' very good, I'll come cheer for you."

"It would be my pleasure. Goodbye Monsieur Lipnitzki. You're an expert on Molière!"

"Goodbye, Mademoiselle de Lignières, the pleasure is entirely mine."

Given the present situation, she was actually relieved that her busy schedule kept her from feeling too depressed. Let's see, after the photographer, the costume studio for her first fitting as Célimène. What a joy to put on that magnificent black velvet dress with elaborate silver slashing that had made such a sensation at the premiere in December 1936! A dress right out of the movies, they had said at the time. When it was first created, Bérénice had seen it worn by Marie Bell, who had the idea to add an outrageous, bright red wig. Marie Bell was so criticized for it that she stopped wearing it after the second performance. That was already three years ago. At the time she was just starting her third year at the Conservatory and was cursing Jouvet for not wanting to let her take part in the July competition! They laughed about it today. "Wasn't I right, little mama?" he said to her, pleased with her success, even if he kept mocking her passion for the House of Molière: "Now that you're part of the company, aren't you tired of it?"

As soon as the elevator stopped at the Rachel level, she knew something had gone awry. It wasn't the first time she had noticed this. It was as if the walls of the Comédie-Française were alive: they breathed, they spoke to her, revealed their secrets to her, carried her, warned her. What were they warning her right now?

Her feet stumbled against an obstacle. She leaned over to see what it was. The Parma violets that were supposed to be pinned on the hand muff of her Célimène costume. The bouquet was lying on the floor—a bad omen. She picked it up and headed down the hallway. Once in the costume shop, she let out a scream. Her costume! Her beautiful black velvet costume! It was torn to shreds, slashed by long scissor cuts, from the bodice to the train, even the silver tassels had been ripped. Bérénice had a vision of a bestial rape, it was as if her own body had been savagely attacked. She recoiled, leaning against the doorframe. Her face went pale. Sensitive to signs, she wondered about the meaning of this omen. What more awful event could befall her? The seamstresses couldn't figure it out, the night before the costume had been in perfect condition. They had placed it on the mannequin, as they always did, it was truly unheard of, who could have done such a thing? Weeks of labor wasted, hundreds of hours lost in an instant of madness. Édouard Bourdet was called immediately, he could only survey the damage. The dress was unwearable, nothing of it could be saved. "This is truly a crime, I'll do everything in my power to find the person who did this," he said in a voice choking with emotion.

Béatrice Bretty also ran in, enraged. Of course she had no proof, but she remembered that just that morning, when she had gone to the costume shop to give the seamstresses last-minute instructions for her Arsinoé costume, she had run into Florence Hégué. It was strange to find her in the hallway so early in the morning. The young woman explained to her that she was looking for a hairpin that she'd forgotten the previous evening with Georges, the hairdresser. Bretty kept quiet about her suspicions. She was reluctant to denounce a colleague despite the wrong done to Bérénice.

"Don't you fret, honey, there isn't time to remake the dress for the opening, we'll never find enough velvet that quickly, but we'll definitely come up with something for you," Mademoiselle Magnard tried to console her—she was the lead seamstress of the costume department. They would take the white, seventeenth century dress from *The Imaginary Invalid*, and alter it as best they could for the role of Célimène. The head of the costume department explained that it would actually be more realistic, since widows at that time wore white, not black. The poor man bit his tongue when he realized his blunder. Bérénice was almost having a nervous collapse, she had an awful foreboding that wearing a widow's clothing would bring bad luck, that something terrible would happen to Nathan if she wore it. "No, I won't have that dress, I won't have that dress," she bawled. Sensitive to the distress that his principal actress was experiencing, Édouard Bourdet escorted his protégée himself to her dressing room, begging her to lie down, even suggesting that she might want someone else to play this role. No, she responded forcefully. They wanted to clip her wings, but she wasn't going to let them. They left her alone to rest for an hour, and afterwards the stage manager came to get her for the rehearsal where she would wear street clothes, blessing the training that allowed her to act under these sorts of circumstances.

That evening, exhausted, she slept for the fifth night in a row in her dressing room. Toward four in the morning, she awoke with a start, terrified by a nightmare. They had abducted Nathan, Florence Hégué phoned to tell Bérénice something she couldn't hear and suddenly her father appeared, pointing an accusatory finger. It was during the insomnia that followed that she had an idea. All that black velvet, impossible to find for her dress ... How foolish could she be! There was velvet all over the theater, on the seats, on the benches for visitors, it was even used sometimes as tablecloths ... she would go talk to Gouaillard, the head upholsterer.

In fact, they found in the workshops a large bolt of red velvet intended to replace the worn out side curtains that hide the wings. The curtains would have to wait, Célimène's dress took priority. And while they were at it, as long as they were completely changing the color of the dress, instead of the silver tassels of the original dress, they would use the gold tassels of the curtains. Quick, quick, get to work! There were only three days left before the first performance, and the seamstresses took charge, working night and day and even

Sunday to create Bérénice's new costume. It was because they liked her so much, their little principal actress, they took to heart the project of repairing the wrong that had been done to her. And this time, they wouldn't leave the gown unguarded for even a minute.

Opening night, all was ready. While putting on her costume, which she got at such a cost, Bérénice feels the uncanny power of the fabric. The velvet grabs her, it hurts her a little at first, as if pins had been left in the dress, but then the material is wedded to her body with the softness of a caress, it becomes one with her, part of her, the same as her arms, her legs, or her hair.

She found out later that Béatrice Bretty was watching the reaction of Florence Hégué in the theater. If she really was the member of the troupe who had committed the crime, how enraged she must have been to hear the audience gasp with admiration when Bérénice appeared in her red and gold dress. But at that point, no one yet knew what other harm Florence would cause in spewing her venom to the reporters.

· 5 ·

"Mademoiselle de Lignières burns with an inner flame," wrote *Le Jour* the next day. Jean-René Daunat enthused: "Yesterday evening a very curious performance of *The Misanthrope* took place, very far from any presented since 1936. And yet it was the same director and almost the same actors, with the notable exception of Célimène, played for the first time by Bérénice de Lignières. If Aimé Clariond presented a *Misanthrope* as neurasthenic as when he acted the part three years ago, Bérénice de Lignières has transformed from top to bottom the concept of her character. In the past, Marie Bell gave us a flirt; Florence Hégué, a scatterbrain. With Bérénice de Lignières, Célimène has become a romantic heroine. In doing so, she has perhaps put herself on a collision course with tradition, but she has imbued her character with that suicidal *je ne sais quoi* that we didn't know about her. Her serious voice, the dark rings under her eyes, her diaphanous face evoke nights of agitation, her intentionally artificial intensity suggest a young woman marching toward her doom. One might say she was caught in a frantic quest for self-punishment or to make the world pay for an ontological error that it had committed. Literally possessed from the play's first scenes, Mademoiselle de Lignières manifests incomparable gifts. She is decidedly a pillar of that House, the future of French theatrical art."

With the exception of those two newspapers, the critics unanimously attacked Bérénice. "How can one help but notice that her contralto voice, sometimes hoarse, doesn't in the least correspond to the character of a flirt? It is a serious error on the part of the executive director to have cast her in this role." "Mademoiselle de Lignières showed us last night the limits of her talent." "Bérénice de Lignières has created a character very far from Molière's intention."

While the critics were hastily scribbling their polemics, rushing to finish and send them to the night desk at their papers, Bérénice returned to her dressing room and sat down at the table where she took off her makeup. She herself was astonished by her performance. She couldn't quite realize precisely what had taken place. It seemed to her that the fabric had bled into her, that her red and gold costume had forced her to act differently, the cloth had communicated with the stage and it had opened its arms to her, recognizing that they came from the same source, delivering then its praise, giving its soul over to Bérénice. An imponderable force had brought about this magical moment where intellect, intentions, and self-reflection are nothing. The theater alone spoke. It was almost frightening to feel herself possessed, as if the body were nothing more than an envelope of flesh in the service of art and that it no longer actually belonged to you.

That's when she saw him appear in the reflection in the mirror. Paralyzed by surprise and the fear of deluding herself, it took her several seconds before she turned around and threw herself into his arms, completely giving in to her emotions, not giving a damn about his eight-day beard, his dirty and wrinkled clothes, his scruffy hair, blessing this gift from the heavens or perhaps from the theater that was rewarding her for having acted so well, for not having given it up despite her anxiousness, for not allowing herself to be replaced by Florence Hégué or Marie Bell who would have been delighted to take her place, or of course it was the Comédie-Française which in exchange for her fiery performance had made him appear, handsome despite his hobo appearance, dripping with life and energy. They could go back home now, she would wash him, caress him, cover him with kisses, her free darling, her handsome *yekke*, she had been so scared but now everything was back in place again.

Talk to me, tell me. Inhaling the perfume of her hair, Nathan told Bérénice that he had been summoned a few hours ago. "We've just received from the minister of the interior the order for your release," they had announced to him. He never knew what factor had contributed most to his liberation: the measures taken by Bérénice and by Alain Béron; Mandel's intervention; or those of numerous well-placed friends, intellectuals, and artists. Suddenly he was torn between surprise, relief, and guilt for abandoning the companions of his misfortune. He left promising to visit their wives. He was free.

Before going back home, she asked him if he would agree to stop by the lobby, where they had organized a party to celebrate opening night. She had ordered three cases of champagne to thank the seamstresses. She told him the story, he saw her become animated, take off the costume whose color was so good for her, he became giddy watching her put on her slip, he became annoyed when she pushed his hands away, "Later, later, when we're home," despite it all she kissed him, put on a stocking, kissed him again, too bad, she was dressed again. They made a triumphant entry in the lobby. People were already rushing toward them, welcoming them warmly, Édouard Bourdet shed his usual aloofness and vigorously shook Nathan's hand, everyone from the company congratulated the two lovers who were radiating happiness, their love deepened by the experience of almost losing one another.

They left the theater very late that night, kneading each other's hands in the taxi that carried them home, taking advantage of the darkness to kiss on the lips. "Rue Guy Lus-sac, you are here, M'sieur-dames." Since he had no money on him, she was the one who paid, despite the driver's disapproving glance. In the elevator, Nathan asked Bérénice if he had seen the guy's stern expression, she called him my gigolo and they went into the apartment laughing. They suddenly became serious when they found the portrait of Bérénice lying on the bed. In Lipnitzki's photograph, the young woman was captured in three-quarter view, her face turned so far away from the lens that it seemed almost a profile. Her translucent left eye, the ear finely fringed with hair, her right hand resting imperially on her left arm, and a long string of pearls. He saw again in this portrait the grace and sensuality of Lou, the majesty of Doña Sol, the candor of her first opening night, and already something more serious that was budding and had crystallized since his arrest, his many-faceted woman, his Bérénice.

· 6 ·

Nathan left his internment more shaken by the experience than he would have thought. He was given assurances that he had nothing further to worry about, that he was being looked out for at the highest levels, but he feared another arrest. It even became an obsession. He wrote to the American Guild for German Cultural Freedom to ask for help in emigrating. Several of his compatriots had been able to settle in the United States thanks to help from this institution. He saw himself working at the Metropolitan Opera in New York where Bruno Walter was willing to welcome him. He didn't speak to Bérénice about this, suspecting that she would refuse to leave the Comédie-Française. It was more difficult for an actress than for a composer to become an expatriate, because of the language—he was well aware of that. Despite all that, as a precaution, he sent the letter.

His *Kaddish for Deceased Parents* dated from this period. In Roland-Garros Stadium, he thought intensely about his family, murdered during Kristallnacht. Mahler's *Kindertotenlieder* never stopped going through his head during his time there, surfacing daily in his musical memory, perhaps because his parents had been dead almost a year and the thought of that terrible anniversary made the memory more painfully acute. This connection between music and the unconscious often struck him: a melody passed through his mind and he realized it was not appearing by accident. When it was a *Lied* or an aria from an opera, the lyrics echoed in his thoughts. When it was instrumental music, it was often the context in which he had heard it for the first time, the person or the situation connected to it that made that particular passage resurface. It even happened that the music that insisted on entering his thoughts revealed his state of mind to him. For instance, toward the end of his liaison with Agnès, it was because he continually found himself thinking about Kurt Weill's "I Don't Love You" that he realized he no longer loved the soprano and that he was thinking all the time about Lou/Bérénice.

The thought that his family had not had a proper religious burial tormented Nathan during his lonely nights at Roland-Garros. "I want to write a kaddish for them," he announced one day to Bérénice. "My father often sang it, he was a remarkable cantor. I think he passed down to me his love of the voice, the desire to write opera. Ravel wrote a kaddish—do you know it?" No, she'd never heard it. He sat down at the piano. "You also have a beautiful voice," she told him, flooded with emotion. He stopped and took her in his arms, an unhappy man and an unhappy woman, both overwhelmed with guilt, he, for having survived his parents, she, for having disobeyed, realizing nevertheless that they couldn't have done otherwise, that if history, by some miracle, could repeat itself, they would do it exactly the same way again.

Kaddish for Deceased Parents premiered on January 6, 1940, at the Théâtre des Champs-Élysées as a benefit for prisoners of war. Bérénice had requested and obtained from the executive director permission to read at the beginning the translation of the words of the kaddish. Nathan preferred to let a colleague take his place in the orchestra pit. In writing the score, he had the feeling that he had paid a part of his debt, but it was impossible for him to go beyond that. The performance of the baritone—who had a register very different from his father's—was deeply moving. For a long time, Nathan remembered the quality of the silence that followed the final note. You write in your little corner, you have an idea of the effect the performance might create, but that silence, that emotion—no, there was no way to anticipate it.

During the course of the evening, Daunat came to congratulate Nathan, remarking on, "the richness of your musical imagination," "the poetry of your orchestration," saying that he had undoubtedly attained in this demanding work the truest expression of his style.

"And your new opera? They say that Rouché has agreed to include it in the repertoire without having heard a single note."

"Yes, he's told me they're drafting a contract, but it's not written in stone yet."

"I've heard it said that you intend to completely reinvent the genre of opera."

Once more, Nathan understood that his project, which he rarely spoke about, or maybe *because* he rarely spoke about it, without his realizing it had given rise to exaggerations that made him uncomfortable.

"I *am* actually thinking about different ways to combine text and music."

"Ah! The eternal question! Beaumarchais hit a brick wall with *Tarare*. Well, Wagner didn't do too badly, I don't think you'd deny that."

"That's true, but he created dramatic opera, I'd like to achieve operatic drama. I hope you don't think that I'm playing rhetorical games—the two aren't the same at all."

"I think I see what you're saying and I suppose that the charming Mademoiselle de Lignières has something to do with that idea. After all, why not? Besides, you have in Béron your Da Ponte to assist you. Let me know when you're farther along. I'm sure it would interest our readers."

Was the librettist at this premiere, taking advantage of a special leave of a few days? What's certain is that shortly afterwards, Nathan, Bérénice, and Alain were all involved in a conversation about the basic points of Nathan's new opera. For several years, the composer had been thinking about the relationship between music and drama, as he had confirmed with Daunat. Up till then he had more or less stayed within classical lines, saving his musical audacity for his pieces for orchestra. His first opera, *Theseus*, made quite a sensation, after its debut in Berlin in 1929, because of its "rhythmical aberrations" and its "orchestral chaos." Besides, the Nazis had banned his music once they took power, labeling his scores "cultural Bolshevism"—it's true that at the time Nathan was still a member of the Communist Party.

Now the composer wanted to go farther. This project was intended to bring together all his aesthetic ideas on lyrical music. The number of performances of classical tragedy that he had attended since he had begun to go out with Bérénice had led him to raise questions about music on stage and its relationship to text. Rejecting the process that consisted of artificially introducing a musical phrase while the actors continued to recite their lines, he dreamed instead of a gradual progression of the word from spoken/chanted to sung. Inspired by the Jewish liturgy that he was steeped in during his youth, he was convinced that opera could, in the same manner, blend reading, prosody, and song.

"What exactly do you mean by *prosody?*" asked Béron, eager to grasp his friend's thought process.

"I'd like it if a character, or better still, several voices, a chorus, for example, spoke the text in rhythm, backed up only by percussion. I imagine this taking place during the most dramatic passages, in a way that creates a sort of rhythmic lament, or, on the other hand, an immense joy that would rise to a swelling crescendo, like the ocean in a storm. That would create the same effect as chanting in a monotone or sobbing—you'd find yourself swept up by a fabric of sound."

"I think the best way to put this into practice would be to apply it to a biblical story. At least that's the image that comes to mind when I listen to you talk about it."

"What would you say about using as a subject David's early life, from his battle with Goliath to his accession to the throne?"

"I was just thinking about that. The war with the Philistines—now that would resonate with our situation!"

"If I understand you correctly, Nathan," Bérénice interrupted, "your opera would be at the very edges of theater."

"Exactly. That's what I call operatic drama. I think it would require real actors to perform it, and not necessarily professional singers."

"That's a terrific idea. Then I could be part of it."

"You could play Michal, David's first wife. I can imagine what a sublime aria that could create. To weave the musical texture I was just describing, it would require adding instruments that aren't usually part of a symphony orchestra. The *kinnor*, for instance, that ancient lyre that some people say was David's harp."

"*David's Harp*—that's your title!"

"*David's Harp*—why not?"

They set to work, rereading the Book of Samuel, decided on a general structure for *David's Harp*, the sequence of the scenes, cuts to make to the original text, they omitted certain characters to make the action more complex, they worked on the material to make it work as theater. In four weeks, Alain Béron had written a preliminary draft. Galvanized by Nathan's enthusiasm, stimulated by the project's potential, he chiseled verses that suddenly came to him, as if he'd been touched by grace. "It's bewildering," he confided to them when he showed them his work, "it's as if I went to sleep and then woke up to find the text written by someone else."

After that it became a true collaboration, you couldn't separate the text from the music, and the challenges of the performance, the diction, and the transitions from spoken to chanted determined the direction they took. The opera became Nathan's obsession. It was almost unhealthy. He only worked on this project, neglecting the composition classes he taught at the Conservatory, refusing commissions to allow himself free time, getting annoyed if anyone spoke to him about other things. All his energy was concentrated on elaborating on the formal structures of the new aesthetic that he'd begun to develop with his *Kaddish*. His ambition was to introduce in *David's Harp* new techniques from a modified Dorian scale in the responds, borrowing from Hebrew cantillation, injecting into his opera his liturgical heritage, working toward this synthesis in a more significant manner than what had been attempted up till then by several Western composers.

Bringing together these three types of vocal art: prosody, recitation, and chanting, constituted to a great extent a utopia. Even before the score became public, articles began to appear in music magazines denouncing the folly of the project. The most conservative were already screaming for Nathan's head: "After Wagner, Stravinsky, and Schoenberg, when are we going to get back to real music?" To which Nathan, on the advice of Jean-René Daunat, answered in *Ars nova* with an article putting forward his theory of musical aesthetics, "On the Operatic Drama," by Nathan Adelman. Who would have predicted that this text would become a reference work for generations of students in musicology? Despite its impact, the critics did not let up, taking as an established truth a remark that went beyond the topic of music. The collaborationist newspaper *I Am Everywhere* wrote: "Judaic liturgy on the stage of our Opera? Just how far does the impudence of these Jewish swindlers go? Not content to infest our musical circles, the kikes now want to corrupt our national Opera by transforming it into a synagogue. Their desire for domination knows no bounds. Following in the footsteps of the Jew Halévy, Monsieur Hadelmann [sic] seeks to expand the influence of his race by …"

"Nauseating," commented Alain Béron crumpling up the newspaper. "They no longer even respect Marchandeau's law against hate speech."

All of this only increased Nathan's anxiety and reinforced his haste to finish his opera as soon as possible. The American Guild for German Cultural Freedom responded positively to his letter, he was just waiting for the right moment to bring it up with Bérénice.

"What's the matter, Nathan? Your opera is going well, I'm going to appear in my first movie soon, and you don't seem happy … Nathan? What's going on? Why are you looking at me like that?"

"Mademoiselle Bérénice de Lignières, will you marry me?"

· 7 ·

She won't be able to tell how the chauffeur came to pick her up very early, at the stroke of six in the morning, to take her to the Joinville Film Studios. It took almost three quarters of an hour to get there. She went straight to her drafty dressing room, they made her up, dressed her, did her hair before she went on set. Several months before, she had gone to see the executive director:

"Please have a seat, Mademoiselle. You asked to see me?"

"Yes, Monsieur, I wanted to ask you ... Monsieur Duvivier offered me a part in a film of his next February."

"Would you like to take the part?"

"Well, I've never been in a movie, and he's offering me the lead, opposite Jean Gabin."

"My child, I congratulate you, but a starring role is out of the question. You know that half the troupe is leaving in February for the Balkans. I have to have actors who will stay in Paris during the tour. I need you here then."

"I understand, Monsieur. Then I'll say no."

"Well, maybe they could cut back on your role so you could shoot in the morning and come back here in the afternoon?"

That's how, in order to keep Bérénice, whom he absolutely wanted to be the first to feature in the movies, the director completely rewrote his screenplay: he cut down the principal actress's appearances and changed the ending of the film. It was a story of revenge against a backdrop of social conflict. Bérénice played a mysterious anarchist who coaxed a humble clerk of the court (Jean Gabin) into assassinating the attorney general. At the end, both of them are shot by a firing squad. Morality is preserved—any other outcome would never have made it past the censor.

"Quiet, we're rolling!" It was the last day of shooting. As on every day since the filming had started, Nathan came to pick her up in his car. Although he almost never went out since he had returned from Roland-Garros, for fear of being arrested in the street, he claimed he wanted to spare her the inconvenience of a long taxi ride. She suspected it was just a pretext, because of his jealousy. It's true she was playing opposite the most seductive actor in all of France, who—war or no war—was far from forgetting the bewitching Lou from The Masked Owl. And he was the one who had suggested her name to Julien Duvivier for the role of the scandalous nihilist.

"Look, here comes your fiancé," said Gabin to Bérénice when he caught sight of the composer.

"Hey, lovebirds, are you coming to the party tonight to celebrate the end of filming?" called out another actor.

"You should take advantage of your last day of being single," added a technician.

And others yelled out:

"You poor things! The good life ends tomorrow."

"Bérénice, there's still time. Marry me instead, gorgeous, and you'll be happier than with that guy who massacres sounds!"

They got themselves ready for the party celebrating the wrap, he had already put on his tuxedo, she was wearing her silk gown with the sparkly tulle, the only thing left was for him to choose her jewelry. That's when they heard about Édouard Bourdet's accident. The executive director had been dining at home with his wife when he got a phone call to say that Jean Meyer, who was appearing in Pirandello's Each in His Own Way, was ill. Wanting to encourage Antoine Balpêtré, who was standing in for him with no notice, Bourdet rode his bicycle back to the theater, but while crossing the Avenue des Champs-Élysées, which was darkened by a blackout, he was hit by a car. Bourdet was taken to the hospital and the diagnosis revealed a triple fracture of the left leg.

"My friends," he said the next day when Nathan and Bérénice came to visit him, "I won't be able to attend your wedding later today. I know you'll believe me when I say I'm terribly sorry. You see what a bad influence movies have on theater people: it was a film producer who hit me!"

Bérénice and Nathan were married in the civil registry office for the 5th Arrondissement. They had an intimate ceremony—the only guests were Madame de Lignières (who gave her consent to her "daughter," still a minor), Alain Béron, Colette, Véra Korène, Béatrice Bretty, Louis Jouvet, a few friends of Nathan, and then Denise Bourdet, who came without her husband, still in the hospital. That was it.

The two of them, a serious and handsome couple as they exchanged their rings, their eyes shining with love, hand in hand, sealing their union, knowing that together they were the world, two orphans who had made themselves or almost, shaped by the art that they pledged themselves to completely, not knowing how to live in the only reality that they absolutely had to transcend, having become one, not doubting the importance of meeting the love of their life, the necessity of their marriage, recognizing in each other those two halves finally reunited as in Plato's myth, furiously eager to live and create, feeling between the two of them the strength of ten Samsons, persuaded by the telluric force of their marriage, and with those around them looking on with admiration and awe, didn't so much excessive love invite the wrath of the gods?

As if to give credence to their friends' sense of foreboding, that very night odd incidents took place at the Comédie-Française. Bérénice was recreating her role as Célimène. When the dresser was lacing up the stays of her red velvet dress, the actress had the distinct sensation that the fabric, which was the color of blood, was contracting, shutting her inside like the maw of a carnivorous plant. Suffocating, anxious, she tried to reason with herself—in vain: all night there were incidents on stage. Her dress bruised her back because of a hook-and-eye in the wrong place, the leading man playing opposite her slipped and fell, another forgot his lines, the prompter gave the wrong cue, the audience never warmed up … She forced herself to attribute all that to Édouard Bourdet's accident, which had shaken up the company. But at heart, she knew that wasn't it. A terror was haunting her, so strange she didn't dare tell Nathan about it. Bérénice was afraid that the Comédie-Française, jealous of her infidelity with the movies, was avenging itself by having its administrator run over. And now that she was Nathan's wife, and she had violated her oath to be married only to the theater, what other elements would be loosed upon her?

Her superstition was not entirely baseless, as evidenced by what she wrote to Yonnel, then on tour in the Balkans:

Dear Jean,

I hope that this letter arrives at the Ritz before you leave for Bulgaria. I was so pleased to hear of your success in Zagreb in *Andromache* and *The Coach*—that will silence the German propaganda smugly spreading the rumor that our friends appear before empty audiences.

You tell me that you have no connection to Aimé Clariond except the daily reports you write. You know that I make a point of staying out of the factions that are a sore spot of this company, but if we want to support our dear Bourdet effectively, I think we really need to get involved in this. You know the saying: "Don't shoot at an ambulance." Clariond violated this rule—he sent a report to the minister criticizing the executive director's management. And only two weeks after his accident!!! Clariond rallied around himself several friends. Naturally, that little Hégué had a hand in it, all too happy to attack the "extravagant production" of *Cyrano*, which our friend Pierre Dux had the nerve not to cast her in! You know as well as I do that the expenses for this play were largely made up for in box office receipts. There's nothing in this but jealousy.

I feel for Bourdet, his recovery seems to me compromised by all this commotion. Did you know that he asked Jouvet if he would take his place for six months? The boss refused, the Athénée takes up too much of his time … From his army barracks, where he sometimes seems better informed than I, Dux writes me that Bourdet has sent Copeau a telegram also asking him. They're waiting for his response from Ankara, where he's now giving a series of lectures.

I'm so eager to see you again. Acting tragedy isn't the same without you and I feel so untalented without my favorite leading man … Au revoir, dear Jean, Nathan sends warm greetings and I give you a hug.

Bérénice

She didn't know that Bourdet had added in his telegram to Copeau, to make sure he accepted: "Just between the two of us, this provisional appointment could become permanent."

Copeau was not long in replying:

"April 1940—Bourdet—Alma Clinic—8ᵗʰ Arrondissement Paris
I accept 6 months. Return 15 May. Telegraph Istanbul if you agree
and send news.
Jacques Copeau."

Everything had changed. Édouard Bourdet was replaced by Jacques Copeau on May 14, 1940, the day before the invasion of France and one day before the Dutch army surrendered to the Nazis. Once the tour of the Balkans had ended, Yonnel resumed his place on the board of directors, which decided to continue performances and to modify the program in response to the state of war.

First speech of Copeau to the assembled troupe, May 15, 1940: "This is war, and we have a duty to fulfill. I am here today because Monsieur Édouard Bourdet asked me to be; but I will remain here only on one condition: let it be said no longer of the Comédie-Française, *It's a terrible company, but it's a great company*. Changing that depends on all of you, and I know I can count on all of you."

That evening, Bérénice told Nathan how outraged she was by these remarks: "What nerve! He sounded like he was disavowing everything that Bourdet has done, but it's thanks to Bourdet that Copeau even has this position and that he's been able to stage shows at the Comédie for the last three years!"

Nathan listened distractedly. "I have to talk to you," he said. His seriousness alarmed Bérénice. "The news is bad. The Germans are getting closer and closer, and if it continues at this pace, they'll soon be in Paris. Don't argue, just listen to me. I've got to get out of here, at all costs. Look at the type of posters that have been appearing on the walls the last few days, yes, I know you've read them, they ask that German nationals in the Department of the Seine, ages seventeen to fifty-five, report immediately to the assembly point at Buffalo Stadium. If I don't do it, they're going to arrest me. Let me finish. I'm not asking you to leave with me, I know you couldn't stand to leave the theater in such a hurry. You'll stay here. They can't do anything to you, you're Bérénice de Lignières, daughter of a French Christian, nobody knows you're Jewish, and whatever happens, no one must know that. Let me finish. I have a visa for Spain. Depending on how things go, you'll join me or I'll come back here."

She listened to her husband in tears, unable to believe his oracular predictions, in tears they made love one last time, in tears they fell asleep clasped in each other's arms. They said their farewells the next day, May 17, 1940, the day French national radio announced that Brussels had been abandoned to the Germans.

· 8 ·

When she opened her eyes, it was as if she had sunstroke. The burning was still there, a stinging sensation. The night before, going to the Comédie-Française, the Rue de Rivoli was deserted. And that flag slapping in the wind, too new, too red. It wasn't the red that Nathan had hoped for, the red of singing tomorrows, of the great eve. In this red a hideous black spider had taken up residence, smack in the center. This red that the facades displayed from now on, brightened by the June sun, had wounded her eyes. The Germans were here.

Nathan, who was on his way to Spain, had not lived through this insane week where their world had stopped functioning, each day a little more. How many gears have to jam before a clock stops running? On Sunday, June 9, the theater had posted the notice of its annual closure after the last matinee of de Musset's *You Can't Think of Everything*. The gloominess of the goodbyes, the unaccustomed silence of the audience as they filed out of the theater.

Then the actors were notified they were being placed on indefinite leave and were authorized to proceed as their individual needs required. Everyone left.

"What are you going to do?" Bretty asked Bérénice. "You're not staying here?"

"Where can I go? I don't even know where Nathan is."

"Join your mother in the Loire Valley."

Bérénice shuddered. "No, I prefer to stay here. At least Nathan knows where to find me. And you, Béatrice, what are your plans?"

"Me? My fate is tied to Georges. I'll go wherever he goes."

Everything unfolded rapidly. On Monday, the board of directors had its last meeting and decided that each artist, as soon as he or she had found a place of safety, should send the address to the treasurer Fleury, in Toulouse. That same day, they heard that Robert Manuel's older brother was among the casualties, a lieutenant in the infantry who died for France at Climbach in the Lower Rhine. On Tuesday, Reims was occupied and millions of the French people joined an exodus of refugees. Among them were Yonnel and Bourdet, headed for Bordeaux. Wednesday, the campaign to defend France was lost, Pétain and Weygand offered an armistice while Georges Mandel advocated resistance to the last. Copeau and his daughter left Paris driving a little Simca that a general had loaned them. On Thursday, Paris was declared an "open city." On Friday the Germans invaded the capital while Jean-Louis Barrault and Madeleine Renaud got married in the Billancourt City Hall.

"It is with a heavy heart that I inform you today, we must cease to fight ..." It was over. The old man with the quavering voice, General Pétain, had surrendered. Bérénice remembered the tears of joy when he had been named head of the armed forces. "We're saved," she had exclaimed, like thousands of others, trusting in the victor of Verdun. But he had stopped absolutely nothing, the impregnable Maginot Line had protected nothing, just as the Munich agreement with Hitler had protected only war, there was no miracle of the Marne this time, one of the world's greatest empires had crumbled in barely three weeks. There it was. The Germans were here. The phony war was over. From now on, things were going from bad to worse. The panzers. The powerlessness. The rout, the surrender at Rethondes, the terrible and dishonorable conditions imposed by Hitler. Bérénice thought of her father, so happy on the day of the Treaty of Versailles that was also the day of her birth. Rethondes 1918. Rethondes 1940. The surrender was in the same clearing in the woods but this time they were the ones who were screwed. They were the ones humiliated, who had to drink the cup of humiliation to the dregs, history repeated, but the opposite way. How could they have trusted Pétain? It should have been enough to listen carefully to his voice on the radio, that trembling voice could never convince anyone, let's face it, that voice would be a flop on stage!

Bérénice felt terribly alone in her apartment. It wasn't possible they had lost, that from now on they lived in a world where the Nathans didn't have the right to live … Bretty had left two days before on board the *Massilia* with Mandel and twenty-six other members of parliament, among them Jean Zay, who had done so much for the House of Molière. "I'm leaving with them," Bretty had announced, kissing Bérénice.

"But where are you going?"

"To Algiers. We don't want any part of this armistice."

"But why Africa?"

"We'll continue the fight from the colonies. We'll form a new government in Algiers. Are you sure you don't want to come with us? There's nothing more you can do here. Believe me, the independence of the Comédie-Française will be threatened sooner or later," prophesized Béatrice Bretty before saying her farewell to her young friend. Bérénice didn't want to believe in this hypothesis, even after another departure, that of Véra Korène, who wanted to offer her modest services to the French government that was about to be formed in North Africa or London.

So, Bérénice stayed alone in Paris. She was one of the first to return to work, notified by Édouard Bourdet's brother, Michel Bourdet-Préville, who had remained the head of personnel, that the German general staff wanted the theater to reopen quickly. As of the end of June, that hadn't happened. They were still waiting for Copeau to return and they only had meager resources: six stagehands, four electricians, one upholsterer, three dressers, four principal actors. A bit short-handed for reopening.

In this period of uncertainty, the actress was delighted to find Alain Béron again, who had already been demobilized.

"I had business to attend to here," he explained to the young woman, who was astonished to see him again in the capital when everyone else was fleeing Paris.

"Where are you staying?"

"I have a little pied-à-terre in L'Isle-Adam in the Seine-and-Oise Department, just a few kilometers from here."

"Oh! If not, you would've been welcome at our place. The apartment has become too big for me. … I'm glad you've come back, you know, we can talk about Nathan, and the *Harp*, about your writings …"

It was from the poet that she heard about the failure of the *Massilia*. They lost those noble hearts, those courageous heroes who had attempted to save France's honor, not wanting to surrender, not wanting to lose hope, thinking they could fight on, continue the struggle from the colonies, persuaded that in leaving France they could better serve it, that it wasn't over yet. They had lost this chivalrous attempt to save the dying Third Republic, these Don Quixotes jousting with Nazi windmills, they had lost, Georges Mandel, Jean Zay, Édouard Daladier, Pierre Mendès France, Pierre Vienot, Alexis Wiltzer ... They were arrested in Casablanca, accused of "abandoning their posts in the face of the enemy," those initially designated enemies, these so-called deserters. From then on Mandel would languish in household arrests and prisons, Bretty would follow him to each new location: Chazeron, Pellevoisin, Vals, Portalet Fort, a terrible litany of detentions, she, doing her best to improve conditions for the former minister, constantly intervening on his behalf, a thorn in the side of the collaborationist Vichy regime till the end, that end that Bérénice will not be able to tell, so we have to tell the tale of his fate here for those who don't know it, who don't know that Mandel was shot by the Milice, the French adjunct to the Gestapo, on July 7, 1944, in the Forest of Fontainebleau.

· 9 ·

Bérénice now went every morning to join her friends for breakfast at a sidewalk table of the Café de L'Univers to escape as soon as possible the nerve-wracking silence of the apartment on the Rue Gay-Lussac. That July 12, 1940, several were back in Paris: Le Roy, Chambreuil, Alexandre, Brunot ... She realized they were all learning to look at the world at an angle: if you raised your head, you were bound to see the Eiffel Tower topped by the horrible black and red spider. And yet, she refused to lower her head. The defeat was humiliating enough without that. Learning how to adapt to the situation—wasn't that already a sort of surrender? She was among those who made it a point of honor not to let things slide. That day, she had dressed as elegantly as possible in her severe suit, brightened by her little straw hat ornamented with tea roses. That day, she might even have worn a little lipstick.

What did it matter that it was insignificant in the face of that sinister summer: after Nathan's departure, the failure of the *Massilia*, now they had denounced the "Judaization" of the Comédie-Française. A rag had just been published called *To the Pillory*, "a weekly to fight against Judeo-Freemasonry." Gracing the first issue, a very refined poem attacked the Comédie-Française:

When you see on stage
Alexandre, Véra Korène all the rage,

Hiéronimus and Ventura,
Tania Navarre, et cetera,
It's just like a garland
Of kikes, not to mention Escande,
Who all share their success
With Bell (Marie) and Robinne,
Don't say "Comédie-Française,"
Say instead, "Comédie-Palestine."

This pro-Nazi rag was passed from hand to hand at the café until an actor grabbed it, stood up, and declaimed the verses with sobs in his throat, ironically, in the manner of an old-fashioned tragedian, very "grand style." Around her, Bérénice heard the comments: "But Marie Bell isn't even Jewish! Neither is Escande!" "Oh, don't kick up such a fuss, it's just for the rhyme."

"Aren't they missing a few? Meyer—isn't he Jewish?"

"No, he's Alsatian."

She quickly left the table. What was that conversation all about? Jew, Jew, Jew, that's all you heard anymore! She went to her dressing room, where she found a letter from Nathan. He had arrived in Barcelona, she could answer him via General Delivery. Finally, some good news!

Unfortunately, bad news always seemed to follow a positive event. That's what Bérénice thought when, a few days later, she saw a German uniform entering the office of Copeau, who had finally returned to Paris. Suppressing an impulse to retch, she sought out information from the secretary general, Cardinne-Petit. The gray-green *feldgrau* uniform belonged to Lieutenant Radenmacker, a former actor that the Kommandantur had placed in charge of overseeing Paris theaters. Blond, as he was supposed to be. Blue eyes, of course. What was he doing here, she wondered. Bérénice couldn't help thinking of Bretty's final words about the independence of the Comédie-Française. Under the seal of secrecy, an indiscreet principal actor confided to her the reason for the German's visit to the House of Molière:

"You remember the article in *The Pillory* ten days ago?"

"Of course.

"So, Radenmacker came here to find out who's Jewish."

"And what did Copeau answer?"

"That he had no information on the matter, that there certainly had to be some Israelites in the Comédie-Française but that he knew neither their names nor how many there were."

So many rumors followed! It became known that René Alexandre had a meeting with the director that afternoon. Was it because of the article in *The Pillory*? People said he had explained his situation to Copeau, that he had converted to Catholicism in 1918, that he and his three brothers had fought in World War I from 1914 to 1918, that one of them had died in the war, that another had left a leg on the battlefield, and that he himself had been wounded.

So many things were said in the turmoil of those days. People said the Comédie-Française was going to reopen in September. They said that theater personnel in the unoccupied zone were going to obtain safe-conducts from the Germans to return to Paris. They said that Béatrice Bretty had asked that the director of fine arts for the Vichy regime communicate to her Copeau's instructions concerning her. They said that certain officials had reservations about her returning. They said that Véra Korène had escaped arrest in Casablanca before embarking for Rio de Janeiro. They said that, along with her son, Mary Marquet had witnessed the vote that granted the Vichy regime full powers from up in the stage riggings of the Grand Casino. They said that any French person who left French territory between May 10 and June 30, 1940, without a legitimate reason would lose their citizenship. They said that Radenmacker was living with a small-time actress in Bourdet's empty apartment.

On July 24, Copeau held a press conference to announce that the theater would reopen. The only newspapers present were the ones that Nathan held in contempt: *Le Matin*, hostile to the Popular Front; *Paris-Soir*; and all the anti-Semitic and pro-Nazi tracts that proliferated from then on, like *France at Work* and *The Sheaf*. Bérénice was furious with Copeau for referring to "the courteous visit that he had received from German headquarters." On July 28, the board of directors decided that the case of Madame Bretty would be "submitted to the minister at a later date by the director." None of that boded well. Bérénice felt paralyzed: the actors weren't returning, the possibility of playing Chimène in *The Cid* seemed more and more remote.

During this period, rumors kept circulating. They announced the nomination of Copeau as director of the Chaillot National Theater. They corrected that. They claimed that Pierre Bertin, a principal actor of the Comédie-Française, had stated in the newspaper *L'Ouest-Éclair* his "hope for a total peace that would permit us to create, in burying ancient rivalries, the soul of a new Europe." They said that Dux had been demobilized and was back in Paris. They said that Jean-Louis Barrault was going to sign a contract with the Comédie-Française. They said that Marie Ventura couldn't appear in Molière's *The Impromptu at Versailles* because she was an Israelite. They said that Copeau reinstated her in the cast once she had produced her parents' marriage certificate from a Greek Orthodox church. They said that Copeau had visited Hautecoeur, the secretary general of the École des Beaux-Arts, to ask his opinion on the question of the Israelites. They said that the official directive, coming from the Minister for Public Instruction and Fine Arts, Émile Mireaux, was to hold off and not cast any Jews who were too visible in the first productions.

Too visible Jews, Bérénice sneered. What does that mean, "too visible Jews"? Jews with Semitic features, the way they're depicted in caricatures: hooked nose, thick lips, frizzy hair? Or well-known Jews, like Yonnel, *the* tragedian of the House of Molière? In any case, the rumor must have had some basis because Copeau and his stage manager Mathis reworked the schedule that they had already put together for the first ten days, eliminating all tragedies. A deft sleight of hand: by removing all the tragedies, they didn't have to cast Jean Yonnel.

Yonnel, or rather Estève Schachmann, who went by the name of Jean Yonnel: a too-visible Jew. It didn't matter that the actor had played opposite Sarah Bernhardt in London, that he had enlisted in the Foreign Legion during World War I, that he had converted to Catholicism in 1935. Being Jewish was no longer a belief, it was a race. Nathan had been right. Bérénice had been dismissive of his panic, she didn't want to believe that what had gone on in Germany since the Nazis had come to power could happen in France. We're not like the Germans, we French—but the fact remained that Yonnel was no longer appearing on stage, and this, this was France.

· 1 0 ·

When is the Comédie-Française going to reopen? That's the question you heard more and more often. Rehearsals had already begun: on August 26 the first reading of *The Cid* took place in the artists' lounge. Bérénice met Jean-Louis Barrault again, whom she had first encountered after a show at the Atelier and whom she admired for his passion, his devotion to the theater, and his ideas. He had just been signed as a member of the company, which many in his circle had criticized. They accused him of betrayal, he, a member of the avant-garde, joining the temple of tradition, they branded him a coward, they said he was afraid of the very freedom he had advocated, even if they understood that Madeleine Renaud, now his wife, must have played an important part in his decision. Bérénice realized that the role of Rodrigue wasn't quite right for him, he was too slight for that character, but what a stimulating leading man to play opposite … True moments of grace when the young principal actress succeeded in forgetting the war and the Nazis.

And yet, each morning she saw Cardinne-Petit, the secretary general, leave for the Propaganda-Staffel, at 52 Avenue des Champs-Élysées. Each time he returned, she managed to get some information out of him—he could be quite talkative if you knew how to handle him. Bérénice's spirits rose or fell depending on what he reported. The Germans seemed to favor a return to a normal cultural life. Sometimes everything seemed to be moving in the direction of a quick reopening. On the other hand, sometimes things got bogged down.

One day the secretary general reported to her a remark that was particularly alarming. At the Propaganda-Staffel, he had run into Lieutenant Lucht, who confided to him something to this effect: "Once we've rid you of your Jews—which you're incapable of doing yourselves—you're going to thank us for the service we've done for your country." He then ordered Cardinne-Petit to bring him a list of the Jewish actors in the troupe.

"But why?" asked Bérénice. "What do they plan to do with it?"

"They say that not a single one can appear on stage anymore."

"And what did you say to him?" The young woman feverishly lit a cigarette. "You smoke?"

"A little, since Nathan's been gone. His absence makes me anxious. What did you say to him?"

"That we don't know who the Israelites are, of course. Questions of religion aren't taken into account here!"

"Of course. And how did they take your statement?"

"Badly." The secretary general scratched his chin. "They want the list and they're holding me personally responsible for delivering it." He tried to appear detached.

Seeing the swagger in his manner, Bérénice understood that he was pleased as Punch about his role with the "occupation authorities." She suddenly felt overwhelmed with fatigue.

"I'll see you later, Cardinne, I've got to rest in my dressing room."

Unable to confide in Nathan, or in anyone else, tired of spinning in circles, and having no rehearsal that day, she called Alain Béron and agreed to meet him at his house in L'Isle-Adam in the early afternoon. If only everything could go back to the way it was before, at the time of The Masked Owl, everything seemed so much simpler then, you could take the train without being afraid you would end up sitting next to a German, you could come home as late as you wanted without worrying about the curfew, you didn't see those signs written in Gothic letters, you felt so at home that you didn't even think about it.

"What a stylish place," she said, entering the poet's home for the first time. "A bit monastic, but fashionable. Am I bothering you, are you working?"

"Very poorly. I can't write anymore since the defeat. I feel sullied … Let's talk about you instead. Is the Comédie reopening soon?"

Bérénice told him about her conversation with the secretary general. Alain shook his head. "Things are very bad. If we don't give them what they want, they'll requisition the theater. Can you imagine, Bérénice? A German Comédie-Française? But to give them that list? That is shameful … Unless …"

"Unless?" she asked eagerly, hoping that the lawyer would find some legal loophole that would save them.

"I doubt that the Germans know the bylaws of the Comédie-Française. Maybe they'd be satisfied by a promise that no Israelite artists would be cast, and they won't demand that they leave the company."

"Not appear on stage?"

"Bérénice, could I possibly ask why all this seems to affect you so deeply? You're not Jewish, and in general you're not much interested in politics. Or am I wrong?"

"Me? I'm thinking of my friends, especially Yonnel, who's Jewish—he's also the leading man I most often play opposite."

The poet's glance pierced her. Bérénice became flustered.

"Nathan didn't say anything to you? You are so high-minded. I'm ashamed to lie to you … . Do you swear this will stay between us? All right, then: my father's name was Moishe Kapeluchnik …"

Copeau and his secretary general took an indirect path. They did actually send the Germans a list of the actors, but they provided the names of the entire troupe. Yes, the whole troupe with its fifty-six members and principal actors!

To Lieutenant Lucht:

> Following our annual closing, which was planned and which was prolonged as a result of the recent events, the Comédie-Française, in accordance with the directives of the Minister under whom we operate, will resume its performances on the 7th of September, 1940.
>
> Monsieur Cardinne-Petit, secretary general of the Comédie-Française, is accredited as the sole individual acting as a liaison with occupying authorities.

Bérénice joked a great deal with Cardinne-Petit about the reaction of Lieutenant Baumann of the Propaganda-Staffel to this letter that he was charged with delivering to Lieutenant Lucht. She won't be able to describe the raised eyebrow of the officer in his field-gray uniform as he read the list—his panicky "*Juden?*" at the thought that all fifty-six actors might be Jews. What followed was much less amusing: when the German realized that Copeau had given him the name of every single member of the troupe, he lost control, stamped his foot, spit out his cigar, and loudly bellowing, demanded the names of the Jews. It would have been all over for the secretary general if Lieutenant Lucht hadn't arrived in extremis, taking him out to eat scrambled eggs at the Colisée Café-Restaurant, flattering him for being a "good Frenchman."

Everyone knew that it was a strategic withdrawal in order to better attack. The Germans were not going to leave it at that. In the meantime, the House of Molière was in an emotional uproar: Cardinne-Petit was shouting from the rooftops that Copeau had given him full responsibility for dealing with the occupying authorities. Puffed up with his own importance, he hadn't realized the actors resented that this excessive prestige had been conferred on the secretary general.

Finally, Copeau had to capitulate in person. He paid a visit to Lucht to confirm that he himself was the one responsible to the Propaganda-Staffel. From then on, Bérénice had a much more difficult time obtaining information. She did hear, however, that "someone" had communicated to Lieutenant Lucht the status of the actors of the Comédie-Française. This "someone" had become very convenient, the same source confirmed they had seen "some actors" at 52 Avenue des Champs-Élysées. As if by chance, the Germans were then extremely well informed that the company of the Comédie-Française was run by a board of directors that included certain "undesirables." The occupiers were pulling the noose tighter and tighter. They were no longer satisfied with Jewish artists not appearing on stage, they wanted them excluded from the theater: "We cannot give permission for you to reopen your theater until you have eliminated all your Jews. *If* Berlin agrees!"

· 1 1 ·

She missed the beginning. It was more difficult than she had imagined to find a pretext to get the reliable Émile to leave his post, allowing her furtively to sneak into the vestibule between the two sets of doors that led to the board-room. If they found her there, what would happen? How could she explain her eavesdropping outside the door? How shameful that would be! Too bad, she would figure something out, she would improvise, she didn't want to think about the consequences, she just had to find out, at any cost, what was being said at the board meeting. They were going to discuss the status of the Jewish members of the company, and the reopening of the Comédie-Française, that much was certain. She wanted to hear every single word. The whole night, she had tried in vain to reason with herself, to tell herself that it was undigni-fied for a principal actor to spy at the door, but her need for information was as uncontrollable as an alcoholic's craving for a drink. So, there she was, hidden between the two doorways, holding her breath, her ears and her senses primed in order not to miss any of the meeting. From behind the doors, the sound reached her in muffled tones. She couldn't always recognize the voices, and certain words didn't quite reach her, but she recognized the voice of Copeau, who opened the meeting:

Copeau: Esteemed members of the company, now that the Committee has authorized the Théâtre de l'Oeuvre to give a series of performances of *Hedda*

Gabler featuring Madame Bogaert, I am reporting to you on an extremely distressing situation with regard to the reopening of our theater. This is indeed a dark hour. You know the situation as well as I. The program for the fall season is ready, but we are still waiting for the Kommandantur to give us the authorization to reopen. I recently visited the Propaganda-Staffel. Lieutenant Lucht made it perfectly clear: the Comédie-Française cannot reopen until the board of directors is purged of all its Jewish elements. Excuse me, Jean, and you, René, for expressing myself so crudely, but this is the position of the occupying authorities.

Pierre Dux: My dear Copeau, the Germans' demand is perfectly clear. Our own should be equally unshakable: let's abandon the idea of performing under these conditions. We cannot sacrifice our friends to the demands of the Nazis.

... That's very generous, Pierre, but you know what that means: the theater will be requisitioned. Maybe even pillaged. Can you imagine? Our invaluable collections, the costumes, the sets, our patrimony in danger of being plundered! That is unimaginable. We can't let Molière be massacred in that manner.

... We are all upset by the fate of our Israelite friends. But ... and ... because, can we sacrifice all of the theater's personnel in the name of a few? Keep in mind that the whole staff here will be out of a job.

Pierre Dux: What are you proposing? To give in to the German's contemptible coercion? Act like the barbarians they are showing themselves to be? Our honor is at stake here. La Comédie-Française cannot be under Berlin's boot.

... Now, now, gentlemen, it must ... stopgap solution that would not compromise our honor ... while allowing the theater to reopen.

Copeau: We already tried proposing that the principal actors should remain part of the company while not being cast during the period of the Occupation. They refused this solution. Whatever the case, it's not up to me to decide the status of actors who are principals of the troupe. This question falls under the minister's domain, and he hasn't given me any instructions ... and I'm not even sure it's under the minister's jurisdiction, since the Israelites, if they were excluded, would be within their rights under the current laws of France, to appeal to the Council of State and to demand compensation.

Jean Yonnel: Gentlemen, gentlemen, this situation is impossible. I can't bear the idea of being the cause of serious damage to the company ... Since this is the price for reopening the theater, I will put up with the violence that has been done to me and I will submit my resignation as a principal actor to monsieur the executive director.

René Alexandre: I believe it's my turn to speak. I was baptized in 1918, my daughter was as well, my family had the honor of serving France and, at the risk of being immodest, I will remind this body that I was wounded in 1916, that I was awarded the Croix de Guerre, that I serve as president of the veterans' association, and mayor of Grosley. I don't think I need to prove my patriotism to anyone. Like my friend Yonnel, I love this theater too much to bring harm to it. The Comédie must continue to … that's the only thing that matters. Monsieur, the director, I will resign this very day my title of principal actor.

Exclamations, regrets, a unanimous expression of sympathy. Bérénice left her hiding place. What had happened in the last few months left no doubt about what was to follow. Everything had been surrendered. Exclamations, regrets, a unanimous expression of sympathy. That's as far as it would go. In the end, didn't that suit everyone? What better solution than the Jews excluding themselves? There weren't that many of them: Véra Korène had left France at the start of the war, Yonnel and Alexandre had thrown themselves on their swords, so to speak. Robert Manuel was only a company member, not a principal actor, and he was thinking more and more about leaving in order not to cause harm to the theater. Only one case remained: her own, and no one even knew about it. Mademoiselle Bérénice de Lignières, Mademoiselle Bérénice Capet, Mademoiselle Kapeluchnik, what are you going to do?

When the resignation letters written by René Alexandre and Jean Yonnel were made public, she pretended to be as surprised as the others.

September 5, 1940

To the Executive Director

Dear Friends,
The authorization to reopen the Comédie-Française was agreed to by the authorities with the condition, *sine qua non*, that I withdraw from the Company, and, not wanting to cause any difficulties for the theater that I have served with devotion and love for 32 years, I ask that you accept my resignation as a principal actor of the Comédie-Française.

With sincere devotion to the executive director and to my dear friends, I remain,
Yours truly,
René Alexandre
Principal Actor of the Comédie-Française
President of the Association of Actor Veterans
Officer of the Legion of Honor, Croix de Guerre 1914/18

September 5, 1940

To the Executive Director

Dear Friends,

The authorization to reopen the Comédie-Française was agreed to by the authorities with the condition, *sine qua non*, that I withdraw from the Company, and, not wanting to cause any difficulties for the theater that I have served with devotion and love for almost 14 years, I ask that you accept my resignation as a principal actor of the Comédie-Française.

    With sincere devotion to the executive director and to my dear friends, I remain,
Yours truly,
Jean Yonnel
Member of the Association of World War I Actor Veterans
Knight of the Legion of Honor
Croix de Guerre

Those who had the opportunity to read the statement of the board of directors of September 5, 1940, were fewer in number:

"The board members, in accepting this solution that they cannot avoid, are unanimous in expressing the profound regret that it causes them, and a deep emotional sympathy for the two artists, both of them veterans of World War I, both of them honored with the Croix de Guerre and members of the Order of the Legion of Honor, and who both, for numerous years, have contributed with talent and devotion to the illustrious reputation and prosperity of the Comédie-Française."

As for the speech that Jacques Copeau made to the press, it did not allude in any way to the sacrifice that had just been made in the House of Molière.

· 1 2 ·

She had gone back upstairs to her dressing room. Her hands frozen. Astounded.
What to do? She couldn't believe it was possible that such a thing could happen in France, at the Comédie-Française, that two of the best actors, who had
given everything for their country and for the theater, their sweat, their blood,
in the literal sense of the word, could be excluded and the sun would still set,
that this scandal could take place without it truly shocking anyone since if it
had been really shocking it would not have happened, it could not have happened. Yes, there were Dux's honorable attempts not to yield to the Occupation at the risk of having the theater closed down, but the majority preferred to
let the black sheep leave in order to go on with their day-to-day existence. But
were they so much to blame? What were the lives of two men when weighed
against hundreds, the lives of all those who worked at the Comédie-Française:
actors, scenery painters, stage managers, machinists, makeup artists, hair styl-
ists, dressers … Even Yonnel and Alexandre had believed that their own fates
weighed less than those of entire families. *But were they so much to blame?* she
would have wanted to ask Nathan. She knew what he'd say. He would've said
that you're lost once you begin to sacrifice your principles.

Sacrificed, Yonnel and Alexandre, sacrificed, declared Jews even if they'd
converted long ago, even if, like her, they really had no other religion than

the theater. Neither Jewish nor Catholic, simply artists, but considered detrimental because they were born to Jewish parents, and because of this, they had to be excluded. If the actors hadn't done it themselves, they would have ended up getting rid of them. And She who said nothing. She who let it happen, wasn't She at all grateful for the glory that they had brought Her? They were a family, maybe even a community hallowed by the bonds that linked actors, from Mademoiselle de Champmeslé in the sixteen hundreds to Adrienne Lecouvreur, Clairon, Lekain, Préville, and Molé in the seventeen hundreds, all descended in a direct line from the august Molière. Bérénice had thought that the troupe's solidarity was something sacred. Where were those lofty values today? They had excluded two of the most brilliant principal actors because they were Jewish, and no one reacted. And what did She do? All religions have their martyrs, Nathan would have remarked with irony.

The relief, the relief—she could sense it even through the closed doors when they announced their resignations, the protests were just perfunctory, but in fact, the situation suited everyone. Yonnel and Alexandre's gesture was grand, even theatrical, you might even call it tragic, their renunciation. Perfect, those resignations, they satisfied everyone, they could all see themselves doing it. Were they in the theater? Yes, of course, so they acted accordingly. Their sacrifice was beautiful, it was powerful, it was something all actors could understand: tears welling in the eyes, vehement protests, a touch of grandeur, the hand of fate, oh yes, they had all played their roles to perfection.

After all, wasn't tragedy a common occurrence at the Comédie-Française, well beyond the stage? Think of those notorious December committees, committees where principal actors could be excluded by their peers for reasons that were more or less artistic. How many illustrious glories had she encountered where the services they had rendered no longer prevented their heads from rolling? The cynics claimed that for a troupe to live, certain elements had to die. The December committees were Malthusianism applied to the theater, so to speak. It was only now that she could understand how they must have suffered, those poor excluded principal actors who were encouraged to "take advantage of their right to retire," a euphemism to mask their being put to death. That permitted the executioners to feel less like the sons of Atreus, sometimes they were even given, to soothe their collective guilt, the title of "honorary principal actor," which permitted them to come back and perform on the stage of the Comédie-Française. Who knows, maybe even Alexandre and Yonnel had been among those executioners, maybe they too had decreed, one day, as part of a December committee, that so-and-so had to leave, after all, those are the rules of the game, you know when you sign your contract with the troupe that once every ten years you run the risk of being laid off, it's just that no one believes it, you know it the way you know that you're going to die, the idea remains an abstraction, you think it only happens to others. But this was different, this wasn't the normal procedure, just the opposite, this was as abnormal as can be, and yet this abnormality had just been set down in black and white in the statement by the board of directors as if it was a common occurrence, on a par with the announcement that there would be a series of performances of *Hedda Gabler*, on a par with the mundane events of life in the theater, and no one protested that it was a scandal.

And Robert Manuel, excuse me, Robert born Bloch, her dear Robert, her friend from her first days at the Conservatory, her good buddy, the one who had first assured Bérénice that she was part of the family, he too, was getting ready to leave. He had been warned about his friends' situation. "I'm Catholic, baptized, but I still have Jewish blood in my veins," he said sadly, bidding goodbye to his friend. His expression when he left, full of so many things, a sort of envy of her, *You're lucky not to be Jewish*, and also nostalgia, which was a kind of bidding farewell to their youth. You couldn't be young anymore after what had happened.

Any moment she expected to be unmasked. Putting behind him the emotion of the drama that had taken place within the board of directors, Copeau seemed to have made up his mind. He was like an alcoholic who has made tremendous efforts to avoid taking the first sip, but who, having fallen off the wagon, no longer counts the drinks: he might as well drink liters, since in any case, he swears that tomorrow he'll quit. According to Cardinne-Petit, Copeau had asked Deninx, a young member of the troupe whom he suspected of being Jewish, to open the fly of his pants. Was that even possible? Was is possible that Marie Ventura had submitted to the executive director a letter intended for the Propaganda-Staffel attesting to the fact that she was not Jewish:

To the Executive Director:

As you requested, I am reiterating the statements that I made to you in person concerning my racial situation, at the same time that I showed you the marriage certificate of my parents, proving that they were married by an Eastern Orthodox priest according to the tenets of the Christian faith.

You must be aware that in the Orthodox religion, Jews are not permitted to receive the church's sacraments.

My father's family being one of the oldest in Romania—his mother was born the Princess Rosetti—I can attest that his ancestors, as far back as one can go, even as long ago as the Crusades, were of pure Aryan race.

On one of the principal arteries of Bucharest, there is a statue of one of my uncles, Lascar Catargi, considered one of the country's greatest men.

My father died, having received the sacraments of the Orthodox Church, as well as at his baptism, and he is buried in Christian ground.

In Romania there are special cemeteries for Jews.

My mother, née Vermont, was of more humble origins, as I mentioned. Therefore I cannot go as far back in her lineage to affirm the purity of her race. I was seven years old when she died, but I do remember that she was buried in Christian ground, having received the sacraments of the Orthodox Church, as well as at her baptism ..."

Et cetera. It was enough to make you vomit. Would it have turned out this way under Bourdet? Would he have acted like this, her dear director? The worst had to be the smirk of triumph that she thought she could detect in certain people's expressions. Difficult to tell the source of that evil joy. What were these actors rejoicing in? The departure of a rival or the departure of their Israelite brothers?

By the evening of September 5, there were no more Jewish actors in the Comédie-Française. Yonnel had resigned, Alexandre had resigned, Véra Korène hadn't returned since the war had begun, Robert Manuel, Henri Échourin, and Paul Bonifas had left the theater. And all of them barely thought of themselves as Jewish. They only thought of their art, they only lived for the House of Molière, to serve the texts and the most French of any stage in the theater. All of that meant nothing. With them gone, the yellow and black posters mushroomed again on the kiosks. Copeau announced the reopening to the press. The box office sold tickets as fast as they could print them. No reaction. No protests. No resignations in solidarity. The Comédie-Française was finally going to reopen its doors.

There were no more Jewish actors—except Bérénice. Oh, the temptation to leave, to show solidarity with Yonnel and Alexandre, solidarity with the

Jewish people. Oh, the temptation to make a grand gesture, to reveal her true identity. Yes, me too, the great principal actress, the tragedian of the House of Molière, the young female lead who does honor to the Comédie-Française, Mademoiselle de Lignières is Jewish, ha ha ha, that takes the wind out of your sails, doesn't it? The caress of that idea. The panache of that gesture. To see Copeau's face, all their faces. Having to reshuffle the assignment of roles all over again. Serves them right.

"You're forgetting that you don't choose to be Jewish—it's something you carry *in* you." She remembered her father's words on that terrible day when he disowned her. It's true: just look at the fate of Yonnel, of Alexandre, whose conversion to Catholicism and status as war veterans were no help at all.

"You're forgetting that you don't choose to be Jewish—it's something you carry *in* you." But no, Maurice Kapeluchnik was wrong. You always have a choice. Yonnel and Alexandre made theirs, the choice to resign, but they didn't have to. It was their way of doing things. *She* would stay. She had too many projects that she wouldn't miss for anything in the world. Playing the role of Chimène in *The Cid* opposite Jean-Louis Barrault. That project of Claudel's that the young man had talked to her about: to play Dona Prouhèze in *The Satin Slipper*—if they could convince the poet to stage it. She couldn't say no to that. She couldn't refuse the promises that life offered to her. She couldn't say no. She wouldn't say no.

There, now she knew. She wasn't Abraham. In Abraham's place, she wouldn't have sacrificed Isaac. She wouldn't have placed her Jewish identity above everything else, she wouldn't have held it up as the moral compass. For her, the theater transcended everything. She had given herself body and soul to the Comédie-Française. Her place was there. Too bad about her origins. To hell with everything that hindered her passion, to hell with all obstacles. In the name of Thalia, she had abandoned her father and mother, lied about her age and her name, let her husband escape to Spain alone, what was one more sacrifice? Too bad about her Jewish identity, she'd never chosen to be Jewish, she'd never asked to be born into a Jewish family. She wouldn't sacrifice what she loved most on this earth. It was the theater that she had chosen once and for all, it was the Comédie-Française that was her nurturing mother and her entire family, she wouldn't sacrifice herself like Yonnel and Alexandre, she didn't have the soul of a victim. She had to act, it was vital to her, it was the only thing that mattered, she had to continue to honor the House of Molière that had gathered her to its bosom. My name is Bérénice de Lignières, and I am of pure Aryan race.

· 1 3 ·

Saturday, September 7, 1940. Two days had passed since the terrible day of the meeting of the board of directors. The Comédie-Française officially reopened at 7:30 p.m. For three quarters of an hour, throngs of invited guests and the public poured through the ticket gate, happy to be back in their theater. The pillars of the colonnade were resplendent, dazzling with the aura of the sick who have emerged from a long convalescence, delighted once again to be mixing with the world and life. The ushers taking tickets in tuxedos displayed the solemn expressions reserved for red-letter days, the secretary general mixed in with the general hubbub, liberally dispensing smiles, handshakes, and witticisms.

Bérénice was not on stage that evening. Only men participated in the reading of texts selected by the author Edmond Pilon for the opening performance. The principal actress sat in the theater next to Alain Béron. Tomorrow it would be her turn to go on stage. She looked at her friend, guessed with a single glance the somber thoughts he was harboring at the sight of the German uniforms taking their seats in the orchestra. As a sign of friendship, she pressed his hand, which he quickly withdrew. The lights dimmed. In the gathered silence, the poet and the actress could detect murmurs of disapproval. Traditionalists of the Comédie-Française criticized Copeau for going on stage—this was contrary to custom.

The executive director, very pale, began to speak: "The actors of the Comédie-Française are about to appear again before you."

"Not all of them," Bérénice whispered furiously in Alain's ear.

"This great company, whose roots go back three centuries …"

"Damn, if he insists on giving us the whole history, we're in for a long night," said a longtime subscriber sitting next to Bérénice.

"This House of Molière, as it's called, has always, in the course of its existence, withstood the crises of our nation. The most recent of those crises, which I would not say we have yet seen the end of, which I should say rather is just beginning, is one of the most severe, most serious, most extreme in our history."

"*Die Franzosen*, always talk, talk, talk," sneered a German.

"How can it happen that, even for those who are the most hard hit, something stirs, something begins now to shine and well up, which we hesitate to name, but which we will indeed have to call tomorrow by the name of Hope? It is because we first acknowledge our errors and our faults, confess them, condemn them …"

"After his *mea culpa*, I'll bet my right arm that he's going to start talking about the fatherland and the French spirit," whispered Alain to Bérénice.

She couldn't help smirking when she did actually hear those predictable words, but she blanched when the executive director went on to describe the Comédie-Française as "the guardian of ideals, high culture, and professional honor." They were so badly tarnished, those values, since the exclusion of Yonnel and Alexandre. And now, after a long tirade on "the French sense of organization," the privilege of actors, the perfection of their art, Copeau finally seemed to be on the verge of winding things up:

"It seemed to me that the setbacks of our country would not prevent me, that, on the contrary, they *compelled* me, to renew tonight, in the presence of the public, in the name of the principal actors and other members of the company, in the name of all those who work here, our oath to make this House of Molière, which the centuries have shaped and have left to us as their legacy, more beautiful, more prosperous, and more vibrant."

Alain and Bérénice exchanged glances as a burst of applause followed this address. A strange speech, strange guilt. "It reeks of collaboration," commented Béron. "Hypocrite," grumbled Bérénice. And then the academician Abel Bonnard followed with his talk on "The Value of the Ordinary Man," followed by the reading by members of the company and Copeau himself of texts by Hesiod, Montaigne, Marmontel, Mistral, Rétif de la Bretonne, Péguy, and still more Péguy. They left the theater at intermission, nauseated, disheartened by these reading passages that had been forced into saying too many things and blatantly tied to the national revolution.

The next day, Sunday, September 8, Bérénice was scheduled to play her cherished role of Célimène at the matinee of *The Misanthrope*. Finally she would be back on stage, finally she would be given a new lease on life, to forget while she was surrounded by the décor of that Golden Age salon the vileness of the twentieth century. She contemplated again her beloved red dress. This time, right away, before she had even put the garment on, the fabric turned out to be docile. Bérénice took this as a sign of approval for her decision, the theater's acquiescence in her choice. On stage, the actress was incandescent, with a mix of gravity and lightness, a reflection of her real-life emotions, since she was overjoyed to be acting again, but at the same time shaken by recent events. The audience gave her a resounding reception, enthusiastic about viewing again a principal actor whom they had seen grow up as an artist. In short, all she had to do to persuade herself that nothing had changed was to ignore those *feldgrau* uniforms.

When she exited the theater, a crowd of admirers was waiting for her at the stage door.

"Mademoiselle, when will you be appearing next?"

"Next Friday, in *False Confidences*."

"I've reserved my tickets to see you in *The Cid*."

"Could I ask you for your autograph, please?"

At the edges of the crowd, Bérénice recognized Alain Béron, who was pacing up and down on the pavement in the empty area of the square. She managed to make her way to him. "At last I escape this unwelcome pleasure/Of many new friends now mine to treasure," she spouted her lines from Racine's heroine in *Bérénice*, laughing and grabbing his arm so he would take her far from these annoyances, leading him with rapid strides away from the Palais-Royal. She was almost happy. She missed Nathan, and this war was turning her life upside down, but as long as she could act, the world, even if falling apart, even if absurd, even if unjust, was bearable.

"Why are you looking at me like that?" she asked Alain, who was staring at her.

"Because when I see you like this, so fervent and happy that you've acted, you're almost inhuman. But still, to act the way you do, you have to be the most human of all of us."

"Do I seem monstrous to you?"

"Almost, in the etymological sense of the word, in any case, like someone who's outside the norm. Surprising, in any case, but that's just a euphemism ..."

Surprised—she was the one who was surprised the morning of Friday, September 13, when she arrived in her dressing room to find a written summons from the executive director. What did he want? To encourage her in her next role as Araminte in *False Confidences*? To inform her that an actress was ill and that she had to step in at short notice? She wasn't expecting that. She wasn't expecting that he would ask her right away if it was true that her real name was Bérénice Kapeluchnik. She couldn't bring herself to deny it. Everything had been revealed, someone had betrayed her. The director refused to tell her how he'd found out about her origins, she gathered that he had received an anonymous letter. He pleaded with her to resign in order not to put the House of Molière in a difficult position. Never, she answered, never. Fire me, throw me out, do it over my dead body if you like, because I'm not going to be as well-mannered as Yonnel and Alexandre, I will not resign. Do you want me to leave? Make me, I won't do it myself. She stormed out of Copeau's office, slamming the door behind her.

That evening, her fury subsided. Bérénice kept to her usual routine: she put on her makeup in her dressing room, donned her costume with the help of Raymonde, summoned her concentration before going into the wings. On stage, she threw herself into the performance, which might be her last. At the curtain call, she felt as if she was on fire, undoubtedly she had a fever, she bowed like an automaton, leaning on her friends to prop herself up, she was moving in a fog, the trance that had come over her at the start of the performance followed her off stage. Removing her costume, taking off her makeup, her gestures were mechanical, as if she was outside herself. Once she was back in her street clothes, she became aware of her situation again, little by little. Her anger surged back, contained, but very present. She looked at herself in the mirror: her cheeks were red and her eyes shining. She drank almost a liter of water, her thirst was so intense.

Her eyelids weighed a ton, she must have had a fever of 104 degrees. She pretended to leave, then retreated to her dressing room, making use of the ploy that had served her well when Nathan was arrested. She wanted to know who had betrayed her, who had discovered her name and denounced her. When everything fell silent in the House of Molière, when the lights were out, when she could no longer hear a single noise, she slipped out on tiptoe, made her way to the hallway to that led to the director's office, and jimmied the lock of Copeau's door with a hairpin. The lock was old, it wasn't difficult. By the glow of a faint electric lamp that she had thought to bring with her, she ransacked his office. Finding nothing, she opened the drawers, and still finding nothing, she looked under the desk blotter, the letter was there, unsigned, obviously, written in letters snipped from newspapers. Who had sent that denunciation? There was no clue whatsoever. While putting everything back in its place without being able to prevent the paper from wrinkling because of her clammy hands, her glance fell on a little notebook, half open: "September 10: this morning I brought this little notebook to my office at the CF, in order to be able to record succinctly, day by day, what transpires before my eyes." She realized it was Copeau's private journal. She quickly turned to the page for September 13: "All day long dizziness caused by bile, strongly tempted to leave." He had to have written that in the morning, after their meeting. Tempted to leave? Yes, he might have felt ashamed. But what exactly had he decided to do? He hadn't written anything, and she hadn't seen him that evening.

The next day she still had a fever but she went back to the theater as if nothing had happened. She wasn't able to enter the building. The concierge denied her access. He didn't dare look at her, and only repeated over and over, "I'm sorry, Mademoiselle, I'm sorry, I have my orders." She felt no compassion at all for that man who had to follow such deplorable instructions. Hatred had penetrated her heart. So, that's how things stood, that's where *she* stood. Banished, excommunicated, *herem*. She restrained herself from slapping the concierge, retraced her steps, planted herself facing the Comédie-Française, gazed at Her for a long time, went down on her knees, still gazing at Her, the nourishing mother who was murdering her, who had cast her out from her bosom. Throwing her hat on the ground, suddenly proclaiming, still gazing at Her, her beloved mother, never lifting her gaze from Her, struggling against Her, an imploring rebel, an angry daughter before her mother who was now killing her after having nourished her and given her life and glory, Medea, you are Medea, she shouted—from now on a double orphan, cursed by her father and cursed by her mother, doubly *herem*, cursed in the daytime, cursed at night, cursed while she slept and while she was awake, cursed when she entered and when she exited, the door of her home forever shut against her, may the Eternal one never forgive this, may the Eternal one set forth all His wrath against her and pour on her all the evils enumerated in the Book of the Law: may her name be erased in this world and forever and may it please God to separate it from all the tribes of Israel, and inflict on it all the maledictions contained in the Law. And you who cleave to the Eternal One, your God, may he preserve you and keep you.

A crowd had gathered around her while the actors and members of the staff watched her from the balconies, the windows. When she fell silent, everyone applauded, thinking that she was rehearsing a new role, not understanding that they were applauding someone being put to death, they were applauding Medea slitting the throats of her own children, they were applauding the Comédie-Française killing her for some obscure betrayal. Bérénice stood up, a wounded bull rushing against the façade, and letting out a savage cry, she left, stumbling, lost, her face livid, disheveled, feeling the life ebbing out of her heart, her long black hair coming undone in the air that had become gelid. She wouldn't act the part of Araminte. She wouldn't play Chimène opposite Jean-Louis Barrault.

· 1 4 ·

The return to her apartment, the temptation to kill herself, to write a last letter to Nathan and be done with it, to end it all by throwing herself out the window or by opening her veins—she preferred the idea of opening her veins—to feel the life flow out of her little by little, to live fully that ultimate experience, to understand what it is to die, to realize, even too late, that perhaps she had not acted well enough when she tried to embody the agonies of Doña Sol or Ophelia. In a fit of temper, she realized she was thinking about theater again, always theater, roles, characters, what good was any of it now? Act somewhere else? But where? Who would take the risk of casting a Jew today? Weren't all the other theaters also going to clear out all their Jews? Besides, few other theaters had reopened. The Madeleine, the Odéon only recently, but without its director, Paul Abram, who was a Jew. Jew, Jew, Jew. It always came down to that. They had entrusted the direction of the Odéon to Copeau. So, no chance whatsoever there. The Athénée, maybe ... They hadn't reopened yet but Jouvet had returned to Paris in August. Yes, of course, the boss.

She immediately picked up the phone, dialed the number at 24 Rue Caumartin. While waiting to hear that familiar voice at the other end of the line, she panicked and immediately hung up. How was that possible? What had happened? That voice ... She had recognized the voice of Jean, the concierge of the Comédie-Française. It took her several minutes to figure out what must have just taken place. Yes, automatically, Richelieu 22–70, automatically, without thinking, she had dialed the number of the Comédie-Française, either unconsciously or by a Freudian slip, her fingers so accustomed to dialing those numbers, it happened without her realizing it. Upset, she examined her hands, as if that part of her body had betrayed her, had tricked her. Her entire body breathed Comédie-Française, lived Comédie-Française, thought Comédie-Française. Richelieu 22–70. She was completely possessed by it. She needed to slap herself. How to exorcise this demon? She grabbed her address book and crossed out the fateful number several times, ripping the thin page, she was pressing so hard on the paper with a pencil. Get out of my memory, Richelieu 22–70, clear out, get the hell out of here! If you could only erase a number from your mind as easily as you can cross out a line in a notebook. She flung the little address book across the room and collapsed onto the bed, pounding the pillows with her fists.

This abortive phone call raised her fever. A lethargic week in bed, no energy for anything. And then youth, the life force triumphed, she managed to get a grip on herself, to call the Athénée, to dial the right number this time, after taking a thousand precautions and holding the digits written large right in front of her in order not to risk making that mistake again. At the other end of the line, a voice that was not Jean's, the concierge of the Comédie-Française. Yes, she had definitely called the Athénée. They connected her with Pierre Renoir, "Bérénice, sweetheart! It's a pleasure to hear your voice. Too bad, the boss just left for his class at the Conservatory. Of course, just go there, he won't mind at all!"

Rue de Madrid. What a strange feeling to return to a place that was once familiar and that she had so passionately loved. In her personal geography of Paris, certain streets were no longer neutral. Reading the plaque outside number 14, that name once so desired, coming back to that street where she had had her routine, her joys, her superstitions, before performing a difficult scene for Jouvet, for example, her heart beat much harder, her hands became as sweaty as when she was there before. She had not returned to the Conservatory since she had left in 1937. Seeing herself through the eyes of the pupils she passed and who recognized her, the principal actress measured the road she had traveled. She was no longer the anonymous student, certainly full of promise but still uncertain of her own destiny. Now she was Bérénice de Lignières, the tragedian of the Comédie-Française, looked at with a fearful reverence colored by envy and fascination. She became aware of what she represented now that she was on the other side of the fence. She experienced for the first time the temptation to pass along what she knew.

She walked up the grand staircase and quietly entered the classroom, which by chance was not locked. Nothing had changed. The platform where they performed, the piano, the corner for the auditors, and him, Jouvet, his expression slightly more anxious, perhaps, his cigarette held more nervously, his eyes bulging slightly more. Seeing again his familiar silhouette, she felt a surge of tenderness for her professor, remembering how he had asked her, "How old are you?" on the first day of class, all of it came back, the aroma of his cologne mixed with tobacco; the ironic pout of his lower lip; his high, bare forehead; his staccato speech. Even now, she still found him somewhat intimidating. She slipped into the back of the room silently, waving to the boss so he wouldn't interrupt his remarks. She recognized Elvira's scene, Act IV, scene 6 of Molière's *Dom Juan*: "Do not be surprised, Dom Juan, to see me at this hour and in this dress …" She closed her eyes, immersing herself in Molière's mechanics, the script that she hadn't acted since her school days came back to her intact. She was at home. All was well. And then, suddenly, Jouvet's voice, commenting on the scene:

"I think you've made enormous progress since last time, especially everything you've taken out of 'I loved you.' When you say without emotion, 'Once more, Dom Juan, I ask this with my tears,' it's so much more moving. But if you indulge yourself and say, 'I *loved* you with the utmost *tenderness*,' it's the actress doing her tremolo number, showing off her virtuosity."

Bérénice opened her eyes. Suddenly she didn't know anymore if it was 1940 or 1934. The voice, the speech, were so familiar, but it felt as if she understood better now. Since her first year at the school, she had had the benefit of her audition for the Comédie-Française, years of experience, numerous roles, and even if she had never played Elvira on stage, her personal experience had enriched her, her knowledge of love, and even her discovery of the Mozart opera *Don Giovanni*, thanks to Nathan. She didn't want to leave. It was so reassuring to be back there, among the sounds and situations that she knew so well, rediscovering the fundamentals, moved like an adult who hears the first melody that had stirred her deeply as a child. She was certain she had knocked on the right door.

· 1 5 ·

Barcelona, September 18, 1940, eleven a.m.

Sweetie,

You asked me to write you what I do, hour by hour. Time goes by slowly, I'm riveted to the newspapers, I inform myself about the situation, and I'm enraged that I can't do more. Above all, I miss you. Each day I feel I love you more even if each day that seems impossible. I go to bed after conversing for hours and hours with your photo on my bedside table. When I wake up I kiss it but … it's your body that I want to press to mine.

The café where I've settled in to write to you is the place I go every day. I have a drink with Ruben, who receives and brings me my letters. I wait for him, wondering if today he'll bring me a letter from you and then my day will have sunshine. I've had the blues for five days now. Not a single letter from you. What are you doing, then? I read the work schedules you sent me, but I would like to have some real news. How are the rehearsals going for *The Cid*? When will the Comédie-Française reopen?

The endless line of refugees here seems to get longer every day. The port is like a hobo encampment, there are so many of us waiting for a visa, a money order, a ship. Funds are running out for all those poor folks. I'm making progress on our *Harp*. I think I might even finish it. Yesterday I started working on a long chorale. It must be this seaside landscape that's inspiring me. The horror we're living is sometimes beautiful, it's so tragic. Do you remember the movie we saw in Montparnasse in '37, I think it was? There was a couple killed in a car crash. In real life, this drama would have been horrifying, but with Schubert's music in the background, it became beautiful, precisely because it was dramatic.

I'm looking out at the sea, this sea and this sun resemble you, they have a Homeric sweep that makes me think of you on stage, my savage, my beautiful Greek tragedian. A little while ago I went back upstairs to look at your photo again. My young neighbor asked me, "Who's that beautiful madonna?" The boy is charming, he's eight years old and his innocent statements would make Alain a fortune. I can't stop talking to him about you, I forget sometimes he's just a kid.

Noon.
My treasure, my dear one, I just received one after the other a card and two letters from you. I was so happy, but I read the one from the 14th and my joy turned to sadness and shame. So, it's come to that. Yonnel, Alexandre ... and now you! What is this time that we're living through? And my sweetheart who is going through all this alone, *dein Mann ist nicht da*. I want, *I demand* that you come here immediately. Together we can find a solution. Come meet me here, let's leave for America, it's time. I'm convinced you could act there, I've heard about tours of South America, we'll find a way, even if it takes time, but come to me. Stop hoping, you don't even know what they might be capable of. Don't think you're protected because you're not a *greenhorn* like me, think about what's happened to you, believe me, this is only the beginning, the fact that you're French will soon mean nothing. Let's get out of here! I'll pass along instructions to you through Alain so you can leave. I won't be calm until you're by my side. Be strong, I'll take care of everything. Kisses, kisses, kisses.

Nathan

He's right, I should go and join him. Besides, Jouvet can't reopen the Athénée—he doesn't have enough actors at hand. He confirmed that. He's not sure he can do anything for me, he's says I'm too well known. He's not even sure he's going to remain in France. So, why not leave and join Nathan? If Jouvet organizes a tour abroad, he'll find a way to meet up with me, he promised. You know that at the Comédie-Française they've given the role of Chimène to Marie Bell? Ha! She's twice the age of that character. I know her well, she's going to play it as a bourgeoise, she's going to swallow whole that poor Jean-Louis ... And Florence, if she's the one who betrayed me, the joke is on her, she didn't even get the role she wanted. You think I'm bitter and malicious, right? If you knew how Copeau deceived me, he's only the shadow of the man he once was, the founder of the Old Dovecote Theater is no more than a Decrepit Old Dovecote. So spoke Bérénice to Alain Béron, pouring out her rancor to the poet, who was pained that he couldn't help her.

So, she was going to leave. Nathan and Alain thought of everything, in one week they had obtained for her, God only knows how, false papers. For the second time in her life she was going to use an ID that had a name other than her own. She withdrew the maximum amount she could from the bank, she had hidden the bundles of bills in fabric sewn into her corset, she had announced to the maid that she was leaving for two weeks to rest, in order not to arouse her suspicions, she left the keys to the apartment with Alain Béron, she took with her the jewelry that had the most sentimental value to her, she had to sacrifice most of her books and clothing, hoping for better days to come. She was to go to Bordeaux where a smuggler was waiting for her, she was to join Nathan in Barcelona and then they would board a ship heading to the United States, he had pulled a few strings, all was arranged, a new life would begin.

· 1 6 ·

She won't be able to tell what happened next in a tremulous voice, the doorbell ringing right at the moment when she was getting ready to leave, and behind the maid the apparition of her mother, yes, her mother, as pale as the statue of the deceased commander in Molière's *Dom Juan*, shrugging off Bérénice's attempt to hug her, her face frozen, finally resolving to unclench her teeth to announce in a voice weighted with reproach Your father is ill, he's asking for you. And Bérénice suddenly sobbing, not knowing if she was crying because she had reconnected with her mother, because she had heard the news of her father's illness, or because she understood that he wanted to see her, Bérénice's sobs, she who for all these years hadn't shed a tear when she thought of her parents, trying not to think about them since she then had another family, a family that she'd chosen, and the shame of acknowledging that this family had exceeded her expectations, making her selfishly happy.

"Now, now, as if this was the time for tears! Is that your husband?" asked her mother, motioning with her chin in the direction of Alain Béron.

"No, he's a friend, Mama. Mother, this is Alain Béron. Alain, my mother."

"Uh huh," said her mother, without taking the hand that the poet offered her.

That "Uh huh," full of contempt, as if the presence in Bérénice's apartment of a goy who wasn't her husband confirmed that her daughter was actually a fallen woman.

"Hurry, we've got to go," said Madame Capel impatiently. "You're making your father wait."

"I could take you in my car—you'll get there sooner," offered Alain.

Despite what they expected, her mother made no attempt to decline, so they all got into the poet's car and drove to the Rue d'Hauteville, where the Capels still lived. From the back seat of the car, Bérénice surreptitiously scrutinized her mother's profile, noticing that the skin of her face had lost its firmness, that a double chin was taking shape, that her hands were swollen now, that her wedding band had sunk into the flesh of her finger, that it must now be hard to take off, maybe even impossible to remove. No one spoke. Bérénice could sense her mother's preoccupation and disapproval, Bérénice didn't know what to say, she was so shaken by this unexpected turn of events. Alain Béron kept silent, out of consideration, no doubt, concentrating on avoiding bumps so as not to frighten her friend's mother. What did her father look like now? Bérénice wondered. Had he also aged? What illness had struck him? Her mother hadn't said anything about it, leaving her to conjecture: cancer, heart attack? Would she find him changed, paralyzed, senile? Was there any hope for him? If he had sent for her, it had to be because he was gravely ill, maybe in agony. Her mother left her to worry—on purpose, no doubt, to make her pay a little more for her decision to leave home. And now that she'd lost everything, how guilty she felt! What would her father say to her? More reproaches? Would he curse her one last time before dying, leaving her only a legacy of remorse?

"I'll wait here for you, Bérénice," said Alain Béron to the young woman, taking her hand gently but firmly to remind her that they had to take the train to Bordeaux that very night.

"See you in a little while," she answered in a serious tone.

She wanted to light a cigarette, but didn't dare smoke in front of her mother. The street looked just as it did in her memories, perhaps it didn't seem as narrow, now that she had removed herself from the family routine that had so repelled her. How strange to find herself here again, walking up the stairs behind her mother: she had walked this way so many times before, after shopping or after school, a little girl scampering after her parents, but today she felt like an adult and oddly more grown up than her mother, despite her severe manner and her silence. What would it be like to see her father again, when she never thought she'd return to the home where her parents had driven her out?

Her mother opens the door, the sharp smell of medications suddenly fills her nostrils. Bérénice follows without thinking, it takes her a while to realize that they are not headed to her parents' bedroom, but to her own room. Which is no longer her room. Maybe because of her father's illness, it has been transformed into a sick room, unless the transformation was done at some much earlier time, maybe around the time she left, perhaps, to wipe out all that it might remind them of, her, the cursed daughter. No dolls are left, or her children's books, her theater posters—no doubt all that adolescent clutter had been tossed out long ago. In the bed that is no longer Bérénice's, there is her father, stretched out. She can't make out his features clearly, they are masked by the semi-darkness.

"We need to speak privately."

Her mother leaves, after an imperceptible moment of hesitation.

Bérénice feels her tears well up at hearing her father's voice as it always was—impressive—despite the years that have passed.

"Come closer."

His breath has changed, it's no longer the neutral exhalation that she'd always known, but a sharper one, as if coming from organs that are decomposing—an old man's breath. She is bothered by these thoughts that she can't stop. *Be quiet, be quiet already* she wants to yell at her brain, don't spoil this moment, don't notice his three-day beard, don't notice the veil that has fallen over his reddened eyes and that makes them almost tearful.

That thick album that he's hiding under the mattress, that he insists she take out from its hiding place, painfully, since his bodyweight makes it difficult to remove, Open it, he says to her, and she can't quite decipher what is in that voice, she's so unsettled, so fearful of a second curse, a third if you count the *herem* of the Comédie-Française, so shaken she can't imagine for a second what she's going to find there, in this thick album that her father shows her, trembling as she braces herself for the monster that's going to leap out suddenly from that album.

She can't believe her eyes. "Bérénice de Lignières, a name to remember," "Bérénice de Lignières Triumphs in *Hernani*," "The Reflections of Mademoiselle de Lignières," "How I View Andromache," by Mademoiselle de Lignières, "Principal Actor After One Year!" Her entire theatrical biography is there, the press clippings meticulously pasted in chronological order, starting in summer 1937, the articles that began when she joined the Comédie-Française and even the notice in the paper announcing her marriage to Nathan. They aren't just from *Le Populaire*, the newspaper he read daily, but mastheads she'd never seen in their home, like *Le Figaro* and *Ars nova*. … She imagined her father secretly slipping out to go downstairs to the newsstand, maybe he even made a long detour to find another stand farther than the one right near their home, to avoid questions or comments from the salesman, "So, Monsieur Capel, not sending the errand boy tonight?" or maybe, "*Le Figaro*? What's the matter, you don't believe in your Blum anymore?" and furtively smuggled into the house, like a small treasure, the articles about *her*. When did he find the time to read all that, when did he have a moment to take out scissors and glue, at what time did he perform these little tasks, sheltered from the eyes of others? Astounded, she was astounded, not even daring to look at him, her emotions were so strong, taking time to notice that with his finger he was pointing out a specific page, from which fell two tickets to the Comédie-Française: Racine's *Bérénice*—11/12/1939, Racine's *Bérénice*—11/26/1939, stupefied, looking at him in disbelief, understanding that he had come to see her, see her in *Bérénice*, that play of all plays, the one that Louis the school teacher had told him about, the one that was the source of her given name, he had seen it, he had paid for his ticket one Sunday matinee, what pretext had he given his wife to be absent for several hours? He had seen her act, he had heard her, he had come back, another Sunday, two Sundays later, he had been there in the theater and she hadn't suspected a thing. She held him in her arms, no longer able to speak, suffocating with sobs, she had never felt so close to him, he says to her, "*noch besser als* Sarah Bernhardt," making that supreme comparison in Yiddish, *even better than Sarah Bernhardt*, and those were his last words.

PART THREE

· 1 ·

"How do you live if you're not an actor? My whole life headed in that direction, I never thought that my life could be anything else," she repeated over and over to Alain Béron. Bérénice didn't leave, she stayed in Paris for the seven days of *shiva*, in the apartment that had been hers from the time she was born till she was fifteen. She stayed for her father's burial, sobbing when she saw the blue velvet cloth adorned with the Star of David over the coffin, a nervous wreck when the rabbi tore his clothing as a sign of mourning. Mostly she was dazed, lost.

And now she was staying with Alain Béron, in his pied-à-terre located in L'Isle-Adam, a few kilometers from Pontoise, just north of Paris. He had discovered the town in the thirties thanks to a letter that Balzac had written to his sister, Laure Surville: "You know that L'Isle-Adam is my earthly paradise." One day he just had to see with his own eyes this corner of France that the author of *The Human Comedy* had made such a strong case for. Then he fell under the spell of a charming little house that was for sale, Rue Poupart, and bought it a few weeks later. Its proximity to the Parc de Cassan, swimming in the Oise, and above all the calm of that bourgeois town suited the Aixois more than the frenzy of Paris.

Night and day, Bérénice remained in bed in the semi-darkness of the upstairs bedroom where he put her up, lacking the strength to get up, crushed by the fate that had turned against her since the debacle. She had lost everything: Nathan, her work, her father. No longer taking care of herself, not even putting on makeup, barely eating, making an effort to swallow a few mouthfuls of soup that the patient poet brought her. Lethargic—as France itself had been since the Germans occupied it—suffering from a "nervous and organic disorder," according to the doctor's diagnosis.

Sometimes, when Alain Béron, with his reassuring hand, took hers, she found the strength to speak and then words poured out of her in an obsessive flow that was only about theater, recalling her first year at the Conservatory, when she spoke on her landlady's telephone and said, "I'm going to my diction class," too loudly, too loudly on purpose, she was so proud of her new student life and, seated in the metro, like all the apprentice actors, recognizable as they were by the perpetual motion of their lips that kept going back over the lines they had to learn with their eyes riveted to the script resting on their knees and then glancing upward toward the heavens, as if you had to go that high to retrieve your memory.

She had given up, incapable of getting out of bed, what was the point since it wasn't to act, since no one was left, not Nathan and not her father, not Yonnel or Alexandre, not Bourdet or Jouvet. I'm right here, murmured Alain Béron in his deep voice with its soothing harmonies. Why are you taking care of me, let me die already, I'm not good for anything anymore, and he taking her at her word, explaining to her very seriously, almost pedantically, that he was helping her because she herself helped people with the light that she radiated. She was too worn out, too defeated to understand. He was preaching into a void and yet the sweet singsong of his words did her good.

Nathan wrote to her every day, anxious, jealous of her being alone with Alain, unhappy that she wasn't coming to meet him, so much so that he imagined the most awful betrayals, and to some extent he was not completely wrong since he had never been so blind as not to notice the poet's attraction for Bérénice, even though the poet reined in that attraction because of his friendship for Nathan but even more for other reasons, deeper, that he himself didn't fathom and resulted in his never having lived with a woman other than his mother, even though he was over forty.

Do you know what I think about? I think of everything I haven't acted yet. All those roles that were reaching out to me. In the classics, for instance, the Countess in *The Marriage of Figaro*, Silvia in *The Game of Love and Chance*, or Agrippina. And even more—few people know this—I wanted to act in contemporary plays. I was criticized so often for belonging to the Comédie-Française instead of being part of the "avant-garde." But I needed that institution because I started out so far from there. That institution was my way of legitimizing myself as an actress. In my own eyes and in the eyes of other professionals. It's so far from my natural destiny, that world, you saw the Rue d'Hauteville when you took me there the other day. Still, I never acted in a "classical" way, I believe. And if I like Jean-Louis Barrault a lot, despite his faults, it's because he understood that I wanted to do some Claudel, and he encouraged me. He made the introductions so I could audition for *The Satin Slipper*, but what good is all that now? Claudel didn't want anything to do with Véra Korène, he thought she was beautiful but she had a wooden voice, and since I was such a coward, I wanted the role so badly that I didn't defend her, although I'm still trying to figure out what he meant by "a wooden voice." You see, I'm not any better than Florence. The day my father disowned me, despite how completely ripped apart I felt, you'll never guess what I was thinking. I was thinking about Hugo's *The King Amuses Himself*, about the curse placed on Monsieur de Saint-Vallier, and I said to myself: I could play that role so well if I were a man. That's horrible, isn't it? My father banished me from the family home, by tearing his jacket he disowned me, and there I was and I heard that voice, not his, no, my own voice, telling me: look, look, listen, you'll use this later, to act. Is it the same for writers? Do you also feed on people? We think of ourselves as more human, superior, because we create art and only humans create art, but we end up forgetting all our humanity, we become worse than vultures. My heart can't be simple anymore, my parents were right when they said that books made me strange.

Calm down, Bérénice, try to rest. No, no, I have to talk, I have to tell you what crossed my mind the first time I met Véra Korène in her apartment … You're going to think I'm completely ridiculous and naïve, but I was only fifteen. Of course I thought she was magnificent, but what really stunned me, what literally rendered me speechless as soon as we met, do you know what it was? It was her hands. They were so fine, so very distinguished, but they had bulging veins. That's when I realized—it hit me like a lightning bolt—that she was a human being, a real flesh-and-blood woman. Up until then I think I believed that actors were gods. You probably think I'm very childish, don't you? I saw her hands, one vein in particular that stood out a bit more than the others or that beat a little harder, and it seemed sacrilegious to me: this actress was a member of the Comédie-Française and despite that she was a woman like all the rest, who breathed like the rest, had the same bodily functions as the rest, who must have eaten like the rest, gone to the toilet like the rest, and didn't smell of roses like the rest!

He took her hand and with one finger traced her veins, so gently, one at a time, ending this gesture with a long kiss on the back of her hand, before leaving the bedroom to let her sleep, and then he went to write—maybe.

· 2 ·

Now the two women were on the platform, embarrassed, not knowing what to say. Alain had gone with Bérénice, who was still pale and weak, to the Gare de Lyon so the mother and daughter could say their farewells. How different her relationship with Madame Capel and his ties with his own mother! His mother was his pillar, they had been partners in crime for as long as he could remember, had become each other's confidants, as precious to each other as they were necessary, calling one another almost every day, astonishing those in their circle who couldn't share enough malicious gossip about the tight couple they formed, so tight that the others around them often seemed like strangers. So he marveled at how this mother-daughter couple were so dissimilar. No physical trait connected them, unless it was a certain fineness in the joints and that determination in their expressions. But Bérénice had a perfection about her features that you couldn't find in her mother, who was marked by a high forehead that took up a good part of her face. Still, you wouldn't mistake them for strangers: the excessive disharmony of their relationship betrayed the filial bond.

He observed the expressions stamped on their features. The recent loss of Maurice Capel could be seen in their worn faces, even if Bérénice's twenty-two years made the rings under her eyes less visible. Her mother seemed nervous, she clutched her identity card and her *Ausweis* obtained thanks to the illness of Grandma Mathilde, who had returned to Provence since the exodus—"thanks to" and not "because of," since that illness had allowed her to get a pass from the Kommandantur. She wasn't planning to return to Paris. The Valabrègue woman was going back to be with her family in the region where she had grown up. Her family would help her mourn for her husband, that at least was what everyone was saying, and what, in order not to create a stir, she was pretending to believe.

He had placed himself at a discreet distance from the two women. While smoking a Gitanes, he was observing Bérénice's mother, who looked older than her years. Despite her coolness, or perhaps because of it, because of her unyielding expression, or the distance between the bodies of the mother and daughter, he could read their thoughts clearly. At the moment she was saying her farewell to Bérénice, she was drawing up a balance sheet, a fairly bitter balance sheet, in truth, that of a mother who had never really connected with her daughter.

What could I say to her? I shouldn't have arrived so early, here I am stuck on this platform having to say goodbye to her, while I'm really only waiting for one thing: to find the best seat I can in my compartment. Tell her I'm going to miss her? She knows that's not true. At heart, all these years, it didn't mean all that much to me not to see her. It would have pleased me if she'd been a normal girl, if she'd been like all the children I knew: a profession or trade, a husband with a good job, not a composer, some kind of circus acrobat just like she is, I don't even know what he looks like, he didn't come to the funeral, in any case, I wouldn't have approved of his coming since he hadn't even asked Maurice for her hand, what kind of manners is that? From the start she never did anything like other children. Even her first name ... Although, it was Maurice who chose that. May God keep his soul, but I never resigned myself to it, with us you were always named Sarah, Myriam, Rebecca, now *those* are kosher names, not Bérénice. That set everything off on the wrong track. In any case, I would've preferred a boy, sons are sweeter to their mothers. I don't know ... they love them more, they're grateful. Me, I only had her. God didn't want to give me other children, and that one always disappointed me. I wanted a daughter with blond hair, hers was black, I wanted her to have a sweet voice, she has a deep voice, I wanted her to have looks that were just right, but she's too pretty, we Valabrègues aren't like that, I was always embarrassed any time someone got all excited about how beautiful she was, people, they thought they were making me happy, but they only made me uncomfortable, you get noticed too much when you're too pretty, who needs that? Like my grandmother used to say, it's better to have a plain face and a good fate. But with her, what good did it do her? It gave her ideas about the theater, she wanted to be like those actresses you see in the movies, and for what? She told me they threw her out of the damn Comédie-Française, doesn't surprise me in the least, it's not a profession for Jews, actor, *tsss*, we always told her that, but no, Mademoiselle didn't listen to us, she always did whatever popped into her head, and it didn't do any good when Maurice threw her out, it didn't bother her at all that people talked about her, she had her photo in the newspapers, he kept his little scrapbook hidden and he thought I wouldn't notice, what did he think, that a Valabrègue wouldn't know that kind of thing? Men! They're so naïve sometimes, did he really think that cleaning house every day I wouldn't run across his hidden treasure? I didn't say anything, it's not for women to create scenes, and I didn't want to humiliate him, the clock is ticking, I'm going to get a lousy seat on this train, why did she have to come, I didn't insist on it, if she hadn't come I'd already be in the train, now I'm sure I won't find a window seat, those are the best, everyone wants those, if she had been normal there wouldn't have been any problem, she could've continued to practice her trade, she could have come with me with her husband and not that stranger, true he seems like a gentleman but he's a stranger, she only spends time with the goyim, God only knows what she does with them, Pétain is right, there's no more morality, that's why we're in this mess, she would've come here with her children, at least I could've talked to *them* but I don't know what to say to her, how old is she again, twenty-two and still no children, that's not normal, what will people think? they have to be saying that she's sterile, it seems she's been married more than a year so why no children? We've always had children. She's so much like Maurice, they've got the same eyes, exactly the same color ... At this age, I should already be a grandmother, and poor Maurice, he'll never have grandchildren, and he wanted them so much, good, now it's almost time, I can tell her I need to board the train ...

On the railway station platform, the mother and daughter face one another. Bérénice seems completely lost under her little hat, she waits for words that won't be spoken, that will never be spoken, the words of gratitude that her father uttered before dying, words that had reconciled them. Alain Béron would have liked to yell at the young woman: stop believing the words will be said one day, he wanted to yell that at her so that she would stop wasting the little bit of energy she had left in this impossible quest, still, it's clear to outside observers that the mother who is facing her is expressing—in her posture and her grudging kisses, and in that forced way that she holds her against her body before boarding the train—"I never loved you." I never loved you, cries her mother's whole attitude, but Bérénice refuses to acknowledge it, and yet she knows it, and as if testifying to that, her shoulders are hunched as she leaves the station. He wants to gather her in his arms like a father. Perhaps out of modesty he stops himself and it's she in tears who seeks refuge against his chest, drawing close to him, the one who understands her, for a few seconds she finds comfort in his arms until the sight of a German uniform makes her stand up straight, suddenly upright and ready again to confront the world as best she can.

In the car on the way back to L'Isle-Adam, Alain thought it was time to speak to the actress: "Bérénice, there's someone I would like to introduce you to."

· 3 ·

"The tragedy of democracies is their weakness. France and Great Britain let Czechoslovakia fall, like Léon Blum with the Spanish Republic." For ten minutes Bérénice had listened, smiling, to this blond, blue-eyed kid reel off his political analyses in an extremely serious manner. Seeing that his audience was with him, he recounted every step of the defeat, starting with President Wilson's angelic naivete—he was the first one to blame—right up to Hitler's lies. In the end, Chamberlain's appeasement policy was excusable: how could an Englishman from the gentry imagine for one second that Monsieur Hitler would not act like a gentleman?

"This kid is amazing," she says to Alain. "How old are you?"

"I just turned eleven, I'm going into sixth grade in the fall. I finished third on the entrance exam!"

And so it happened that she met her neighbor on the Rue Poupart, a boy by the name of Guy, a young Jewish Parisian with a Dutch last name, fair-haired and blue-eyed, who had found refuge in L'Isle-Adam with his family since the start of the Occupation. He had first taken a liking to Alain Béron because he wanted to be a lawyer like him.

"My father doesn't want me to, he says it's a profession where you starve to death."

"Your father sounds like he has very good sense," answered the lawyer-poet.

After school started again in the fall, every day after he returned from the municipal middle school of Pontoise, after a long walk and a train ride—the commuter railroad that ran from Beaumont-sur-Oise to Pontoise—the boy came to visit Bérénice.

"Look at my German textbook. Of course, you know this poem by Heine:

Ich weiß nicht, was soll es bedeuten,
Daß ich so traurig bin;
Ein Märchen aus alten Zeiten,
Das kommt mir nicht aus dem Sinn ...

"Well, now look at the signature: *Unbekannt Dichter* (Unknown Poet). Hah! As if nobody in Germany knows that 'The Lorelei' is by Heine! But Heine is Jewish, and so ..."

Alain knew what he was doing when he introduced the young man to her—his anecdotes always amused the actress. What a lesson, this kid managed to laugh at the news, to not let himself be crushed by the darkness of the world they found themselves in. At his age, the gusto for life is at its strongest. This meeting did wonders for her health. She became ashamed of her own defeatism, she had to shake it off and make a decision. A German decree had just been issued, requiring a census of all Jews in Paris and the Department of the Seine. What to do? According to the laws of the Occupation, she had to declare herself: anyone was considered Jewish who had more than two Jewish grandparents. Like most Israelites, the father of little Guy went to the police station to fill out his declaration. Even though all his ancestors were without exception Jewish, he decided not to declare one of his grandmothers, after which he said to his wife and two children: "She must be spinning in her grave." His lie was undoubtedly absurd, and since the Germans occupied Holland, they could easily ascertain that it was false, but wasn't it even more absurd to require Jews to turn in their radios to the police? Wasn't it even more absurd to forbid them to ride bicycles and to talk on the phone, *even in a public phone booth*?

Once again, as she did after the board of directors meeting on September 5, Bérénice found herself having to make a choice: register with the census as Jewish or refuse to obey this unjust law. This time the choice was clearer. Defying anything that wore the German uniform or the Nazi symbol, she knew almost immediately that she would not submit. No doubt it was easier for her to make this decision since this new diktat came from a foreign authority.

She probably wouldn't have been able to violate this law without the support of Alain Béron. Bérénice never knew if his connections consisted of ties with the administrative authorities or with former "clients" who had somewhat shady pasts and were grateful to the lawyer for having gotten them off. In any case, Alain's friends arranged things well: in addition to getting a new identity card, she obtained a certificate of baptism and all the ration coupons she needed. Her name was now Bérénice née Pascal, married name Béron. Their neighbors were already convinced they were married, and it was simpler to let them go on thinking that.

In October 1940, the authorities struck another blow against the Jews. The national radio announced that the government was taking new measures, and that the full text of the law would soon be published in the *Journal officiel*. They explained that everywhere, but especially in public service, the "insidious and destructive" influence of the Jews had been felt. One could almost sympathize with the government, because they had to shoulder "the woeful task of restoring France." They assured that, "the entire government, with absolute serenity, has asserted that it is not taking these actions in the spirit of reprisals. They respect the persons and property of Jews. They merely prevent them from performing certain functions, whether relating to information, management, or education, since experience has shown them, and all impartial minds as well, that the Jews exercised these functions with an individualistic tendency that led to anarchy." Blah, blah, blah, Bérénice turned off the radio. She had a thought for little Guy—his father had preferred to smash his radio rather than hand it over to the authorities.

Now it was official that Jews were excluded from certain professions. This didn't (yet?) affect actors, but for certain, she was better off passing as Bérénice Béron.

Nathan, who continued to be well informed of events, sent his wife messages that were more and more anxious and pressed her to come and join him: "Alain writes me that you're doing better, I beg you, come, I can't stand this waiting for you any longer. The situation worries me more and more, I won't have any peace of mind until we get to America." At this point she knew that he had been right, from the start he was right to be alarmist. So often she had made fun of him, of his predictions, of his obsession with decoding every sentence in the newspapers, attributing sinister meanings to them. She thought she was safe. Never did she think that France's greatest theater and France itself would discriminate against French people. They're making second-class citizens of you, the way they did under the Ancien Régime, Alain stated bitterly. I'm not even talking about the Germans: did you know that the Otto list, which censored Jewish authors, freemasons, and communists—just to name a few—also banned Pirandello? He's not even Jewish, he's not a freemason or a communist, but his translator is Jewish, so, *verboten*!

For the first time, Bérénice was glad that her father had died. At least he wouldn't see this. At least he wouldn't read in the newspapers, "Jews cannot take part in public duties or perform them," followed by an enumeration of the forbidden professions, as if that were a normal state of affairs, as if nothing in that would elicit indignation. Maybe her father saw what was coming and left in order not to see it, she even started to think. The France that he loved and that he had taught her to love, where was it now? It had reached the point where they were stripping people of their citizenship. Bérénice thought of all the Jews of Eastern Europe who had come to France as he had to escape pogroms, certain of finding in the homeland of the rights of man a land of refuge, revering France, proud to shed their blood for her. She thought of her father's friend Michel Hoffeld, also a Russian Jew, who had fought all four years of the Great War while his wife had subsisted on a soldier's wife's stipend, and who, when he returned, when he had just started to earn a better living, had returned his veteran's pension to the State, explaining that he was getting along fine and that undoubtedly there were others who needed it more than he. Even her father, who was the soul of integrity, found that excessive. Michel Hoffeld was one of the first to be deported, God knows where, the Germans yanked out of bed "the Hoffeld Jews" and pillaged their apartment, including a first edition of Schiller's poetry that was the jewel of their library, leaving behind them only a chamber pot.

Even for those born in France like her, and even those like the Valabrègues, who boasted a long lineage, proud to have nothing in common with the rough-mannered immigrants of Paris's working class neighborhoods, who yammered in French and got lost in the metro, even they were downgraded professionally. They ripped off the epaulets of Dreyfus, they broke his sword in half, all the children of France had etched into their memories the image of that humiliation, everyone had seen the drawing in *Le Petit Journal* of that "traitor Dreyfus," standing straight as an arrow in the courtyard of the Military Academy, his uniform stripped of its decorations while facing him an officer caparisoned in medals and bars broke his weapon with a rage that bordered on delight. Now many could feel what that innocent man had experienced under the impassive glow of the dome of the Invalides. All of them innocent as he was, except for the crime of being Jewish, they were wounded to the heart. To what Devil's Island would they now be dragged?

She looked at little Guy, so brilliant at age eleven, whose ambition was to become a lawyer and showed obvious talent: already he spoke with authority, knew how to frame an argument, had a certain presence. Not very long ago, his future would have been clear. He would have passed his baccalaureate exam, would enroll in law school, and would have been sworn in after earning his graduate diploma. Today, if things kept going in this direction, he could banish from his mind any such ambitions. Bérénice's heart bled for him, she felt so guilty to belong to this world of adults that allowed no hope to children that she spoiled him as much as she could, giving him bread she had obtained with her ration card or the last squares of chocolate that remained in the kitchen cabinets. Enough to improve on the usual fare allotted to children with J2 ration coupons.

She no longer held out any hope of acting again in France, and Nathan's America didn't tempt her. Her pessimism encompassed the whole world ever since her own world, that of the theater, so full of certainties and joys, had crumbled. Leave? Stay? Of course in Barcelona there was Nathan, but what horizons could the United States offer her? Here there was at least the French language and this young boy whom she was teaching elocution, and with him she felt at least a little useful. For Nathan it was different: his music constituted his world. Even in prison, even uprooted, even deprived of paper and pencil, he could still compose in his head, his mind was full of notes. While with her, without a stage and an audience, how could she practice her art? She was nothing but a tree without fruit, *Yerma*, barren, as the Spanish say, and the most poetic of them, Federico García Lorca. Another role she would never play.

· 4 ·

Alain Béron was no longer writing, except for a journal that he kept regularly beginning in the fall of 1940. The defeat had drained his morale, the Occupation had paralyzed his muse. This conquered and dejected France left him literally disarmed, guilty, maybe about having the luxury of writing poetry. There was still his calling for the law. The courts reopened on October 1 ("We both go back to school the same day," he joked with Guy). That day, the president of the bar association, Jacques Charpentier, gathered all the judges and lawyers in front of the bronze plaque listing those in the legal profession who had had died during the Great War. Oh, yes, he gave a stirring speech, the president of the bar, imbued with the mentality of sacrifice that seemed to have become the new credo of the national revolution, describing an ideal and bucolic France. How he crafted his conclusion: "Teach us, as the school-children of yesterday were taught, to cherish the homeland that our forefathers built and for which you gave your lives, our vineyards, and forests, our meadows and our wheat fields, the land that stretches from the Rhine to the Ocean and from the North Sea to the Pyrenees, France one and indivisible, that will not die."

In truth, the lawyer hardly had any confidence in his peers at this point, he who had held in such high esteem his profession and the honor of wearing its robes. The law of September 10, 1940, regulating access to the bar, had just forbidden the profession to anyone who did not possess "French nationality and origin, defined as being born to a French father," a xenophobic law that even excluded from the bar some French people who were born in France. "Read the *Journal officiel*," he recorded in his notebook. "I already can't stand the sight of, 'We, the Marshall of France, head of the French state.' So it was true, the rumor that circulated yesterday. I didn't want to believe it. What a disgrace, for racism to be enshrined in the law. It breaks my heart that at the Palace of Justice, no one is reacting. Even the leading lawyers, usually so quick to become impassioned, remain quiet as mice. How naïve of me to have thought that the legal profession would erupt in protest. When the law on Jews was entered into the legal statutes, it was treated as just another day at the office. I'm waiting for it to be taught soon in law schools by our eminent professors."

But Alain Béron wasn't wet behind the ears, he knew that xenophobia and anti-Semitism had always been in good taste at the Palace of Justice. It wasn't an accident that a Jew had never been elected president of the bar association. And yet the lawyer wouldn't have bet on the silence of his colleagues. You would have thought that military defeat had petrified everyone, contaminating even the bar, a natural rampart of freedom. He did not rule out that many were secretly relieved by the project of regenerating France that the collaborationist ruler Pétain promised. So what if two hundred lawyers, give or take a few, were the price they had to pay …

What was the price of their honor? Where had their sense of morality gone, their ideal of justice, their faith in a republic and equality? They talked about a letter from the lawyer Pierre Masse, officer of the Legion of Honor, awarded the Croix de Guerre, senator from the department of the Hérault, who wrote to Marshall Pétain, his former friend on the general staff in 1917 during the First World War, to ask him, after the decree declaring that Jews could no longer serve as officers, even those with strictly French ancestry, if he should return the stripes earned by his brother, killed in the battle of Douaumont in 1916, and those of his nephew, killed at Rethel in May 1940, if his brother could retain the military medal he was buried with, the stripes of his son wounded at Soupir in June 1940 and even the Medal of Sainte-Hélène awarded to his great-grandfather? That was an insolent letter, no doubt. To write it and have no qualms about sending it, you would need to be named Pierre Masse and possess his lofty independence, you would need above all the power of his indignation faced with the outrage of an unjust law. What answer would he receive? Would they even answer him? Undoubtedly Pierre

Masse himself had no illusions about the effectiveness of his action, despite his ties of friendship with Pétain. The latter, at best, would have a suitable letter written by some lowly pencil pusher who would grumble about this added paperwork. The upright lawyer didn't deserve that, Alain thought sadly. He had met Pierre Masse several times when he was clerking. The man seemed to him the very embodiment of the Third Republic, he had impressed him with his air of authority and his qualities as a jurist. At the time, Pierre Masse was about the same age that Alain was now.

One thought led to another, and the man of law now went back over the years of his apprenticeship, his move north to Paris to enroll in law school. Parting with his mother had been difficult, he had spent his entire life with her, never separated from her for more than a day. His relationship with his father had always been cooler—he had never supported Alain's career as a poet and his father's absence during the Great War had ended up stretching their connection even thinner—and then death found him in 1917. In Paris, the young Béron proved to be a good student, he quickly earned his law degree, had gone on to finish a doctorate, which never prevented him from writing poems, some of which were published in *Cahiers du Sud* and praised by Paul Éluard, who was ten years his senior. The two most moving events in his life as a young man were taking the oath for the bar under the benevolent gaze of his mentor, the lawyer Albert Willm, and seeing his name on his first collection of poems.

Pierre Masse. Bérénice. It seemed to the lawyer as if France was a compass gone awry, whose needle, directed by a Nazi magnet too strong for it, had become useless for indicating direction. French law was now being dictated by the invader, but was it necessary to obey them so timidly? If he could no longer write, at least he had to speak about all this with trusted friends who would share his distress and his impulse to revolt. And then maybe, if inspiration returned to him, to publish this revolt in a magazine, that of Pierre Seghers, for instance, *Poets in Helmets*, which had published him at the time of the mobilization, and which was now becoming *Poetry 40*, under the editorial direction of several writers.

Meanwhile, even if it had let him down, the judicial sphere seemed to him the only place where he could defend those who needed help. But how much longer? He didn't know. Maybe in the midst of this cacophony it would reach the point where victims no longer had the right to legal representation, maybe there would soon be only summary proceedings, for the sake of appearances— they might even do away with all trials. Alain Béron's natural melancholy found a powerfully combustible material in the world around him. To shut himself up in an ivory tower would have been the most natural response for him, but that inclination seemed impractical at this stage. So he would send the president of the bar association the proof required of all his colleagues that his father was French on the day of his birth, and then work, plead cases, help those he could, first of all Bérénice. For the moment, the ends justified the means, but he knew that this formula would rapidly reach its limits, that it would soon be of no use if he did not want to compromise himself.

· 5 ·

The day began badly. In the morning, returning from the center of town where she went to buy newspapers, revolting rags that she bought, despite their bare-faced propaganda, to get the latest information on food supplies—when the new milk ration cards would be distributed, which coupons on the "assorted foodstuffs" card would be accepted, she chanced for the first time on a red poster. It announced that, following the killing of a German officer in Paris, hostages had been shot. She felt a dark foreboding.

When she got back to the little house in L'Isle-Adam, she found, balanced on the cast iron radiator of the entry hall, a letter from Nathan. It had taken quite a journey to reach her: since there was no more postal service between Spain and the occupied zone, it was necessary to use roundabout means. Mailed in Barcelona, the letter in a double envelope arrived in the unoccupied zone of France at a general delivery post box where a friend had picked it up. He passed it to another comrade who had an *Ausweis*. That man had hand delivered it to Alain Béron, who had received the letter for Bérénice before leaving for the Palace of Justice. The letter was now in her hands, very thick. Why did the young woman again have this sinister foreboding when she felt the letter? Ordinarily she would tear open the envelope without hesitation, she was so happy when she received a letter instead of a postcard. A card was too quickly read, while with a letter, there was first the pleasure of weighing it in your hands to estimate the number of pages, the perusal of the stamps and the postmarks, slitting the envelope with a letter-opener, very neatly, the finger that caressed the edge of the triangle that sealed the envelope, thinking, "Right underneath this, he used his tongue to fasten the flap." And then removing the pages, guessing from Nathan's handwriting the state of mind he was in at that moment: writing with a definite slant with large spaces between the words = fatigue. Regular writing = calm. Many words crossed out = nervousness … Here, the writing was cramped together, the margins neat and straight. It was a letter of ripe reflection, it was an ultimatum.

Bérénice,

I've been waiting for you for four months now and I don't know what to think anymore. When you had to cancel your trip because your father was dying, naturally I understood your decision, you had a legitimate reason. You needed time, and I gave it to you. But today, why are you still attached to France? You can no longer practice your art, your mother is far from you and doesn't need you, your life is in danger in the occupied zone—what is it then?

Do you want to die or even suffer for an anti-Semitic France that threw you out like a dog? Do you want to remain in a France that couldn't do any better than to dump your husband in some damn camp instead of protecting him from the Nazis?

I know what you're thinking, your father brainwashed you with his republican ideas, his romantic vision of France. If he were still here he would treat me as a shirker because I'm not enlisting in London or in the ranks of the Free French, and maybe even you think that as well. But I'm no hero, I'm a composer. My years of military service were wasted years, the soldier's profession runs contrary to my physical and mental constitution. My work on this Earth is to compose music. To march in line, live the life of a private in the army, peeling potatoes—I've already paid my dues. Sign up again? No, thank you. I don't want someone informing you that I died in combat, I don't want you putting my photo on a marble mantel like all the families who lost a husband, a son, or a brother during the Great War, I don't want my final piece of music to already have been written and not to come, I don't want to die at thirty-five because of the cowardly politicians who failed to figure out in time how crazy Hitler was, when they could just have read *Mein Kampf* and understood it all, I have no intention of adding to this deadly delirium when all I want is to live peacefully from my music. Is it a crime to want to accomplish what you are born to do? History is too big for me, I'm not up to it.

As a communist, I was thrown out of the party. As a German, I was kicked out of my own country. There are only two labels left to me in this world: Jew and composer. Jew, because we are reminded every day that we are members of that group and it would be useless for me to convert or deny the law of my fathers, I can't erase my circumcision or cancel the generations of Jews who came before me. A composer, because even in banning my compositions, even in declaring me a "degenerate composer," they still recognize that identity: composer. My way of talking about it would undoubtedly not have been the same in '36 or '37, when I was still caught up in the communist ideal, but today, I only believe in the reality of two things: anti-Semitism and music.

The only solution to anti-Semitism that I see today is America and if one day that haven also turns out to be a trap then there will always be Palestine for me, where I wouldn't hesitate to go if I had to. As for music … I put it above all because I know its power, because it's my reason for living, because they can take everything from me, but not that, because if they took it from me I couldn't live anymore, I'm certain of that.

Bérénice, my wife of music, I'm not waiting any longer. A freighter is leaving in two months for America. There is ample time for you to receive this letter and make the journey to join me.

One word from you and we leave together as we should have done from the very start. Soon it will be too late, my transit visa will expire shortly. I still have enough connections to extend it, but what's the sense in that? I'm only staying here because I'm waiting for you. I don't want to wait any longer.

So, join me, forgive the tone of this letter that might seem high-handed to you, but imagine my state of mind, far from everything, far from you. I miss you, you can't imagine how much I want to see your blue eyes, how much I want to touch you, to … I don't understand anymore what's holding you back. It makes me crazy to imagine that you, with Alain … No, I don't want to go down that path. You see, your absence is making me ramble, come to me my beautiful actress, join me. Think of the life we'll have together in America. We'll make the trip full of hope like the pioneers of yesteryear. The Statue of Liberty will open her generous arms to us. Just seeing the boat will fill our eyes with tears of joy. We'll live in New York or Los Angeles, we'll be friends with the artists who have already gotten to America: Darius Milhaud, Lion Feuchtwanger, Pierre Monteux, Otto Klemperer, Bruno Walter. We will recreate the Paris that we love, the one before the war where every café held the promise of meeting a new brother, where artists could share beautiful sunshine, a poetic idea, instead of talking about restrictions, bombings, and shelters. It will all be the way it was before, in that Eden with its infinite skyscrapers, we'll quickly learn to speak American, we who are so used to adapting ourselves to the whims of persecution, we'll celebrate July 4 and we'll eat turkey on Thanksgiving, I'll finish *David's Harp*, which is already complete in my head, we'll stage it at the Met or the San Francisco Opera, there will be plenty of conductors who will want it, it will be your first role in America, you'll be known and celebrated, no one there has seen an actress like you, you'll be the new American heart-throb, you'll erase their memory of Sarah Bernhardt, you'll be the queen of the stage, if you want you could even sing on Broadway, sing Kurt Weill like in The Masked Owl, remember, my Lou, you had the perfect *mi*, your *mi* sharp on the "don't" of "I don't love you," oh, my love, our meeting at The Masked Owl, you rushed your eighth notes a bit in the first couplet, that drove Agnès mad but you were right, it was more theatrical like that, and for me, the success of the *Harp* will bring me commissions, they'll make me conductor of an orchestra, I'll be free to compose as I hear it, I'll record all of Mozart's operas, or better still, all of Wagner just to piss off the Nazis, I'll have a chair at a university, I'll give lectures, I'll write music for films if I fancy it, maybe we'll become rich but above all we'll be free, far from the war, far from Europe that has nothing more to offer us and which wants nothing more to do with us, we could even start a family if you want, we'll give birth to real Americans, they'll be good-looking like their mama and we'll be proud of them, we'll learn how to drive, we'll buy a Ford and we'll go on vacation in Canada or Mexico, we'll be free, we'll be happier than ever.

· 6 ·

Two days had passed since the arrival of Nathan's ultimatum, but Bérénice still hadn't been able to make a decision. She showed the letter to Alain but she found him strangely distracted, unavailable. Every time she tried to talk to him about it, it seemed like an inopportune moment. Either the lawyer had to be at the Palace of Justice, or he had clients visiting, or he had shut himself in his office—an important file, a complex case—those were his only explanations. On the afternoon of the second day, or rather at the end of the day, after examining and reexamining the problem in her head without finding a solution, she felt the need to reread Nathan's letter. Where was it? It wasn't in her bedroom, or in the living room, or in the kitchen. Bérénice finally remembered that her friend had taken it with him to his office while trying to find the right moment to read it carefully.

After a slight hesitation, she decided to enter his sanctuary. It was the first time she had gone in there by herself. Except for the living room, it was the largest room if not the lightest in the house. An elegant Empire writing desk, which undoubtedly had come with the house, served as the poet-lawyer's worktable. Some chairs, a settee, and a Thonet lectern, provided a more modern counterpoint. The walls, covered in wainscoting and panels of bottle-green leather gave the room a warm albeit dark touch. It was a winter office, meant for electric lights and for gathering your thoughts, away from the sounds of the street.

Bérénice flicked the switch. Everything on the writing desk was impeccably arranged, the very image of the methodical Alain Béron. Several files sat not far from a little pot that held pencils, blotting paper, and a page-a-day calendar, but no letter. To the right, on a wide table, other files leaned against a pile of books whose pages had not yet been cut. A few papers, a few letters, too, stamps, postcards for interzone mail, small change, newspapers, corrected galleys, copies of the *Nouvelle Revue Française*. This table was the sole element of disorder in this neat universe, "Flaubert had a private corner where he could roar his writing—I have a dumpster where I store my writing," Alain Béron liked to say, triggering in Bérénice the memory of a phrase that Jouvet often repeated: "The work of a poet is disorder."

Where the devil could he have put that letter? It had arrived too recently to already be buried under the clutter of the large table. Maybe he had locked it in a drawer of the writing desk? Too bad, Bérénice could not bring herself to rifle through it, she would wait for him to come home. She collapsed onto the settee, a bit discouraged. Her hands wanted to be occupied with something.

Mechanically, she grabbed one book and then another, just long enough to glance at the title, in an effort to calm her nerves. At the top of the stack of files, a thick folder was labeled: Bergeret v. de Staël. Clippings from newspapers were sticking out of it, and folders inside the folder. That had to be what was giving the lawyer such a headache. Continuing to pick up books to read their titles, she happened on *The Epilogue* in the *The Thibault*. The last volume in the series by Roger Martin du Gard that had just been published. Since she had read the earlier novels, she wanted to browse the opening lines of his new opus:

"'Pierret! The phone's ringing. Can't you hear it?"
"The office boy, taking advantage of the early morning hour when doctors and patients, occupied with medical care, left the ground floor vacant, inhaled the aroma of the jasmine, leaned over the bal …"

"Bérénice, what are you doing in here?"

Absorbed in her reading, she hadn't heard Alain Béron come in. She recovered: "Oh, excuse me." She blushed at the idea that he would think she'd been indiscreet. "I was looking for Nathan's letter, I was waiting for you and …"

"You were going through my papers?"

"No, of course not!"

"No one can enter my office." He had lost his temper. "You know that, you know this is the only room that no one has access to unless I'm here, not the cleaning lady, no one! In Aix, even my mother doesn't go into my office. Who do you think you are?"

"I'm so sorry," she stammered, disconcerted. It was the first time she'd seen her friend angry. She could understand his reaction, if someone had entered her dressing room while she was getting ready, at the moment when she was summoning her character, she wouldn't have appreciated the intrusion, but he'd never spoken to her in that tone of voice, he'd never wounded her before.

"I promise you, I'll never do it again," she said, defending herself and beating a hasty retreat.

His only response was to slam the door.

Alone in the hallway, she remained stunned. What had gotten into him? Despite all the kindness he had shown her, Bérénice couldn't help finding the poet's anger out of proportion, and terribly unfair. She swore to him she hadn't opened even one folder, and hadn't moved anything except the volume of the *Thibault*, he could at least take her word for that, couldn't he? All she'd wanted was to get Nathan's letter back … and after all that, she still hadn't gotten the letter!

"Hi, it's me! I brought potatoes. Maybe tomorrow there'll be meat in the market. Corinne, the butcher's wife, was the one who told me."

Gigi had just arrived. The concierge's daughter came by every evening to tidy up for a couple of hours and make dinner. She always had a bit of gossip or a funny story to recount. She heard lots in the houses where she worked. Her arrival defused the tension. Bérénice heard her in the kitchen railing against the war that made it impossible for her to cook the dishes of her native Burgundy: "not the way they should be made." "Oh la la, it's terrific: milk with no cream, coffee without sugar, dishes without butter, how are you supposed to cook?" She liked to complain for its own sake, because in reality she was the queen of reusing leftovers and no one knew better than she did how to replace ingredients that had become rare. "Well, stop me if I've already told you this one. There's this rich guy who sees that his wife has bought yet another hat. So, he says to her, 'What? Another new hat? That's gotta be at least the fifth this month.' And she says to him, 'What does it matter, honey, they don't ration 'em!'"

The rationing hadn't inconvenienced Alain and Bérénice too much yet, except for coffee and sugar—they detested saccharine. As for the rest, their little backyard garden allowed them to grow a few fruits and vegetables, and the lawyer frequently received food parcels: there was always a client whose parents owned a farm in the provinces and who showed their gratitude by giving him jams, eggs, and even—that was a feast, when you invited friends and acquaintances to share the windfall—a whole chicken. That evening, it was less formal, "no fuss," as Gigi announced: a leftover rabbit pâté with noodles.

"These noodles, they remind me of when I was a schoolgirl," Bérénice forced herself to say to get the conversation going when Alain joined them at the table. "We had absolutely no money, at home we sometimes were reduced to cooking Lustucru pasta. Sometimes we didn't even have butter to put on it, so we just ate it plain."

"My mother would disown me if she knew I was eating pasta made by someone other than her. She's Italian, so it's sacred for her ... I'm sorry I lost my temper a little while ago, I don't like the idea that somebody can see my writing before I feel it's finished—and some of my files are confidential. It's not that I don't trust you but ... let's just say I'm an old bachelor set in his ways. I just left the letter on the mantel, if you want we can go over it together after dinner. But really, I don't know what advice to give you. I can't judge one of my best friends. Nathan has his reasons. You might call him self-centered in today's climate, but he was one of the first to have a clear idea of what was happening. It's that same absence of illusions that prevents him today from fighting against the disaster we find ourselves in. What he aspires to is complete freedom to pursue his work. In anyone else, undoubtedly we'd find that abominable, but we both know his talent, his musical genius, we know he's incapable of cynicism, which would be hateful, so how could we blame him for putting his work above everything else? Who am I to judge him? I can't write anymore, we're so enslaved that I feel paralyzed and it seems to me I won't be able to produce anything until we lift our heads. Sometimes I start to think that this paralysis is the true sign that I'm not a poet. A lawyer, yes, undoubtedly, this situation makes me want to take action more than ever, to become a militant, me, who never wanted to join anything of that sort. But a poet ..."

In his journal, that evening he wrote, "Long conversation with Bérénice about Nathan. I'm afraid I talked too much. She seemed torn up. Am I mistaken? I have a very definite sense that Nathan's letter caught her off guard: she wasn't expecting him to take a stance that has all the appearances of an ultimatum and, I fear, doesn't match what she was hoping. I still have confidence in her. I know she's strong and solid, far more solid than any of us, though she doesn't think that about herself. Her integrity makes her stand tall."

· 7 ·

Some days, the war seemed far away. This Sunday, for instance. Little Guy didn't have school so his parents had given him permission to go play on the beach of L'Isle-Adam. Before the war, it was a destination well known to Parisians, who filled entire trains to discover the joys of swimming—and only twenty miles from the capital! The beach was the brainchild of Henri Supplice who, in the years after 1910, had begun to turn the place into a true resort equipped with high diving boards, Normandy-style cabanas, a restaurant with half-timbered beams, and even a music gazebo. For just a five-franc coin, you could get yourself a little Deauville along the Oise River.

The beach, that was Guy's kingdom. He had his routines. An excellent swimmer, he often went to exercise there. The sun was so inviting that Sunday that Bérénice and Alain agreed to go with him. At first glance, they could almost pass for his parents, until you realized that Bérénice was too young to have an eleven-year-old son. Nevertheless, if you didn't look too closely, their trio resembled an appealing young family along the Oise River on a beautiful Sunday in October. Guy had asked the elderly local woman on duty for paddles and balls to play ping-pong. Bérénice watched him play against Alain. The sun, the parasols, the cabanas, the sand: the war seemed like a collective bad dream that she was waking up from delightedly. It was her turn to play

Guy. She tried ping-pong for the first time, the balls shot every which way, the young woman's hair came out from under her hat and her laughter rang out. In the little crowd of onlookers who started to gather around them, Guy saw some of his friends out of the corner of his eye. He stuck out his chest, proud to be with such a beautiful woman. With a bit of cockiness, he imagined their comments. Sure that tomorrow, at school, he'd be the king of the schoolyard!

"Who wants ice cream?"

"Me, me!" Guy answered.

"What flavor?"

"Pistachio. That's my favorite."

There were the three of them, sitting on their beach towels, eating their pistachio ice cream that she insisted on paying for, despite Alain's protests, arguing that it might be the last ice cream of the season and he should at least offer her that treat.

Sometimes in life there are perfect moments. In general, they are extremely fleeting, they last at most a second but they are so piercingly felt that they imprint themselves forever on a life. Maybe they are so intense because they appear so unexpectedly, without anything preparing or announcing their arrival. These are not those happy moments, lucky moments that occur in all lives, but brief instants where you suddenly know for certain everything is good. For Bérénice, that time when she was eating her pistachio ice cream in the company of Guy and Alain was one of those perfect moments. The ice cream cooled her warm body after her bracing swim, all sensations were sharp and precise, she was immersed in a sweet well-being and she suddenly was conscious that no one could take this from her: the air she breathed, the water where she'd gone swimming, the sun caressing her skin. That air, that water, that sun would be there forever, no one could wrest those from her or the memory of that October day. The sky overhead bestowed its limitless blue, the horizon stood before her, dizzying. All was good. At that instant, she knew that her place was in France.

She turned to Alain: "I won't be joining Nathan," she announced serenely. His only response was to light a cigarette. Seeing him make such a calm gesture, she wondered how he could have lost his composure when he'd surprised her in his office. Now that she too was in a more peaceful mood, and she was less focused on herself, a suspicion crossed her mind about this scene. But there would be time to think about that later …

"I'm happy you've made your decision. I was afraid of making a mistake if I gave you advice," the lawyer added. And so ended a week of agonizing indecision that had caused Bérénice so many sleepless nights.

And now they rented a little boat to go rowing on the Oise. Letting the riverbank recede behind them, they wanted to forget completely that the Germans were just a stone's throw away, that they had requisitioned the most beautiful houses, that they had established their local Kommandantur in the Castelrose on the Avenue de Paris. The three of them would soon go back ashore and sit on their towels, Bérénice's delicate hands would sift through the fine sand, the onlookers would turn around to gaze at her because she looked so graceful in that pose, in her long white dress, her face half obscured by her wide-brimmed hat. The child and the poet would see who could make her laugh the most, to entertain her. A photographer would pass by. Maybe one day someone will discover, in an attic or a basement, buried under a layer of dust, a memento of that day, and will finally understand it. In the photo, there won't be any pistachio ice cream, it's probable that in that time of rationing there was no more ice cream, it's equally probable that the October skies were not so clement, and yet that day did take place and will remain for a long time a beautiful memory for Guy, who will perhaps recount it to his children.

· 8 ·

Of course he could have hidden the newspaper that day but that wasn't Alain
Béron's style. As a man of great integrity, he was generally in favor of telling
the truth, even at the risk of hurting someone, being of the opinion that the
responsibility of humanity was to know the facts and then to decide on the
right course of action. There was no question that the article would not please
Bérénice. He even wondered how that copy of the *Petit Parisien* dated several
days before had landed up there, in the kitchen. Maybe Gigi had brought it
back when she went shopping, the newsprint serving as wrapping for her provisions, or maybe she pinched it from another employer to cut out a recipe.
However it arrived, the performing arts page contained a story about Florence
Hégué's beautiful performance in *The Cid* at the Comédie-Française. That
would be yet another blow to Bérénice, who just a few days before had to
endure the humiliation of Jean-Louis Barrault recounting to the gossip colum-
nists how he got started at the House of Molière and his experiences during
the rehearsals of *The Cid*. Not a word about her, about her departure, he spoke
about Marie Bell in the role of Chimène as if the role had always been hers
from the start. They were erasing Bérénice's name. That was even more painful
than phone calls from her friends drying up: "You're not part of the House of
Molière anymore, so we're going to forget you," she commented bitterly. She
now heard from no one but Bretty, whose news came from farther and farther

away, but the former soubrette had much to complain about since Mandel had been arrested. Fortunately, the Comédie-Française didn't abandon her, continuing to give her unpaid leaves, which they renewed every three months. The House of Molière was less generous with Véra Korène, whose citizenship was taken away by the infamous decree of October 29, 1940. The theater strictly applied the rules of the Company of Actors of the Comédie-Française that required members to be of French nationality. She, too, was excluded.

"Florence Hégué is not completely devoid of talent," wrote Alain that same evening in his journal, "she simply had the misfortune to be born around the same time as Bérénice. Like all the young women of her generation, she found herself overshadowed by this singular talent, by her new way of reciting text, more natural, by her innate sense of tragedy, by her voice that some call ugly, but that all acknowledge as an exceptional instrument. With Bérénice, you can't compete. The power of her interpretations sweeps aside all those who are lukewarm. Now that Florence has only ordinary rivals, it's easier for her to combat them and to be noticed.

"We heard today that the Bourdets have returned to Paris. Bérénice is dining tomorrow at their home on the Quai d'Orsay."

During the entire train trip to Paris, Bérénice wondered if, as rumor had it, Bourdet would once again become the executive director of the Comédie-Française. In principle, his leave ended on November 12. When he returned to Paris on November 5, he invited Copeau to his home, at 71 Quai d'Orsay. No one knows what transpired between those two men. The most one can say is that on November 13, Bourdet didn't return to his post. It must be added that shortly before this, Georges Ripert, the state secretary for public instruction and youth, informed him that he had named Jacques Copeau as the permanent director: "No point in disturbing you," he concluded, "just submit your resignation." Indignant, Bourdet's response was devastating: "For four years I sacrificed my career as a playwright. I devoted my time and my energies to reinvigorating the House of Molière. I was seriously wounded in its service. It is impossible for me to resign, but I will accede to your decision."

Would the minister of the Vichy government relent? That was the topic of conversation that Friday, November 15, at the Bourdets. Alongside the couple were those who had been their partisans from the start: Bérénice, Pierre Dux, Jean Yonnel, Marie Bell. The first glance exchanged between Bérénice and Yonnel since their exclusion from the Comédie-Française was highly charged, sad, and fraternal. Even if they all hoped for the return of Bourdet, even if, with the wine lifting their mood, it was pleasant to build castles in Spain by imagining the life of the House of Molière with its director back in place—hope was hard to come by. The military tribunal of Clermont-Ferrand had just convicted Jean Zay of desertion in the face of the enemy. Reduction in rank, expelled from the country for life: they didn't pardon this new Dreyfus the pacifist and anti-military positions he took before the war, they didn't forgive the *Massilia* episode. How could they count on Bourdet being reappointed? He was too close to the disgraced Jean Zay.

One question gnawed at Bérénice: what would Bourdet have done in Copeau's place on September 5, 1940? Would he have accepted the resignations of the Jewish principal actors? At the end of dinner, she pulled him aside to ask the question. She gazed at him intently, her face becoming almost childlike while awaiting his response, searching keenly for the slightest expression that would appear in Bourdet's blue eyes. The former executive director equivocated: "It would not be honest for me to answer you today, Bérénice: here I am comfortably ensconced in my armchair, I'm smoking a fine cigar after a dinner that was not at all bad, not to mention being surrounded by the dear friends who have remained loyal to me, I'm looking at you, you and Yonnel, two of the best actors of the House of Molière, and at this moment it would be easy to say that I wouldn't have sacrificed you ... You know me, my entire being revolts at the injustice that was done to these great actors, you among them, only because they are Israelites. Dux is my witness that we discussed this issue extensively at the time. He was of the opinion that we should not give in to the Germans, and that was also my deepest wish. But can I be certain that I wouldn't have taken advantage of Yonnel and Alexandre's offer to resign, as Copeau did? Who can say? We can't rewrite history, my child ..."

When Bérénice returned home that night, Alain noted in his journal, "Bérénice seemed disappointed to me. She would have liked a clear and definitive answer from Bourdet. She seemed very alone tonight. Orpheus must have felt that way in Hades, the one living being among the dead."

The minister's response was issued the next day or the day after: the provisional administration of Jacques Copeau was extended until December 31. At the end of December, after an exchange of letters between the minister and Bourdet; anti-Bourdet petitions at the Comédie-Française; a collective response from Gaston Baty, Charles Dullin, and Louis Jouvet; and then a counterattack from Copeau in the press, the question was definitively resolved by a laconic note from the Fine Arts Bureau: "Monsieur Édouard Bourdet is no longer the executive director of the Comédie-Française. Monsieur Jacques Copeau is succeeding him." Perhaps Bourdet was somewhat consoled by the statement of solidarity by his supporters: Baty, Dullin, and Jouvet resigned from their posts as stage directors at the Comédie-Française on January 2, 1941, while Pierre Dux and Fernand Ledoux left the board of directors.

As for Copeau, he didn't have long to enjoy his victory: the Propaganda Staffel demanded his immediate resignation. On January 7, 1941, the man who had presided over the best days of the Théâtre du Vieux-Colombier posted on the bulletin board of the Comédie-Française a note explaining his departure:

"Ladies and Gentlemen, Principal Actors and Members of the Company of the House of Molière.

Because my son held a high position in French propaganda during the war;

Because I have not collaborated closely enough with German propaganda efforts since the start of the Occupation;

Because I showed too much moderation with regard to the Israelites, the Kommandantur demands my resignation from the Comédie-Française."

Perhaps he was thinking of posterity in concluding with these words:

"I became involved with your company under difficult and even extreme circumstances. Do not forget me completely.

Jacques Copeau."

· 9 ·

Click click click click click, the noise became more rapid from then on, click click click click click, by practicing she had gotten fairly good at it, a little more and the sound of the keys would be completely uniform. The *ding* of the carriage return came at regular intervals, every twenty seconds or so. Now she was typing almost like a professional. "To the people of Occupied France," "France has given up, let's restore her honor," "Raise your heads" … Bérénice had been helping Alain Béron for nearly a year and a half, typing the anti-Nazi propaganda he wrote. She finally understood. That day he had gotten so angry when he had found her in his office … She thought he had lost his temper because she had violated his personal space. But it wasn't the fear that she would find the first drafts of his poems or even his intimate diary. It was his dread that she would stumble upon his clandestine activities.

A suspicion had begun to insinuate itself into her consciousness at the beach in L'Isle-Adam. That memorable Sunday in October, while eating her pistachio ice cream, to be precise. The sensation was fleeting, but after that, Bérénice had paid closer attention, she had paid closer attention to their life in the little house in L'Isle-Adam. First she became aware that Alain Béron was receiving late night visitors despite the curfew. In her room upstairs, she sometimes heard a buzz of voices coming from the lawyer's office below. Then, one night when she couldn't sleep, she went to get a book from the living room. The bookshelves were filled to capacity, thousands of works were available to her, which to choose? And it was there, while browsing a title by Anatole France—it must have been *The Red Lily*—that lightning struck. That imposing yellow file labeled Bergeret v. Staël that was in Alain Béron's office ... what if it was a code name? In his symbolist-inspired poems, Alain Béron proceeded by means of analogies. Bergeret, let's see, that was Anatole France's most famous character. And Madame de Staël, author of *On Germany* ... Was it possible? Bergeret versus Staël, a code name for France against Germany? In her hyperactive, insomniac mind, in the extra-lucid space of her midnight vigils, she couldn't decide if it was a coincidence or an alias to hide clandestine activity under the seemingly trivial cover of a lawyer's file. She went back upstairs to her room, carrying a book with her that she had chosen at random. The pieces of the puzzle seemed to lock into place and form a coherent whole. But of course! The compromising file left in plain sight on the desk could only be an homage to Edgar Allan Poe's "The Purloined Letter" that the poet loved so much.

Click click click click click, the next day she mustered all her courage and asked him point blank. She had dreaded to see the reaction of her friend, fearing that he would lose his temper again. All he did was look straight at her without saying a word. She had the impression of experiencing the look of Jouvet all over again, the first time he had spoken to her at the Conservatory, when he was gauging the depth of her desire to be in the theater. In the same way, the lawyer seemed to be measuring how important the question was to Bérénice. He ended up confirming her intuition. It was true, he *had* joined the Resistance. She had guessed right, that file contained writing that called for the fight to continue. They talked for a long time.

"At the very beginning, I began writing tracts by myself, I secretly left them wherever I went, trying not to make myself conspicuous, on the train, at the bakery, at the Palace of Justice, I even slipped one into your purse one day, you didn't notice? I thought I was being discreet but I ended up being spotted. Lucky for me, it was one of ours who understood my game. He told me to stop, that it was admirable to resist on your own, but that there were organized networks that were much more efficient. So I joined a network, oh, my role is very modest, I limit myself to doing what I know how to do, which is to say, writing. I began with slogans, and then I penned entire tracts, and now I write articles."

It was without exaltation, on the contrary, with great calm, a determination that was almost frightening, that she declared: "I don't want to live and above all to see children like Guy grow up in a Nazi world, in a world that is anti-Semitic, xenophobic, cruel, unjust, I don't know how I can contribute to your activities, I've never done anything in my life except acting, even at the time some people found that trivial, I never did, and I still don't. Probably, if I could've continued to act, in fact, for certain, I would still be on stage at the Comédie-Française or in other theaters, I definitely wouldn't have followed this path, but it was decided for me. I served the theater, and now that I no longer can, I would like to serve freedom. I don't know how to do anything special, I don't have a talent for writing, since all I've ever done was to interpret other people's texts, but I have a voice, eyes, arms, legs, for example I could deliver the tracts that you write, it's possible they'll be less likely to suspect a woman, and if I have to play a role, to pass for someone else, I believe I might know how to do that. What do you think?"

"I have to speak to my group," he answered her. "I have to discuss you with certain individuals but I'm sure that you could already help me by typing what I write. I suppose you've never taken a typing class? Don't worry, you'll learn. Look, you could practice starting right now on my little Royal. Take whatever text—Balzac, for instance."

Click click click click click, for a year and a half, they labored together. Because of his legal work, that plan went smoothly. Wasn't it natural that in wartime when you couldn't afford a secretary, the lawyer's wife would help out her husband and put his legal briefs in order by typing them? She could remain perfectly calm while she sat at the Royal, not like so many others who had to hide in a basement to muffle the noise of the keys. As a precaution, though, in case of a police raid, she always kept at arm's length the text of an actual legal brief that she would place on top of the pile of clandestine leaflets.

Click click click click click, she had started to feel some affection for the typewriter, vowing the same love for it that the techs had for their theater. It was her work tool, she pampered it, regularly changed its ribbon, buffed each glass-covered key, made the golden letters of the brand name shine. She knew her instrument by heart, knew that the *e* was more flexible than the other keys, and on the other hand, that the *m* required more force, since for that key she used her pinkie, which was her weakest finger. Seeing her hands on the keyboard made her think of Nathan's on the piano. Nathan whom she only heard news of infrequently. A good soul told her that he was living with a singer in New York. Thinking of this, her fingers pounded harder on the typewriter keys.

1941. For Alain Béron, that year was marked by certain sounds: the click click click and the *ding* of the carriage return of his Royal, the rustling of the onionskin paper—any other paper was too expensive and difficult to find—Bérénice's little sniffles during that glacial winter when her hands were too busy typing for her to take the time to blow her nose, the sound of air raid sirens that made them take shelter at first—and then no more, either from weariness or recklessness—the sound of planes, the sound of bombs ... Those sounds were for the most part intrusive for the poet, who was hungry for silence, but silence was no longer appropriate, the same with likes and dislikes, it was wartime, you had to live beyond yourself, even your own life wasn't as important, what mattered was the idea, the fight, the Resistance. An exacting way of life, and austere, just as writing had been for the poet before. With the subtle difference that the writer's solitude, even if it was painful, had always suited him, because it corresponded to his deepest nature that yearned for tranquility, contemplation, even daydreams. While this war, on the other hand, precautions, clandestine meetings, the fear of being caught were more in keeping with a more active mode that was less familiar to him—or, let's say it only related to his work as a lawyer. He was only half himself.

1941 was also the year of noise in the theater. Alain Béron had long talks with Bérénice. For the first time since she'd begun working in her art, the actress had the time to stop and get some distance to explore the paths of her artistic work. Up till then acting had felt to her like a vital necessity, but now it might be time to examine its sources and to ask oneself how to practice it, and to what end. She had heard about the case of a company formed by a handful of men. The Caravan—that was the troupe's name—roamed from region to region and brought theater to the most remote villagers. The idea had its appeal, it reminded her of the experience of the national traveling theater led by Firmin Gémier before World War I, or of course Jacques Copeau's traveling theater with his Copiaus in the 1920s. Béron was convinced that these types of experiences were essential: coming from Aix-en-Provence, he knew how difficult it was in provinces to see good quality, live theater. Very often you had to wait for a show from Paris to go on tour or travel to Paris to see it—which was out of the question for many ordinary folks who had neither the money nor even the awareness required. For Bérénice, this idea was even more novel: a Parisian, she had hundreds of theaters within easy reach. Her entry into the cocoon of the Comédie-Française had also insulated her from this type of concern, even if the concept of touring companies was familiar to the members of the House of Molière. Though she had barely participated in them, she understood the importance of tours for the influence of the theater and for spreading their repertoire, but the most successful were the ones outside the country, less so in little provincial villages or the suburbs. Now that she had been excluded from the institution, she saw the appeal of traveling companies, which seemed true to the spirit of the community of that troupe, but also to the spirit of popular theater that the Shakespeares or Molières had known.

"Why don't you try to rejoin that troupe?" Alain asked her. She had thought about it often but had become reticent when she learned that Jeune France was patronizing The Caravan. Jeune France was a sort of private cultural association—a commendable venture that mostly sought to enliven art and culture—but fully supported by the collaborationist Vichy regime and connected to the General Secretariat for Youth. An astonishing fact: several key figures on the Left seemed to be part of it. Bérénice had even heard that Clavé, the founder of The Caravan, was in the Resistance. Undoubtedly this ambiguity could be explained by the spirit of Jeune France, which strove to "combine art and life, the people and the artists." What theater person, who had any kind of principles—and who was part of the lineage of the Cartel, like Bérénice—could dispute such an agenda?

Out of curiosity, she corresponded with a certain Jean Vilar, who was the director of the theatrical section of Jeune France for the northern occupied zone. Despite her mistrust of the association, Bérénice was taken in by the speech of this man schooled by Charles Dullin—he had also been friends with Jean-Louis Barrault at the Atelier. One letter in particular, which she received in the summer of 1941, had inspired in Bérénice the desire to meet him and to speak further with him. He had written to her, "Anything in art that is not currently the expression of a struggle can only be worthless, because more than ever in this slack period there are ideals to defend and the forming of habits we have to fight against."

In 1941, there were not only noises, there was also the exact opposite, namely silence. "You know, Bérénice, what strikes me the most is the silence at night, I'm not talking about those nights when we're startled awake by the sirens, but that silence, almost every night, because it's after the curfew and we can't go out or go walking late at night in the city. I ask myself, when will that day come again? When will that day come when we can go out again at midnight because we're allowed to, because we're free, because it will seem completely natural? When I came and stayed with you in Paris, in your apartment, did I ever tell you what I liked the most? It was smoking a cigarette at the living room window. Inside, there were discussions, there was dancing sometimes when you put on a record or Nathan improvised a fox-trot on the piano. There was this boisterousness inside, and outside, there were entirely different sounds, women's heels clicking on the pavement, a car engine turning over in the street. I took my time smoking my cigarette, I loved looking at all those lives that you see in the lit windows of the buildings facing us, and I imagined—oh, many things, or maybe not much, ordinary lives. I scrutinized them, I didn't look for the why, but I did observe the how, how the woman on the fourth floor clears the table, how the child who can't sleep plays with the shade of his bedside lamp or covers it with a cloth so he won't be caught reading, how the couple on the third floor argues, how diligently the young man on the second floor does his homework … Today all that's gone, the windows are all closed and painted blue, the people living there sequester themselves behind the curtains, the light is stifled, you don't see anything anymore, you can't even guess what those lives are like behind the opaque walls. Maybe that's why I can't write, poetry has been padlocked. All those distant windows with those lives behind them, I would go back to Aix and often in the train I would think about them, my imagination on high alert, you can't know how much I loved those moments when I was alone at your window, me, my cigarette at my lips and all those lives behind their windows. When will that day come again, Bérénice, when will that day come again?"

· 1 0 ·

"I was with Nathan in Venice in 1938, I was given a leave from the Comédie-Française to travel with him for a series of concerts. It was the first time I'd been in Venice, unlike Nathan, who'd gone there many times. I'm telling you this because he took me to the ghetto. He told me—I hadn't known anything about this before—that the word *ghetto* comes from the Venetian *geto*, a place where they threw the waste products from the nearby foundries. Now, this isn't certain—others believe that the etymology is from the Hebrew *ghet*, which is the Jewish term for divorce. In any case, it was fairly late in the day, I think it was December, night was falling, it was dark out and the air was chilly, it seems to me that it had rained during the day, but that it had stopped, we felt close to one another in that silent place, we were moved. I remember that we both thought: if we'd been here in the sixteenth century, this is where we would have lived, in this place with its tall buildings, much higher than the dwellings of Venice, this is where we would have lived, we would undoubtedly have been poor, we would have known all our neighbors' names, we would have talked from window to window, the whole quarter would have gossiped about our love lives, like in those little *campielli* that Goldoni describes, and most importantly we would have had to wear the little yellow patch so it was visible on our clothing. I remember that it was deeply moving to us, that thought brought us together, it was right when we left the ghetto, on the little nearby bridge, that we imagined the children that we might have together one day. I remember that place very well, it's engraved in my memory. It was poignant to talk about how we might have lived there in the past, but that seemed to us like another time, other customs, happily modernity had passed through there, things like that had been abolished, they were part of another era, thank God, they could no longer exist."

And yet tomorrow, it has to be worn. Tonight in thousands of French households, fathers are explaining to their children that tomorrow they will have to wear that star on their clothing, tomorrow the mothers will cut the stars from yellow cloth that they've bought with their fabric ration, in tears they will sew the stars on their clothing: jackets, overcoats, coats, shirts, sweaters, blouses. Tomorrow in the street you will see the yellow stars on the elderly, on children (and the dogs belonging to Jews, do they also have to wear the stars? maybe the Jews would have to bring their dogs to the police stations as they had brought their radios—but of course not, after all *dogs* are innocent).

Certain people, seeing these yellow stars popping up everywhere in the street as if the buttercups had suddenly bloomed, will see in this a confirmation that there are way too many Jews in France, and others, I would hope, will think that even one star is too many, that all French people should wear them in solidarity, but how many will think that? At this moment, how many Jews are still asking themselves what they're going to do tomorrow? To wear it in order to stay within the boundaries of the law (but what sort of law are we talking about—can such a law still be legal?), or refuse to wear it in order not to submit? Maybe some Jews think that they should wear it out of solidarity with their coreligionists or to show that they are not ashamed to be Jewish.

"And you, Bérénice, what are you going to do?"

"Me? I already had to make that choice two years ago at the Comédie-Française when I had to hide my Jewish identity or be recognized as a Jew and risk not being able to act anymore. You know how it went. I wanted to hide it but I was caught despite my efforts. 'Being Jewish is something you carry in you,' my father used to say. But I'm not going to carry around that star. Just as I refused to put myself on that list, I refuse to stigmatize myself. They are sacrificing us, but in the name of what? This is the twentieth century, for God's sake, not the Middle Ages! Can they really be taking such a tired, old routine out of mothballs? It's as stupid as a witch trial, or animal trials, or trials by ordeal. Who still believes in such things? They're trying to resurrect the idiotic barbarities of the thirteenth century. So all the progress of civilization has meant nothing?"

The following evening, Alain Béron couldn't stop writing in his journal, covering dozens of pages, not censoring his pen, sensing in a confused way the vital importance of keeping a record of what was happening. "I think my lips were trembling at that moment. What I love about B. is that sort of innocence—very different from naïveté—that makes her rage against injustice. What if everyone were like her? The world would walk on its own two feet instead of upside down. I was afraid for Guy this morning when I saw him leaving the house with his star. I offered to drive him to school to spare him taking the micheline railcar that the kids all rode. He hesitated a second, both of us were thinking about the big kid in the oldest grade he heard saying on that same train a few days ago: 'If we're in deep shit, it's because of the Jews.' Guy hadn't answered, his parents had urged him not to say anymore that he's Jewish. This morning he looked at me, rubbing his eye: 'It's not gonna be fun, from what I heard the other day …' I thought he was going to accept my offer, but suddenly he raised his head with an air of bravado and said, 'Well, I want to finish my studies, damn all those anti-Semites. They'll see!' I found out he had some swagger, that kid, but I was still worried about him, even more so because half the schoolyard is taken up by ambulances belonging to the Wehrmacht. This evening he came home and told us about his day. When he entered the railcar that took the kids to school, his palms a little sweaty because of his star, the same kid ran up to him:

'So, you're a Jew?'

'See for yourself.'

'You know, everything I said the other day was just b.s. The first kid who bothers you, say the word and I'll smash his face in.'

"Sometimes I'm proud of my countrymen. If B. had been with me, we would've hugged that boy if we'd been there. According to Guy's father, this is what French anti-Semitism is like: 'They talk bad about Jews, but they don't mean us any harm.' I'm afraid I have difficulty sharing his optimism. But I'm proud of that boy. Real courage does exist."

· 1 1 ·

Friday, December 11, 1942

Imprudent act yesterday at the Palace of Justice. I tried to do everything possible to speak about neutral subjects with X, but he went too far. It's already too much to be muzzled, not to be able to write anymore, not to be able to speak anymore, me, who chose two professions linked to the word, lawyer and poet—it's too much.

X didn't realize that his hatred was disfiguring his face to the point where he resembled those caricatures of Jews, that "race of misers," that he so abhors. In the end, exhausted by his sermon, I took him down a peg. His reaction was unequivocal—I made myself a mortal enemy. He issued threats that augur no good.

I didn't want to cause B. any anxiety by telling her about this episode. She was already so stirred by the news: *The Dead Queen*, which premiered Tuesday at the CF, directed by Pierre Dux. Montherlant puts me to sleep, but I realize that he wrote a great work of art. We saw it together not so long ago, on the beach in L'Isle-Adam. B. looked very willowy in her little dress with the floral pattern, she spoke softly but there was so much fervor in her serious voice that it was clear she would've been magnificent as Inès. The irony of fate: Yonnel was permitted to play the role of King Ferrante even though the second statute regarding Jews forbade them from occupying any position in a subsidized enterprise. What one executive director overtaken by the course of events had let happen was now the law of the Vichy regime. In short, our Yonnel has now been reinstated in the troupe. Should B. create, as he did, a file with police headquarters on her Jewish identity so that she might benefit from an exemption? At the time, I advised her to file a claim under Article 8 of the law of June 2, 1941. Yonnel came in person to convince her to do it. I even brought her the permit from the GCJQ so she could hold in her hands the proof that he was reinstated:

Presidency of the Council

GENERAL COMMISSION
FOR JEWISH QUESTIONS

Paris,
1 Place des Petits-Pères

Monsieur Yonnel,
     You have asked us to certify that under the terms of the law of the 2nd of June, 1941, you should not be considered Jewish.
     In view of your affidavit dated the 13th of June, 1941, in Paris and notarized at the Consulate of Romania, we hereby certify that you have brought us proof that all your ancestors on the maternal side are of pure Aryan race and that you should, as a consequence, and as stipulated by law, be considered yourself as pure Aryan, having been baptized in the Catholic religion in 1935.
     We will deliver to you at a later date, as soon as the form has been completed, a standard certificate of Aryan identity. In the meantime, this letter will serve as proof.
Most sincerely yours,

Pr of the Gnrl. Commission for Jewish Questions
Director for Personal Status

Signed: J. DITTE

(I kept a copy of this letter. It's fascinating to see what pains they take to give their work the appearance of legality.) She looked at it with her huge eyes: "I'm happy for Jean, but I couldn't do that." She didn't give any further explanation for her refusal. She often repeated to me Bretty's phrase from the summer of '40: "Sooner or later the Comédie-Française will be compromised." B. almost suffocated on the two occasions when a German company came to perform on the stage of the Salle Richelieu. That had never happened since the founding of the House of Molière in 1680.

I understand now why she doesn't want to take that humiliating step. To claim that exemption is to recognize the law and the authority that promulgated it. Not only that, there's no guarantee of a favorable outcome. Yonnel seems to have had several difficulties, and René Alexandre, despite his certificate of baptism and many letters of support (Émile Fabre, Bourdet, and even Guitry, plus his membership in the organization of actor veterans), did not earn the right to invoke Article 8. I don't know how she can stand it. What a waste! When will the day come again when she can appear on stage?

Alain Béron's journal breaks off here. Bérénice will not tell her children about the gruesome day that followed. She won't tell them that she went out to stretch her limbs for an hour, and when she was on her way home, a neighbor ran to meet her and grabbed her by the arm: "Don't go back home, they've arrested your husband, they're looking for you. Go hide somewhere." It had to happen eventually, it had to happen, they'd taken too many risks. Last week, she had just avoided getting caught. She was hiding two letters destined for the unoccupied zone, one in her undergarments, the other in the handlebar of her bike. A German stopped her and asked to see her papers: *"Schnell, schnell!"* She handed them to him, still fairly calm, but the Boche's menacing attitude didn't sound good to her. As if he'd read her mind, he demanded that she dismount from her bicycle. There wasn't another living soul on that road. Her heart was pounding when he started to frisk her. It wasn't fear, it was her indignation that he was sullying her. She stiffened more and more as she felt the German's greedy hands linger over her thighs, her breasts … The Boche seemed to have had a few drinks, he became more and more insistent, she wondered where this would end. Finally, she became so repulsed that she heard herself say, "Get your dirty paws off of me," at the same time that an inner voice was warning her, "It's no use, he's going to put a bullet in my head because of what I said to him and God knows what he'll do to me." She smelled the wine on his breath, she saw hatred in his eyes, his male excitement fanned by her resistance, he squeezed her tighter and tighter. Luckily, a car full of officers passed by, they knew "Madame Béron," having seen her several times in town. One of them told the *Feldgrau* to leave her alone, which he did, clearly with reluctance, but respectful of the higher ranks. Bérénice got back on her bike and without even thanking or listening to what the officers were yelling at her, she pedaled so hard it hurt her calves, scraping the skin of her legs when her feet slid off. It was only when she arrived at her rendezvous and gave the letter to her correspondent that she realized her hands were trembling. "You get the jitters?" She nodded yes. "I thought he was going to kill me."

After that they were warned that the Kommandantur had its eye on Béron. It seems that the lawyer had been anonymously denounced to the Germans and accused of clandestine activities. They had even decided to leave L'Isle-Adam, but the Germans were too quick for them. Now she had to alert the network as soon as possible. "They've taken Homer," she had to tell them, "They've taken Homer," Bérénice, or rather Mélisande, had to inform them. They had chosen their code names together. Like children, they had spent a long time on it, wanting their pseudonyms to fit them, for the names to evoke something essential about their lives, but also that they should seem larger than themselves.

She only had five hundred francs in her wallet. Panic was seizing her now that their covers were blown. Gone the identity of the respectable lawyer and his devoted wife, from now on she would have to be in hiding. A spasm of sadness doubled her over, thinking of Alain Béron. What had happened to him, what were they going to do to him? His face passed before her eyes, his voice buzzed in her ears. How she would have loved to hear that voice right at that moment saying, "Don't worry, Bérénice, they let me go, they didn't find any evidence," she imagined him with handcuffs on his wrists, his hands could no longer tell the rosary of garlic cloves that he always kept in his pockets, "to ward off the devil," he joked when he was surprised doing that. Would the Germans find them and what would he say if they asked him what those were for? He would be capable of throwing his usual reply in their faces, defying them with his expression or maybe on the contrary, he wouldn't be able to say or think of anything funny.

What would they do to him? What could happen to him? Would he get out of it, would he die, would he be tortured by the Gestapo, deported to the East or sent to a forced labor camp, or maybe shot as a hostage, or possibly shot during an escape attempt, would he go so far as to commit suicide to be sure he didn't talk under torture, or would he die of dysentery or harsh treatment in some prison, as happened to many, or of sheer exhaustion or illness, all those deaths entirely plausible? Again Bérénice was doubled over, her stage fright had never been this intense.

She took a thousand precautions to make sure she wasn't being followed, she took a thousand detours to reach the cistern located next to the path that led to Croix-des-Verts. It's there that in case of an emergency she was supposed to leave a message, according to the procedures she'd been taught. I'm leaving to hide in Paris, she added at the end of her note, breaking the rule, which was to wait for instructions, but too terrified by the thought of remaining by herself in L'Isle-Adam where everyone had known her for two years. Paris seemed safer to her: a big city offered more possibilities for hiding. She'd go somewhere—it didn't matter. A basement, an attic, a back stairs would do. As she approached the Parmain Station, she saw that it was swarming with Germans and gendarmes. Were they looking for her? That surge in law enforcement personnel seemed unusual to her and very worrisome. Just as she turned back, ready to travel the twenty miles to the capital on foot or by bicycle, she felt someone grab her arm: "Don't say anything, just follow me and don't resist." Mechanically she obeyed, the grip was so strong she couldn't resist. The man who was leading her away was about thirty years old, he wasn't wearing a hat, but a brown leather jacket over a navy blue suit. He had brown hair, square shoulders, thin lips, and in his light eyes she could sense an incontrovertible determination. She had never seen him before but something told her that this man was capable of killing in cold blood. With an iron hand, he pushed her into the back of a car. The driver pulled away immediately.

"Who are you?"

· 1 2 ·

They blindfolded her, walked her down a few steps. From the dampness she felt around her, from the stale air, from the loose ground under her feet, she understood that they had taken her to a basement. And yet she was no longer afraid. A week had passed since her "kidnapping." The man who had ducked into the car with her had explained that his name was Gideon—a nom de guerre. She later learned his true identity: Zeev Zilberg. Born in Odessa, he belonged to the Armée Juive (AJ), the Jewish Army, a resistance group founded in 1940, in the wake of France's surrender. Its objective was to fight the Nazis and to establish a Jewish state in Palestine. Bérénice had suddenly pricked up her ears. Before the war, she would've laughed about such ideas, as her father had done when he talked about the meshuganah who broke rocks in the hopes of living like their ancestors. Now she understood the necessity for the Jews to have a place of their own, where they wouldn't have their identity thrown back in their faces at the moment when they least expected it, an identity they had more or less forgotten. Examples all around her, her own included, made her understand that the world considered them a race. Consequently, no conversion, no assimilation, no integration, even totally successful, was sufficient: at any moment they risked being excluded from society. Because of the roundups, which were increasing without regard for country of origin, even the French Jews began to realize that they too had every reason to fear the worst.

In several cities, armed groups of civilians organized to fight openly against deportations, collaborators, and the Nazis. If the choice of violent means raised some fears in Bérénice, who had never handled a weapon in her life, saving Jewish children struck a chord with her. Bringing Jewish children to safety in neutral countries such as Switzerland or Spain? The first image that came to mind for her was little Guy eating his pistachio ice cream on the beach at L'Isle-Adam. To save little boys like him, protect little girls who only wanted to live? The messenger of the Armée Juive arrived at an opportune moment: she was ripe to enlist.

The members of certain Jewish units wore on their epaulettes a blue and white Star of David. Bérénice also wanted to wear that symbol. It wasn't the infamous yellow star that the oppressor had imposed on the Jews, it wasn't the mark of shame that had suddenly resurfaced from the medieval ghettos, it was an honor that they could claim with their heads held high, proud of their history, proud of their biblical heroes, David against Goliath, the wisdom of King Solomon, the dignity of the defenders of Masada choosing suicide. They were hunted everywhere, excluded everywhere, but here, on the contrary, they stood tall as warriors, happy to have found an ideal again. A little later, in the fall, in the shrublands of the Tarn region, they hoisted each morning the blue white red French flag and the blue and white flag. *The Marseillaise* and *Hatikvah* rang out with equal force, stirring in Bérénice, when she heard those anthems for the first time together, an emotion almost as strong as when she first acted at the Comédie-Française.

She was smuggled into the unoccupied zone in the south, they cut her hair and dyed it a light chestnut brown to make her unrecognizable. Not for a moment did she hesitate to sacrifice her beautiful dark mane. It was like playing a new role, her cropped hair helped her become someone else. The worldly actress, removed from all real vicissitudes, yielded more and more to a young woman of her time who grabbed hold of the world with open arms, a soldier whose only objective was the defeat of the fascists, understanding that History was larger than she was, larger than all of them, rendering their individual lives negligible in the face of such high stakes. If she were to die, another would take her place, if she were to do nothing, another would take action in her place, but a mere drop of water in the ocean or not, she had to make herself useful and to fight, her conscience dictated it, she no longer had a choice.

"When will that day come again?" Alain Béron's nostalgic utterance no longer made much sense to her: it was obvious that nothing would ever be the same again. After all that, if she survived, she would act again on stage because it was what she knew how to do best, but no longer in the vacuum of the Comédie-Française. What she wanted to do afterwards, was to integrate herself into society, become part of it like threads woven one by one into cloth, she wanted to bring theater everywhere, into every region of France, to participate in the movement for decentralization that was emerging more and more among the people who thought deeply about theater. Through intersecting networks, she managed to continue her correspondence with Jean Vilar. They had just discussed the possibility of a meeting, each one eager to encounter the other to exchange ideas in person.

But first came the day of her induction into the Armée Juive. Her contingent was based in Toulouse, a city ideally situated on the road to Spain, and thus Palestine. They had judged that she would be a positive addition to the AJ and consequently had decided that she would undergo the initiation for new recruits. So they blindfolded her and took her into a cellar. The point was to make a violent impression on the mind by creating a state of fear—the ingredient involved in any initiation. But she no longer felt fear, it was as if all the pieces of the puzzle had finally come together since her expulsion from the Comédie-Française.

They asked her to take a new name. It seemed completely natural to her to assume different identities: wasn't that an actor's job? Another first name, another role, another story. She chose Judith, the name of the biblical heroine, slayer of the general who threatened her people.

They removed her blindfold: she had to confront her destiny. She blinked: they had turned a spotlight on her, again life reflected the theater. On the stage, two props: the Old Testament and the blue and white Zionist flag.

"Do you acknowledge that the extermination of the Jewish people is already taking place and that it marks the total failure of the ideology of assimilation?"

"Yes."

"Do you acknowledge that the Armée Juive is the movement to prevent the extermination and the suicide of our people and to definitively answer the Jewish question?"

"Yes."

"Do you acknowledge that our goal is the creation of a Jewish state in Palestine?"

"Yes."

"Do you agree to join the Armée Juive?"

"Yes."

"Do you agree to put your life at the service of the Jewish people?"

"Yes."

"Are you ready to swear on the Bible and on the Zionist flag?"

"Yes."

"Extend your right hand and swear!"

Bérénice read the paper that was shown to her.

"With my right hand on the blue and white flag, I swear fidelity to the Armée Juive and obedience to its leaders. May my people revive, may *Eretz Israel* be reborn. Liberty or death."

A great silence followed. Despite herself, the tragedian had gained the upper hand. Her serious voice, her bearing, the intensity of her presence had given this imposing ceremony an even greater solemnity. Everyone had goose bumps.

It was done. She was now an "Armand Jules," as they nicknamed the members of the Armée Juive. She would receive an intensive physical training on top of military instruction, as well as a spiritual education that consisted of biblical passages and classes in Jewish history and Hebrew. Zeev looked at her with his shining eyes. She didn't know what he was thinking, but he was a likeable man. Over the course of these days, she was able to gauge his scientific approach to commanding and also his charisma. Something about his determined look reminded her of Alain, while his feline appearance made her think of Nathan. "When will the day come when I can see them both again?" she wondered.

· 1 3 ·

At heart, she was made for groups. She was the one most astonished by this, it had always seemed to her that her solitary and dreamy childhood had pushed her in the direction of individualism, even egotism. She realized that she loved being part of a community. Undoubtedly it was this solidarity that had made the communist ideal so appealing to Nathan. At the Comédie-Française, she fought alongside her friends to make the texts come to life, so the public would be transported. Here, in the Resistance with the Armée Juive, the stakes were different, it was a battle against the occupiers, but she discovered the same sort of group cohesion, and she found it extremely satisfying.

For several months she had undergone a punishing regimen of physical training. They exercised in the scrubland in Biques, established as a base for French evacuation convoys. Bérénice was assigned to make the trek to Barcelona. Three years after her missed rendezvous with Nathan, she would perhaps get to know the café where he had written letters to her every morning and where every morning he had awaited hers. She would gaze at the sea that he had described so thoroughly in his letters. She might even walk by the hotel where that sweet boy lived—but the boy would have grown up, there was no telling whether he would have kept that sweet innocence, who knows, he might even have joined Franco and the fascists—you saw so many switching sides in France, it could also be happening in Spain.

Barcelona was still distant. They first had to cross the Pyrenees with the children. Then she would return to France while the kids continued on their journey to Haifa, in Palestine. Everyone knew the trip would be dangerous. The craggy mountains, the unpredictable weather, their inexperience, exhaustion, setbacks, the lack of scruples of certain smugglers ... A few days before, two members of a convoy had been intercepted by a German patrol on the platform of the Saint-Cyprien Station, in Toulouse. No one knew what had become of them. With the children, the trip was that much more unpredictable. To minimize the risk, only the healthiest children, the ones with parents in Palestine, were given the green light to make the journey.

The long-awaited day arrived. The smuggler had demanded five thousand francs for each escapee—a lot of money, but they managed to scrape together the total, aided by what they called "the Joint"—the American Jewish Joint Distribution Committee. The children were divided into groups of twelve, an operative discreetly escorted the convoy in order to hand over to the smuggler, at the moment when he took charge, a submachine gun, disassembled in his suitcase. For two days and two nights, they hiked almost nonstop to make up for the delay in their schedule. One of the children stumbled and sprained his ankle. They had to stop to bandage his leg—Zeev took charge of that since he had been a doctor before the war—after that, they couldn't hike as quickly. Despite the delay, the thought of soon reaching Spain spurred them on, they made progress in their journey in an astonishingly good mood.

On the third night, the smuggler pointed out the snowy peaks: "That's Spain, behind there. In normal weather, we'd be there by four in the morning tomorrow. But when it's like this ..." He didn't seem very optimistic: "You realize there are snowstorms, sometimes the mountains are impassable."

Zeev asked him to be more precise. "How much of a risk do you think we're running. The forecast doesn't seem that bad."

Bérénice scanned his face. She knew that Zeev, like her, was trying to interpret the guide's manner: was he telling the truth, or was he just trying to jack up the price? The two men talked for almost half an hour. A little girl named Julie, who had taken a liking to Bérénice, came up to her and squeezed her hand very tightly. Bérénice felt she was close to tears: *I don't trust him, he's going to betray us,* suggested the child's whole attitude. The young woman had to keep from panicking. She was also mistrustful—there were so many horror stories about guides who pocketed the money and then abandoned the groups they were leading, or worse, denounced the ones they were supposed to be helping. Who knew if this guide was trying to make them retrace their steps back to where a German firing squad awaited them? She clung to the sight of

Zeev's shoulders. They were solid shoulders, you could trust him, he wouldn't let anyone take them for a ride. "I spent all my childhood in the mountains," he said to the smuggler. "I'm almost certain we can get past those peaks. Let's get moving, it's starting to get very cold just standing here." The smuggler agreed. He was clearly reluctant, but he said yes and they continued on their route.

She will never know exactly what happened. She was a bit distracted for a few seconds, with her thoughts stuck on a nightmare from the previous night. It was a horrible dream, added to the long line of those that had regularly disturbed her sleep since the war had started: the Germans had captured Nathan, who had come back from the United States. They had also arrested Bérénice and wanted her to give them the names of all the heads of the Armée Juive. "If you don't talk, bitch, we'll torture your husband while you watch. We're going to circumcise him a second time, centimeter by centimeter, so he won't have his cock anymore, that's what we should do to all Jews to keep them from reproducing." She had woken up with a start. Since then, she couldn't stop thinking about that dream: what would she do if it happened in real life? It seemed to her that accepting torture would be less painful than witnessing the suffering of those she loved.

A panicked cry brought her back to reality. "Help, Léon has fallen into a crevasse!" Léon, a twelve-year-old boy, lively, so excellent at chess that he'd beaten all the adults, and who, when you spoke to him, had just the hint of a smile, making you think he knew more than you.

"Léon, can you hear us?"

No answer. Only an echo came back, even more frightening because it seemed immense in the midst of that silence. The guide swept the crevasse with his flashlight but they couldn't see a thing.

"Léon?"

"He's not answering. We've got to go down there and look for him," she said to the guide.

He shook his head: "With all the snow and how deep it is, there isn't much hope. It's too dangerous."

"If you won't go down there, I will," warned Zeev.

"You'll just waste time, it's at least a hundred feet deep," answered the guide. "It's impossible he survived."

"We have to try, we can't just abandon him. The crevasse is narrow, he might have landed on a ledge."

"It's crazy, you can't see a thing. Even in the middle of the day it would be dangerous. Fine, fine, I'll go," he finally said, seeing that they would never start out again if he didn't make an attempt.

They could hear him muttering in the hostile mountains, where the darkness was still dense. By the feeble glow of the flashlight, Bérénice could just make out the guide pulling a rope out of his backpack, as well as other tools, which had to be ice axes, to prepare for his descent. They were up at the rim, waiting for him, everyone holding their breath. Silence surrounded them, only the rubbing of the rope could be heard against the snow-covered wall. Julie's little hand never left Bérénice's.

They never knew if the guide told them the truth when he came back up. He had gone more than thirty feet down and hadn't seen a thing, then the gap became too narrow, there was no chance that Léon could still be alive. There was nothing more they could do, they had to keep going. It was an agonizing choice, and yet Zeev quickly made the decision to continue their journey. The only way they could have been sure that Léon was dead was to wait for daybreak, but they were already behind schedule and the guide's appraisal of the situation seemed realistic. They started walking again, everyone terribly silent, thinking of Léon who hadn't foreseen that gambit. At four thirty, just as the guide had predicted, they set foot on Spanish soil.

· 1 4 ·

Barcelona and then Toulouse. The children had arrived safely. Bérénice returned by herself to France while Zeev had continued with the group as far as Palestine. The night before he was to board the boat, he joined her in her room, and she realized then how much she needed to press herself against him, she had sobbed in his powerful arms, sobs that she could not hold in, not knowing exactly what triggered them, the fact of being touched by a man after months of being on her own, or the guilt of being in a bedroom with someone other than Nathan, the fear of becoming that shiksa her parents had condemned, also maybe the sense of release after months of unrelenting tension, and the furious desire to survive, especially after Léon's disappearance, the encounter with another body as the most tangible sign that she was still alive. She sobbed for a long time in Zeev's arms, so hard that it was no longer possible to think of going farther, and she curled up closer and closer against him, letting herself be warmed by his surprised fingers that gently caressed her, letting the tears flow that didn't want to stop now that the gates were wide open, tears for her husband, tears for her father, tears for her mother, for her life before, for the carefree woman she had once been, for the Jewish children, for the Resistance fighters who had died, for the innocent who had been killed, for the righteous who had been betrayed.

In Toulouse, she received word through her network that a man was trying to contact her. She couldn't believe her eyes when she saw him appear next to the statue they had designated as their rendezvous point, "I was so afraid for you," she murmured, touching his face to make sure he was actually real, "I missed you so much," answered Alain Béron in a voice that seemed to her changed. They held one another and fused in an embrace for several long minutes, both thinking the same thing, dreading that the other was not thinking the same thing, but feeling more and more that it was possible, that their desire was shared and after all they had the right because they were both ghosts. They took a room in the first hotel they could find, while he gently undressed her she clung to him as if she had no one else but him in the world, she didn't cry this time, at least not at the start, but at the end, when they were both lying on their backs, at once surprised by the lightning intensity of their union, and at the same time struck by the evidence of their two bodies together, each one perhaps knowing that this meeting had been inevitable, that desire had always been there between them even if they'd tried to hide it through the artifice of using the formal *vous* with each other and with their extreme politeness.

"Nathan beat me to it," he confided to her, "I'm slower, and I couldn't fight my friend." She didn't answer, she knew that he knew everything: it was this war that made relationships different, deeper, more authentic, as if the hardships they were enduring sealed secret pacts between people. Bérénice now understood the friendships of the veterans of World War I, those till-death-do-you-part friendships. With Alain Béron, as with Zeev, as with all the members of the Armée Juive, it was like that, a powerful complicity, indissoluble, that she had never developed with Nathan because he had left. When the day came, they would all be there for each other, as sure as two plus two made four.

Now she was right up against him, she caressed his torso with her hand while he played with her hair, while he whispered to her that he liked her new boyish haircut, and the sweet smell of her hair, of her skin, her delicate hands, and her body like a tanagra, and her eyes like sapphires, and her expression that moved him so much, and she touching her lips to every scar that the Germans had left on his body as if her kiss had the magic power to erase all those bruises and even the memory of them, passing a finger over his thin lips, astonished to desire them when she'd always been attracted to fuller lips, caressing the underside of his arms where the skin was so soft, furled against him, not wanting to think about anything but the present, not wanting to think about afterwards, about returning to camp, the discomfort and the cold, about Alain Béron's leaving for England, and he thinking of fragments of poems, as if inspiration had come back to him with the return of Bérénice, and the sentence, "When will that day come again?" as the refrain, no doubt it would become the title of a poem or even a collection, he also not wanting to think about the hours that would follow, about their separation, about this concrete world that they had to live in, they would've wanted to stay forever in that little hotel room, even though it was neither very inviting nor particularly well heated, but how they already cherished those faded curtains with their tassels coming undone like the hair of a weary woman, how they loved that squat little armchair upholstered in wide blue and beige stripes, how they loved that purple bedspread with its blue ink stain. It was their languorous bedchamber.

When that day comes again, everything will work out, murmured Alain Béron into Bérénice's ear, we've struggled so much, suffered so much that everything will be miraculous afterwards, everything will be possible, we'll just have to think of something and our desires will be fulfilled, when that day comes even seeing Nathan will be easy, and *David's Harp* will be performed at long last. After so many horrors, art will triumph, humanity will understand that it is the only salvation, that art is all that keeps us from our dark side, that's obvious to me, just listen to a Rilke poem or a Schubert *Lied* and you'll understand love, you can't be completely evil if you write something like that and appreciate it, yes, that's me telling you that, my little Madonna, it's me saying that after having gone through French jails and German torture, there, where I was being held, in Royallieu, some of us managed to preserve our dignity because we believed in the power of poetry and music.

Bérénice listened attentively to the poet's words, astonished by his new-found optimism, since she'd always known him to be ridden with doubts, and yet she had difficulty believing in it, despite how much she wanted to, she didn't believe that the day would come when things would be as they were before, the world had slipped too far into barbarism.

"I need to go, Alain. They're expecting me at camp. Will we see each other again?"

"I'm sure we will. *When that day comes again, starry beauty*, when that day comes again, the world will be cobalt, and your eyes will shine again."

"A new poem?"

"Maybe. Just something that came to mind."

The day didn't come again. No day came again. She won't be able to say why, nor could Alain Béron, since he wasn't there, and there was only hearsay, no one knew for certain if it was based on actual facts or someone's imagination or if it had been distorted by being recounted and repeated time and again. What she will never tell nor could any character in this story, even those who survived such as Alain Béron or little Guy, was that she had a meeting one week later with a man in Paris, part of her clandestine activities. She was also hoping to take advantage of this visit to meet Jean Vilar afterwards—she had continued to correspond with him. They had first tried to meet in the spring, but it had to be postponed because one of them was committed elsewhere. So they had finally agreed on a new date in Paris, where they both had business.

Her rendezvous for the Armée Juive was arranged at a little café near Montparnasse Station. She got there fifteen minutes early, having misjudged how long it would take. She entered the bistro thinking she would warm up inside, also thinking that it would look less suspicious than if she were lingering outside in this glacial weather—also a bit out of vanity, since she didn't want her contact to see her with a reddened nose. She sat down at a table, in the most secluded corner she could find, ordered a hot beverage and rubbed her frozen hands together. She managed to look natural when three Germans entered the café and sat at a table next to hers. She was trying to figure out the best approach to take: leave and risk missing her rendezvous or stay and risk being exposed.

As if that wasn't enough, the door opened and two French gendarmes entered. "Your papers, please." She prayed that everything would go well and that her contact would arrive late, even though she wasn't counting much on it, knowing the discipline of the Armée Juive. When it was her turn, she showed them her identity card. She wasn't afraid it would give her away, it was a real false ID, the best quality counterfeit document.

"Catherine Mulliez," read the gendarme out loud. "That's funny. I have the same last name. You from Lille?"

"No, I'm from the Lower Normandy branch of the family, in the Orne."

"How do you like that? We're almost cousins! Have a nice day, Mademoiselle."

He caught up with his partner and the two of them continued to carry out their duties, they were almost done. Bérénice would gladly have left, but the waiter had just brought her order and it seemed safer not to do anything that would call attention to her. Besides, the gendarmes were just about to leave. They stopped when they saw a woman coming back upstairs from the restrooms.

"Bérénice, I can't believe it. What a surprise!" she exclaimed when she spotted the actress.

It was Raymonde, her former dresser.

"Oh, excuse me, I mistook you for someone else," she corrected herself, reading in the young woman's eyes that she had made a blunder.

"Your papers, Madame," demanded the second gendarme. "Raymonde Domenech. What are you doing here?"

"I'm catching a train in a quarter of an hour to visit my family."

"Fine, you may go."

That's when there was a grating of a chair against the floor. One of the Germans stood up and walked over to Raymonde.

"What did you call the young lady sitting next to the wall?"

"That was my error, I made a mistake," stammered the dresser, "I thought she was someone else."

"Really? You know what I think? I don't think you were mistaken at all, I think you used her real name and that she has a false name on her papers, isn't that true, Mademoiselle." He turned toward the young woman.

"I have no idea what you're talking about, I've never seen this woman in my life," Bérénice answered curtly.

"Really? Well, let's get to the bottom of this, Mademoiselle Catherine Mulliez. Take these two women in," he ordered the other soldiers in German.

That is the last glimpse of Bérénice de Lignières. Bérénice leaving the café in Montparnasse with her former dresser, flanked by three Germans. Maybe her contact saw her from afar, maybe he surmised that she was the woman he was supposed to meet, maybe not. Should we believe what some people say, it seems so inconceivable … Should we repeat the rumor that the man Bérénice was supposed to meet was Nathan. Should we believe it, was it possible that he had left the comfort of America, that he came back to throw himself into the lion's den out of love for Bérénice?

Maybe a few others saw that little group leave, maybe some of them remembered it years later, but who can be sure, it was such a common sight at that time. All that is known is that Bérénice was transferred to Drancy concentration camp in January 1944 along with hundreds of Jews arrested from the four corners of France.

She was deported in Convoy No. 66.

She never met Jean Vilar.

EPILOGUE

And yet I would be remiss if I didn't mention that little blond boy in his handsome sailor suit, didn't mention his sister's demure skirts, in Paris in the courtyard of 32, Rue d'Hauteville, in the 10th Arrondissement. It would be wrong to omit his big blue eyes creased by the sun, not to describe his thick blond hair, rebellious despite the side part that a maternal hand no doubt would have liked more docile, not to depict his childlike arms dangling alongside his body, and how he stands ever so straight to pose for the camera, which he would probably prefer to skip in order to return to his books of adventure stories, certainly Jules Verne, unless it was Alexandre Dumas or Michel Zévaco. Not one of them, not the little boy, not his sister, not his mother, not his father, not one of them knows that in barely three years the war will break out, annihilating all in its path, above all faith in reason, no one can know that the fair-haired child with big blue eyes in his sailor suit will have to wear the yellow star at the age of thirteen, will smoke his first cigarette at age twelve, not bothering to hide it from his mother who won't say anything in order not to add to the hardships of the war; and as for his father, he won't be able to say anything either, he lives clandestinely, carrying a false identity card in the name of Robert Sicard ever since the neighbors warned him that the police were coming to arrest him. I would be remiss if I didn't mention the father's counterfeit identity card, which stated that it was issued in Nantes because the city was bombed and there was no risk of finding the civil registry records, it would be wrong to omit the date of birth inscribed on that identity card, August 24, which, as everyone knows, is Saint Bartholomew's Day, but which, more importantly, is the little boy's birthday, a date his father is sure to remember in case his emotions overcome his presence of mind, or in case of torture, perhaps. I would be remiss not to speak of this little boy who might have been deported because he was born at the wrong time, and Jewish—that little boy: my father.

In my childhood nightmares, the Germans came back, the sound of their boots pounding the pavement terrified my nights. Then there were all those real moments, in the metro, when suddenly the crashing thunder of thousands of Parisians' shoes, amplified by the echo of the concrete vaults and the ceramic walls, remind me of the memories that I actually never experienced: the hammering of the Germans' boots. These still weigh heavily, even recently I've dreamed that they were coming back and I hid, sweating with fear, on the roof of a house they'd surrounded.

There's worse: I believe that I'm guilty of not having been able to do anything for my father. Of course, you find this self-reproach absurd: I wasn't even born, what could I have done, and what does the war have to do with me, born thirty years later? So you find this reproach absurd, like children's magical thinking, unless you have remained partly a child, or if you truly love, because then you understand what I'm trying to say, you understand that retrospective sadness of not having been able to help a loved one, because you were born too late, as you understand those sad and serious children, matured too early into the guilt of not being able to prevent a depressed parent from succumbing to depression. It might be for this reason that the sentence my father used to say to me never seemed the slightest bit absurd, evidence of our complicity, while it made my sister so jealous: "When I was little, you gave me pistachio ice cream." I really believed this. I had really given pistachio ice cream to my father when he was little. I really gave him pistachio ice cream, but I couldn't arrange it so that he would not have to wear the yellow star.

The yellow star is still there, in an old box of business cards printed on transparent plastic, stashed away in the middle drawer of his Empire-style mahogany desk. It's still there, beached, tired, astonished to have endured such a long time. Its points have curled up, a few badly cut threads still hang from it, like the last bit of a scab that won't fall off a battered knee: the stitches that were made before attaching it to garments I've never seen.

Time passes and the eighty-two-year-old young boy is also still there, his blond hair has whitened, but his eyes are just as blue, except maybe during Passover, when they seem to me to redden and mist up with tears held in. What do I truly know about his thoughts then? I would be lying if I said I know how he celebrated the holidays when he was a child, not only because I have no knowledge about whether it was possible to celebrate the ancestral rites during the war, but also because he came from a family of atheists who didn't even fast on Yom Kippur. I only know that after the war, when you could again find matzoh meal, his mother cooked for an afternoon snack some *bubeleh*, or sugared matzoh meal fritters, which filled the house with their fragrance. His mother, they say, was not a good cook, but there is forever the aroma of those beignets, which, when it starts to waft, can symbolize all by itself the Pesach holiday. He loved to roll these large, very hot fritters in a plate of sugar before wolfing them down with utter glee, that's all I know. Still, I believe that today, just smelling that aroma from his childhood and rolling the fritters again in sugar makes him recall the little boy he once was and all those who weren't able to grow up and live as he did. So I, too, catching sight of those tears that my father shoves aside on his restrained face, my heart sinks and I think with emotion of that little boy I wasn't able to help, and of all the others whom no one was able to help, and of the children that those children, who weren't able to grow up, were never able to have. If he had been deported, if he had been a victim of the Holocaust, I would never have known him, he who remains the greatest man in my life, my brilliant and funny father, an ocean of culture, humanist, rationalist, and a man of action. Since my childhood I've dreaded the moment of his departure, sensing that his death would mark the end of an era, the disappearance of a world, like Yiddish, that musical language which is going out everywhere, one light at a time. How many like him died in the camps, who didn't know life, who never became what they could have, who don't even have a grave. Whether their life would have been trivial or spectacular doesn't matter, it would have been, and no one had the right to take it away.

ABOUT THE AUTHOR

Isabelle Stibbe is an important new voice in French fiction. After beginning her career in international law, she became the director of publications at the Comédie-Française, and later at the Grand Palais. She served as the secretary general of the Athénée Théâtre Louis-Jouvet from 2011 to 2016. Stibbe taught at the Institute of Theater Studies at the University of Paris-III, and currently is the theater critic for the magazine *La Terrasse*.

Bérénice 1934–44: An Actress in Occupied Paris is her first novel, published to critical acclaim in 2013. The novel received nine literary awards in France, including the Prix Simone Veil, honoring a book that celebrates a woman of action. Stibbe has subsequently published two other works of full-length fiction: *Les Maîtres du printemps* (Serge Safran Éditeur, 2015) and *Le Roman ivre* (Robert Laffont, 2018).

ABOUT THE TRANSLATORS

Zack Rogow's translations from French include works by Colette, George Sand, André Breton, and Marcel Pagnol. He received the PEN/Book-of-the-Month Club Translation Award and the Northern California Book Reviewers Award in Translation. He is the author, editor, or translator of twenty books or plays. www.zackrogow.com

Renée Morel is a translator and native French speaker. She teaches French at City College of San Francisco. Morel also lectures throughout the Bay Area on French culture, art, and civilization, from the Gauls to de Gaulle. Her translations include *Shipwrecked on a Traffic Island and Other Previously Untranslated Gems* by Colette, with Zack Rogow, published by State University of New York Press.